Not You Again

Patricia Elliott

ISBN 978-1-7380272-8-6

Published in 2024 by Patricia Elliott

First published by Black Velvet Seductions Publishing in 2019

Prologue

With his hands on the steering wheel, he sat outside Emma Praught's house, staring at her. The tanned curtains in the living room were pulled back, and he could see her and her daughter clearly. He could take her out right here—right now—if he wanted to. But no, he was going to wait and torture her a little before making his final move. She deserved it. They all deserved it. Everything was going fine in his world until they botched it.

Looking down on the seat beside him, he let his fingers roam over the rifle. It wouldn't take much to lift it up, aim, and fire, but where was the fun in that? He preferred to watch them slowly realize that someone was coming for them, like he did with his cheating ex-girlfriend. The thrill that had raced through him when he haunted her, stalked her, and finally tortured her to death was like a drug, and now his body was crying out for more—for another. He loved watching their eyes glaze over as their spirit left their body.

Thankfully, his dad was none the wiser to his dark activities. If they ever came to light, his dad would throw a god-damn fit, and he'd be up the creek without a paddle. While he was at home, he was the duty-bound, ever-loving son. Talk about boring. How could anyone live that way?

He was born to be a hunter. Not of animals, of course, but humans. It just took his girlfriend screwing around on him to find his calling in life. Anyone who wronged him was going to pay for their indiscretions, and he would have fun every step of the way. This time, his prey was that damn woman and her daughter. No one was there to save them. They were alone and vulnerable. His favorite type to hunt.

When they moved away from the window, he got out of the car and stretched. His back had a terrible kink from sitting too long. He stared across the street and eyed the garden that ran along the wall of her house as he raked a hand through his freshly cut hair.

"Showtime," he said, shoving a baseball cap onto his head to hide his face from any possible cameras.

He made his way across the grass and ducked below the window to keep out of sight, purposely dragging his feet through her flower bed—crushing marigolds, sunflowers, and tulips in his wake. Grabbing a blue tulip, he quietly walked up the steps and left it on the porch in front of the door, before disappearing back to his car.

He completed phase one of his plan. Now, he'd let her mull over that one for a while before making his next move. His phone vibrated on the passenger seat, and he looked at the caller I.D. It was his mom. He wanted to stay and watch Emma's reaction, but he was being called elsewhere. And like a good son, he'd be there for her.

He turned on the engine and pulled out onto the road. "I'm coming, Mom," he said into the phone, before tossing it on the passenger seat.

Glancing out the rain covered window, he flicked on the wiper blades. The rain filled the air with ominous music as the smell of wet musty dust floated through the slightly open window.

When he could no longer see her house, his fingers tightened around the steering wheel. He hated leaving a job incomplete, and he ached to return and do what he knew was right. But it couldn't be rushed. If he tried to rush, he would screw it up. He had to plan it right to the smallest detail or things would go belly up.

And he had no plans on being the one in the coffin anytime soon. "Bye, Emma. I hope you enjoy my calling card."

Flowers. They were right up a woman's alley.

Chapter One

It was *him*.

Emma Praught fumbled with her phone, catching it before it hit the ground as she walked into her bedroom. She turned it over and looked at the screen again, her stomach flip-flopping.

Out of every person in the world that could have messaged her on online, it had to be him. They hadn't really talked in over twenty years, but now his name—Devon Matthews—appeared on the screen, highlighted in bold in her private inbox.

>I read about what happened. Are you okay?

Tears filled her eyes. She didn't even know how to answer him. He was the last person she expected to hear from, let alone care about what she was going through. After typing a few sentences and then deleting them, she put the phone down. He was the man who held her heart in high school before he walked away. Not that it mattered these days. He was part of her old life. One that didn't exist anymore. All that mattered was making sure that she and her daughter made it through this dreadful time together.

Another ding made her pick up the phone again.

>Please talk to me. Let me know you're okay.

Emma paused before she replied.

>I'm as good as can be expected.

"Please don't write back," she mumbled. Yet a part of her hoped he would.

The most they'd ever said to each other over the years was happy birthday and her heart would pitter patter whenever she saw his name. It drove her crazy. She thought her feelings for him would disappear after she got married, but, instead, they hounded her like a poltergeist. And with everything that had happened recently, his messages were making her feel worse. She hated it and hated herself.

Her phone chimed again. Her verbal plea refused.

>My heart goes out to you. I just want you to know that you can talk to me anytime. You don't have to be alone in this.

Alone? That was her word of the week. She couldn't even gather herself enough to get groceries, and they were down to their last liter of milk. She'd stayed cooped up in her house, hugging his pillow and breathing in her husband's scent.

Her breath caught in the back of her throat, and an all too familiar pain stabbed her in the chest, digging itself deep within her bowels. Putting the phone down, she climbed into bed and pulled the sheets up to her chin, desperate to forget everything. But she couldn't. Emma picked up their wedding photo and held it close to her chest. Nineteen years were gone, disappearing into oblivion in the blink of an eye. As she ran her finger over the photo, a soft knock caught her attention.

"Come in."

Her teary, red-eyed daughter, Skye, walked into the room and curled into a ball on the bed beside her. Emma wrapped her arms around her, pulling her close. "I'm sorry, baby."

Skye cried into her mother's shoulder, hiccupping with each sob. "I didn't even tell him I loved him before he left."

"He knew you loved him, sweetheart," she said, kissing the top of Skye's head.

"I didn't even hug him."

Neither of them had hugged him. They'd been too busy disagreeing over household chores. Emma had given him a quick kiss goodbye, but then went back to their argument about the dishes. She'd wasted their last few minutes together. Minutes they could never get back. She should have spent that time hugging him, kissing him, and wishing him a good day. The argument could have waited until after he left for work.

A life-time full of regrets came crashing down on her. All their arguments over stupid, petty things surfaced like a crashing wave. Things that shouldn't have mattered had taken precedence over things that were actually important.

A heavy weight wrapped around her chest, threatening to pull her under. In silence, she cried out to God, praying that this was all a bad dream. Maybe she would wake up in the morning, and he'd be in the bed beside her, snoring.

"Do you want to sleep in my bed tonight?" she asked her daughter.

Blowing her nose, Skye nodded. Emma pulled the sheets up around them both and held her tight. Her baby girl shouldn't be going through this. She was much too young to be facing the sting of death. At fourteen years old, it was supposed to be all fun and boys, not death and gloom. Depression hung like a dark cloud over their lives.

Her phone dinged again in the dark. She picked it up and saw Devon's message.

>Here's my number, 604-432-5643. Call me. It might help to hear a familiar voice.

She stared at the phone number. Did he really want her to call him? He was probably just trying to be nice and didn't care one way or another. Shaking her head, she put down the phone and cuddled with Skye, whose sobs had finally quietened down. She hoped tomorrow would be a better day, but that was still up for debate. For now, maybe sleep would give her a break from life for a few hours.

"Aw, Mom," Skye complained. "Do I have to?"

"As much as it sucks, we both have to go."

"Can't we just pack up and go somewhere?"

Emma brushed the hair away from her daughter's face, resting her palms on Skye's cheeks. "I'd love nothing more than for us to take off somewhere, but I can't take anymore vacation time until the summer."

"I don't mean a vacation, Mom. I want to leave this house, leave this town. I don't want to be here anymore," she said softly, tears glistening in her eyes.

Emma pulled Skye into a hug. "Oh, hun. I wish we could."

The house was a constant reminder of the memories they'd had as a family. Every room carried its own depressive weight. She wanted to smile at the good times, but she couldn't bring herself to do it yet.

"Let's just do it," Skye begged.

"I wish it were that easy." She didn't think she could handle a move amidst all the estate crap she had to deal with—lawyers, funeral directors, insurance companies. She was so overwhelmed thinking about it all that her throat clogged.

"I'll do anything, please," Skye pleaded.

"We have to wait and see what the insurance company and the police decide."

If they decided it was her husband's fault, then she wouldn't get anything from them and would be forced to pay for all the funeral expenses. She wanted to hide, to disappear, and not have to deal with the ramifications of what the future could hold.

Placing Skye's lunch into a paper bag, Emma held it out to her. "Here."

Skye looked inside and rolled her eyes. "Ham, again?"

"I know. I promise to go shopping after work." She grabbed her own bag and coaxed her daughter out the front door. "Come on."

"You said you were going shopping yesterday."

Fighting to keep control, Emma waited until Sky had moved aside and locked the door. "I know. I'm sorry."

She'd been a failure as a mother lately, unable to do even the most basic motherly duties, like grocery shopping. Glancing down, she saw the blue tulip that had once graced her garden.

Crap. The neighbor's dog must have gotten into the flower bed again. She looked over the railing and stared at the trampled flowers. Her heart sank, and an uncomfortable feeling settled into the pit of her stomach. Someone or something had destroyed the garden. Only a few flowers remained. Why couldn't just one thing from her husband be left alone?

She climbed into their little Honda and turned the key. The engine sputtered, refusing to turn on. *Please don't do this.* She tried again, and the result was not much better. With water pooling in her eyes, she placed her forehead against the steering wheel.

Her husband's voice rang clearly in her head. 'I think you need a new battery before it leaves you stranded somewhere.'

"Oh, Peter," she murmured, her shoulders shaking as everything built up inside her to a breaking point.

Skye wrapped her arms around her. "It's okay, Mom. Please don't cry."

Her entire world had crashed down around her, and there was not a single thing she could do about it. Giving her daughter a quick hug, she grabbed her purse and climbed out of the car. A drop of rain landed on her glasses. Great! Even the heavens appeared to want to join in her misery. Grabbing the umbrellas off the backseat, they briskly walked toward the school.

Once there, Skye plunked herself down on a bench in the covered courtyard, crossing her arms. "I want to stay home."

Turning away, Emma took a slow, deep breath and then let it out. On mornings like this, her patience was shot, and she didn't want to get upset with her daughter. Life was hard enough already without them fighting.

As soon as Skye was safely inside, Emma headed to the bus stop and sat on the bench. Her phone dinged in her pocket, making her heart race. She knew it would be Devon. No one ever messaged her. Grabbing her phone, she looked at the screen.

>How are you doing this morning?

Groaning, she lifted her head toward the sky.

>Off to work.

>That's good, but that doesn't tell me how you're doing.

Persistent son of a gun.

>Why do you want to know?

>Because I care about you.

Her breath hitched, and her hands shook as she tried to type back.

>You do?

>Did you think I stopped?

Emma bit her lip.

>Kind of.

>I never stopped caring about you.

A large vehicle drove by, making her light brown hair fly in her face. As Emma brushed the stray strand away, she looked up and noticed the bus. It was only about a half a block away. She stood up and waited behind an older gentleman, who was standing close to the bus stop sign.

She had remained friends with Devon after they broke up, but that was mostly because they had mutual friends. That was what she had told herself anyway, but her heart had told her something different. It refused to let him go. Maybe that was why she moved away after high school. She couldn't stand to see him and not be with him.

Another message soon appeared.

>I still remember our last date.

Before she realized it, she found herself replying as she took a seat on the bus.

>You do?

>Yes. It was Valentine's Day, and I wanted to take you out to dinner at the place I worked. My boss helped me with my tie and

ribbed me because I had bought you fake flowers. I told him it was because you were allergic to real ones. Afterwards, we took a walk and held hands.

Her face warmed as she read his text.

>I wore my black graduation dress.

>Yes.

>Even though we'd broken up by then, you still kept your promise to take me to dinner, and that meant the world to me.

>You were the one I wanted to spend the day with.

>I thought you did it out of obligation.

>I never did anything with you out of obligation.

Emma placed the phone on her lap and shook her head, unsure of how to respond as guilt flowed through her like a fast-moving river. Her husband's death had only occurred a few weeks ago, and now she was talking with her ex-boyfriend about the past.

>I gotta go.

She shoved the phone in the pocket of her windbreaker. Glancing out the window, she blinked rapidly. The bus was passing a tall, multi-level concrete building with smokestacks on the roof. It looked liked a factory of some sort. Why didn't it look familiar? She took the same route to work every morning. She should remember it.

That's when it suddenly dawned on her. "Crap."

She had missed her stop.

Devon Matthews rested his elbow on the armrest, placing his phone on his lap. He couldn't even imagine the turmoil going through her mind. His chest ached for her in more ways than one.

God, he needed to hear her voice to make sure she was okay. If she didn't make use of his number, he'd pester their mutual friend, Nicole, and find out Emma's address, so he could surprise her in person. He may be twelve hours away, but that wasn't going to stop him. She needed him, whether she realized it or not. And he wanted to be there for her in every way that counted, like he should have been all those years ago.

"Uh oh. I know that look. Who is she?" Adam asked, flicking on the left turn signal to change lanes. They were heading out to the work site to tend to a few trees that had fallen over in a recent storm.

"You wouldn't believe me if I told you."

"Try me."

"An ex-girlfriend."

"Going to have to narrow it down, buddy. You've had like forty."

He slugged Adam in the shoulder, causing him to swerve. Thankfully, the roads were empty this time of the morning.

"Hey, I'm trying to drive here," he said, nodding toward the phone in Devon's hand. "So, who's the girl?"

"My high school sweetheart," he said with a lopsided smile.

"How many of those did you have?"

"She was it."

Adam gave him an incredulous look. "That's hard to believe. So, what happened? Did she dump you?"

"No."

"What then?"

"Me being a teenage ass, mostly."

Adam smirked. "Why doesn't that surprise me?"

"Oh, shut up."

Devon turned and stared out the window as they drove along the flat plains of Alberta. There weren't many things he regretted in his life, but the way he treated her filled him with remorse.

She was the sweetest, most angelic creature he'd ever had the pleasure of holding in his arms. He'd gone over it a hundred times and still had a hard time understanding his old frame of mind. How do you walk away from a girl like her?

When she got married shortly after high school, that was it for him. He went off the deep end and did a lot of stupid things. And if it wouldn't have been for Leila, his ex-wife, he would have done a bunch more.

Even though they weren't together now, he would always be grateful that she pulled him out of his slump. He felt bad that it had never worked out between them, especially since they had two kids together. But he couldn't spend his life with her when his heart belonged to another.

There was nothing he could do to stop it, and it wasn't because he didn't try. He did. But the intensity that had scared him off as a teen was the same one that continued to draw him in Emma's direction.

"Hey, bud. Snap out of it," Adam said, waving his hand in front of Devon's face. "We're here."

"Sorry."

"Man, you still have it bad for her, don't ya?"

Devon shrugged as he pulled out the chainsaw. "What about you? Who was your high school sweetheart?"

"Lisa."

"Your wife?"

"Yep."

Was he the only person stupid enough to walk away from the best thing he'd ever had? He knew he wasn't ready for what Emma deserved back then, but that didn't make him feel any better about breaking up with her. The look on her face had nearly crushed him. He'd almost taken her back when they went out for Valentine's Day. She had looked stunning, and he had wanted to take her then and there. Why he hadn't? God only knows. One touch and she would have melted in his arms.

"Stupid," he mumbled. "Stupid. Stupid."

"What's that?" Adam asked.

"Nothing."

The man shook his head. "Let's get to work, and we'll go out for a beer after."

"Sounds good."

They had a long day ahead of them, and a beer would hit the spot once they were done. He knew something else that would hit the spot, but he didn't think Emma would be game for the idea. And rightly so, she'd be grieving hard right now, and he needed to step back on his desires and be there for her. If she got a whiff of him wanting more, she'd high tail it back out of his life before he even had a chance to earn her trust back. And he wanted to make up for everything. Be the man she deserved.

But first things first. He had to get her to talk to him or everything else was a moot point.

"Hey, dude, you're forgetting about this thing called work," Adam said.

"Right. Sorry. I'm coming."

Mrs. Jackson folded her arms across her chest. "You're late."

"I'm sorry. My vehicle broke down. I had to take the bus."

"I understand life has been hard for you lately, and I sympathize. But I have a business to run, and everyone needs to do their part." After saying that, her boss turned and walked away.

Emma pulled out her phone and messaged Devon.

>Thanks, bonehead. You made me late for work.

>How'd I do that?

>I missed my stop talking to you.

>Lol.

She tightened her grip on the cell phone as she contemplated throwing it across the room. The man was driving her insane already, and they had barely started talking again. She hated herself for the butterflies that flew around in her stomach when she heard from him.

There was no controlling her body where he was concerned. Not even years of separation, nor being married, dulled her feelings for the man. She loved her husband, gave as much of herself to him as she could, putting her all into their relationship. But she couldn't stop thinking about Devon, and that made her feel dirty. She tried to forsake him, as you were supposed to when you married another, but it was like he imprinted on her. And no matter how hard she scrubbed his mark away, she couldn't get rid of it. That bothered her now more than ever.

Why couldn't she hate him, like any normal ex-girlfriend would? It would make things so much easier. But no, he had to keep his promise and take her out for dinner after they broke up, messing with her heart all over again.

She wasn't sure whether to forgive him for that. Yet it was because of that night, she couldn't find it in her heart to hate him, despite the pain that filled her after they separated for the last time. Emma groaned under her breath. Her stupid girly-crush daydreams were going to be the end of her.

>It's not funny. I can't afford to lose my job.

>You could stay with me.

>Haha, very funny.

>Can't harm a guy for trying.

>Stop texting me. I'm trying to work.

>You texted me first.

Emma groaned with half a smile and then paused in shock, her jaw dropping. Suddenly feeling nauseous, she fled to the bathroom, making it just in time to see the contents of her stomach make a re-appearance in the toilet.

Sliding to the bathroom floor, Emma wrapped her arms around her stomach as she wept. "Oh, Peter, how could I have smiled so soon after losing you?" she asked, her voice breaking.

It was a bad idea to come back to work. She wasn't ready to talk to people or to resume her normal life. And she definitely wasn't ready to speak to a man who could turn her into an emotional mess with only a text message.

Glancing down at the ring on her left hand, she made a pact with herself. She wasn't going to answer any more of his messages, even if it killed her.

Chapter Two

"Mom, who keeps texting you?" Skye asked.

"No one," Emma muttered, turning back to the sink full of dishes.

"That no one wants to talk to you like super bad."

Emma had tried to discourage Devon from messaging her by not responding to his text messages over the last week, but he was still going strong. Okay, so she sent the odd text back, but only to tell him to stop contacting her, and that made him respond even more.

Skye picked up Emma's phone off the counter and turned on the screen. Drying her hands quickly, she snatched the phone back.

"Get those prying eyes off to school," she said, snapping the dish towel at her daughter.

Hopping down off the stool, Skye picked up her backpack off the kitchen island. "You're so bossy."

When the front door slammed, she thought about yelling, 'don't slam the door,' but it wouldn't do any good. Skye was already gone. Her phone dinged again, and she looked at the screen.

"Not you again!" she groaned, looking at his message.

>I'm serious. If you keep ignoring me, I'm going to come down there.

>Then come :p.
>Okay.

"Oh damn," she said, resting her forehead in her hand as she shook her head. What if he really came down? The thought of seeing him again rattled her already frayed nerves. Maybe she should take off for a few days, go visit her parents or something. But he would probably sit on her steps and wait for her to come back.

Nausea rolled around in her belly. This was wrong. This was bad. He shouldn't be coming down. And she shouldn't want to see him as much as her heart wanted to, and that flooded her with unease, leaving her mind spinning. Was Peter in the room right now? Could he read her mind if he was? Just thinking about that possibility made an uncontrollable shiver ripple through her.

Why her? Didn't Devon have anyone else to bug, like other ex-girlfriends? Surely, they would be more available than her. Grabbing her purse, she headed out the door to go to her appointment with the lawyer.

Mr. Moore apparently had news about the case and wanted to talk to her in person. His voice had sounded so neutral on the phone, so she had no idea what he was going to say. She should have been able to mourn for her husband without all these other worries reigning in her head. If only she had the money to disappear, to have the chance to think and just be.

Pulling into the parking lot, she turned off the engine and stared at the three-story gray brick building. Emma clutched the steering wheel, her knuckles turning white. Apprehension didn't even begin to cover the emotions churning inside her.

Peter should have taken out life insurance, but he kept on acting like he had forty years left. She wasn't much better, though. It wasn't until after he died, she applied for it herself. Her parents helped her sort it out, as her head refused to focus.

She pulled open the glass doors of the lawyer's office, entering their spacious lobby, her shoes sinking into the luscious red carpet.

Approaching the desk, Emma smiled at the older lady, who looked up at her.

"Hi, sweetheart, you're looking better," Mrs. Fitzgerald said. "I'll let Mr. Moore know you're here."

"Thank you."

Turning away from the front desk, she stared at the furniture that lined the wall. She was almost too afraid to sit in the expensive mahogany armchairs, not wanting to get charged for breaking them. Everything in the room smelled of money. How had she missed noticing that before?

"The chairs won't bite, darling," the secretary said.

"I know, but they are so pretty. I don't want to damage them."

Mrs. Fitzgerald nodded in understanding. "Would you like something to drink?"

"I'm good but thank you."

A short, round bellied man walked into the room, his gray hair thinning in his old age. "Hi, Mrs. Praught. How are you doing today?" he asked, motioning her to follow him.

"Surviving," she replied, "I think."

When they were inside his office, he shut the door and walked behind his large Victorian style desk, pointing toward the chairs in front. He seemed to have a penchant for antiques, not that she could blame him. If she had a lot of money, she probably would, too. Sitting down, she looked over at the man, who looked small compared to his furniture. The chair swallowed him whole.

"I wasn't expecting them to come to a decision so fast, but you'll be happy to know that they decided your husband wasn't at fault," he said.

Emma leaned forward and covered her face with her hands, letting out a soft cry. The tension in her shoulders melted away, and it was like a big weight rolling off her back. Dropping her hands to her lap, she looked at her lawyer. "What now?"

"They've agreed, at this present time, to pay for the funeral expenses, so that your husband gets the burial he deserves."

That was the other thing that had affected her so badly. They'd kept his body because of the investigation. Beyond identifying him, she hadn't been able to see him since it all started. What did they think she'd do, stuff him in a suitcase and run off with him? If she could do one thing, it would be to go back in time and stop all this from happening.

With tears brimming in her eyes, she asked, "When?"

"As soon as you can get it organized."

Numb, she nodded her head. Her life was moving forward, not quite in the direction she wanted, but her husband could finally be laid to rest.

Threading the pen through his fingers, he said, "The police detachment would also like your permission to attend the funeral."

Emma stood up quickly, the chair tipping over backward behind her. "No! I don't want them anywhere near his funeral."

"They'll abide by your wishes, but you may want to consider letting them."

"Wh-why should I let them?" She backed up toward the door, wrapping her arms around her stomach. "They k-killed him. They are the reason I will never see him again."

After she said that, she turned and ran out the door.

Devon pulled up to her house and parked across the street. He wasn't sure how she was going to react to having him there, but when he had heard her husband's funeral was over the coming weekend, he knew he had to be there for her. It was a step in the right direction of earning her trust.

Her white and blue, one-story house was as small and as cute as she was. The front of the house was lined with a garden that looked like a hurricane had whipped through it, but just seeing the garden itself surprised him. Emma was allergic to anything with pollen. For a second, he wondered if he had the wrong house until a car pulled in the driveway and she stepped out, her long hair being tousled by the wind. He swallowed hard when she looked across the road. It made him want to duck, but he didn't.

She was wearing blue sweats and a blue t-shirt. He chuckled. If he didn't know any better, he'd say she knew he was coming. Blue was his favorite color. Granted, if he had his choice, she wouldn't be wearing sweats and covering up what he remembered to be hot looking legs.

When she turned away and went into the house, he opened the car door to follow, but his jelly-like legs wouldn't listen to his brain. His heart was doing a strange thump in his chest, and his hands tingled, itching to touch her. He never thought that seeing her again would pack such a wallop on his senses.

"Oh boy," he muttered. There was something about her that made him wonder whether he was in over his head. Nobody could make his body act seventeen again, except her.

Finally gathering the courage and the leg strength, he got out of the car and trotted across the street into her driveway. Taking a deep breath, he pressed the doorbell. After a few seconds, Devon noticed the curtain in the window move as a set of eyes peeked around it.

"Mom, I think it's for you," yelled a young voice. That must be Skye. He'd seen her pictures on Facebook. It wasn't long before another set of eyes appeared, and then a face, her jaw reaching the floor.

Breathing rapidly, Emma quickly closed the curtain and leaned with her back against the door. He came. He actually came. They hadn't seen each other in decades, but she could still recognize him easily.

"Are you okay?" her daughter asked.

"I'm...umm...I'm—he," she stammered.

"Open the door, Emma," came his deep, familiar voice from behind the solid door. "I know you're in there."

"Who is he?" Skye asked.

"My high school sweetheart," she said breathlessly, as she eyed the back door down the hallway, wondering if she could make an escape.

Her daughter moved the curtain and peeked again. "He looks cute."

"Skye!" Emma pulled her daughter's hand away from the curtain.

"Well, he does...in an old person kinda way."

"I heard that," he said.

Emma's face heated, and she brought her fingers to her lips to shush her pint-sized mini-me.

"Oh, come on, Mom. Don't be a chicken. It's not like you're going to sleep with him."

She was certain her daughter made her voice a little louder on purpose, and it made her want to crawl into a hole and die. Just the thought of having sex with him was enough to make her body wake up in ways foreign to her. And she didn't want that. Not here. And certainly not now.

Emma could still remember playing around with Devon on the trampoline in his backyard, hiding under a blanket. His brother and his girlfriend would be under their own blanket across from them. Occasionally, their little brother would crawl under the trampoline to spy on them, which always riled up the boys. She shook her head at the silliness of her youth. It seemed like a lifetime ago.

She had thought they would last forever, but Devon apparently had other plans. They'd gone from seeing each other every day to him completely ignoring her. He'd left it to his brother and his girlfriend to dump her for him.

She'd been heartbroken, to say the least, but had continued to put on a brave front so she could stay friends with everyone. And when he took her out to dinner, she wondered if he had reconsidered, but he never said anything. His eyes told her he wanted her. Yet when he took her home, everything he said and everything he did reeked of her being in the friend zone.

That wasn't exactly where she had wanted to be at the time, not when she had been planning a life with him. She hated her teenage fantasies. They stuck with her like dirt on the bottom of her shoe. It didn't help that they knew each other on social media, but it made it easy for her to find out what was going on with him. She should have turned away and never looked back.

"I'm not going anywhere until you open the door," he said.

Groaning, she ran her hands down her face. There didn't seem to be any way out of this. He was going to make her open the door. And she knew the moment she did, she would make an utter fool of herself.

Skye reached for the deadbolt. "I'll do it if you won't."

Emma shoved her hand away. "Don't you dare, you little turkey!"

"Geez, Mom, relax. It's just a guy."

Taking her daughter by the shoulders, she turned her toward the hallway. "Don't you have homework to do?" she asked. "Now, shoo!"

When her daughter disappeared down the hall, Emma turned to face the door. She tucked her hair behind her ear and straightened her shirt. "You can do this," she muttered to herself as she turned the lock and opened the door.

Chapter Three

The first thing she noticed was a pair of white Nike shoes. No scuff marks to be seen. His laces were pure white as though they hadn't seen the dirt littering the ground. A pair of black jeans covered the tops of his shoes.

Emma's heart pumped wildly. Her hands clammy. "Nice shoes."

A deep, rich laughter echoed in her ears. "We haven't seen each other in decades and all you can say is 'nice shoes'?"

"I—you," she stammered. Holy heck. She didn't even know what to say. He was standing right there on her doorstep.

Cupping her chin, he raised her face to meet his, his thumb brushing her cheek. "I'm so sorry for your loss."

A lump formed in her throat as her chest tightened. When his eyes locked on hers, a tear slipped down her cheek. *No, don't lose it now! Don't lose it in front of him.* But the second he held his arms open, she couldn't resist his comfort and found herself moving into them.

He wrapped his arms around her and held her tight, resting his chin on the top of her head. "Oh, honey."

"I didn't even get a chance to say goodbye," she cried into his chest, hard sobs racking her body. "It's not fair."

"I know," he murmured, rubbing her back soothingly.

After a few minutes, her weeping turned into the odd sniffle as she focused on the familiar touch of his hand. The way it felt as it trailed down her back and up again. When his fingers brushed the bare skin of her neck, a tremor rippled through her.

She stiffened in his embrace, and Devon knew he had to make a choice quickly, so he slid one arm under her armpits and another behind her legs, scooping her into his arms.

Pushing against him, she cried, "Wh-what are you doing?"

"Making sure you don't fall down." He carried her over the threshold and sat with her on the brown suede couch. As soon as his ass hit the cushion, she scooted off his lap, making a beeline for the farthest side of the couch.

He chuckled but grew silent when he saw the devastation on her face. He'd overstepped his bounds, instantly regretting his actions. Tears were streaming down her face, her chin trembling.

"I'm sorry, Em. I didn't mean—"

"Why'd you come?" she interrupted.

Devon wasn't sure how to answer. He knew his real mission to win her back eventually would scare her away, so he had to think carefully about his response. "You looked like you could use a friend."

"Is that what we are? All you've ever done in the last seven years is wish me a happy birthday."

That wasn't overly by choice. Okay, it was, but he knew if he did anything more, he'd be lost all over again, and she was married. There wasn't much use opening a door that couldn't go anywhere. He had almost given in a few times and had actually typed a message, but then guilt filled him over how he had treated her in the past and the pain he caused her that he couldn't find the will to hit send.

"You made it quite clear that you weren't interested in having anything to do with me," she stated.

"That's not true."

Pulling her knees up to her chest, she wrapped her arms around them. "Then why? Why'd you leave me?" As soon as she finished the sentence, her hands flew up to her mouth. "I'm sorry."

She jumped off the couch and rushed down the hall. He got up to follow her, but she disappeared behind a door, slamming it in his face.

Puzzled, he asked, "Emma?"

"Can you go away, please?"

"I'm not going anywhere until we talk."

"You're so infuriating," she yelled, banging on the door.

He knew based on their texts that the initial reunion would be tough, but he hadn't expected to see such an array of responses from her. She'd gone from hugging him to yelling at him.

Folding his arms, he leaned against the wall. Hanging on hooks across from him were scores of family pictures. It looked like they took one during every stage of their relationship. Devon's gaze paused at their wedding photo, and, for a second, he stopped breathing.

Emma was wearing a strapless, figure hugging, white gown that flowed to the ground, the train trailing behind her. Her hair was pulled back, hidden beneath a crowned veil. Beside her was a man that could have passed for her father, but he knew it to be her husband, Peter.

It should have been him in that picture, and not the man whose arms he had pushed her into. How could he have been so stupid? Next to the wedding photo was their first picture with a baby, who he presumed to be Skye.

When he thought about another man touching Emma's bare skin, a pang of jealousy moved through him. He'd been such a dolt. Staring at her smiling face in the photo, her question echoed in his mind, 'Why'd you leave me?'

Did he even have an answer for that, one that didn't sound stupid or hokey? He knew the one he had would probably get him hit up the side of the head because it didn't make any sense, even to him.

But what he wanted or didn't want, needed or didn't need, wasn't important right now. The love of his life had a funeral to attend, and he was getting in the way.

"Emma, I'm sorry. I didn't mean to upset you. I just wanted to be here to support you at the funeral."

"That's all?"

"Yes." For now, he added silently.

He wanted more, but he wasn't dense enough to think that now was the time to bombard her with his true motive. They did say patience was a virtue. However, that wasn't something he excelled at.

"Why don't you guys get ready to go and I'll take you."

"Fine."

~

Tears blurred Emma's vision as she stood behind the podium, staring down at the closed coffin. She couldn't even see the words written on the paper in front of her. Skye stood beside her with her arms wrapped around Stephanie, her best friend.

"My daughter, Skye, and I would like to thank you all for coming. I never expected to be standing here before you so soon. People always said he would pass away before me, but I thought we would've had at least another twenty years. That was my hope anyway. Peter was an amazing husband and father. Sure, he had his struggles. Ones that made me want to smack him up the side of the head sometimes," she said, chuckling solemnly. "But I know I had many of my own that he put up with. Don't ask me how, but he stuck with me through thick and thin, the good times and the bad. He taught me how to love even during our hardest moments, and I can't believe—"

A sob broke free, and she turned away from the crowd, rubbing at the ache rising in her chest. She took a few deep breaths before turning back to face them again. She recognized most of the faces in the crowd, except for a few.

"I can't believe that I'll never get the chance to hold him again. And all because of a mistake. One that would never have happened had the cops been paying attention. He did everything r-right. Damn it!" She banged her fist on the wooden podium. "He did everything right."

Her legs collapsed, and she fell to the ground in a heap. "Mistake. This is a mistake. We shouldn't be here," she muttered. "We shouldn't be here."

Suddenly, the church bell rang, and in her mind's eye, all she could hear was a doorbell. The chapel auditorium and the large crowd faded away into the distance, and she found herself back in her living room as the doorbell rang again.

"I don't want to remember," she whispered, fighting valiantly against the oncoming memory.

She had got up from the couch and opened the door to find two cops standing there, hats against their chest. Her heart dropped into her stomach, and she knew why they were there even before they said the words.

"Mrs. Emma Praught?"

"Yes."

"Can we come in?"

She motioned them inside. "What's going on?" she asked, her voice squeaking.

"I'm afraid your husband was involved in a fatal motorcycle accident."

Fatal—the word echoed over and over in her head. "What do you mean?"

"He didn't make it. I'm sorry. We have to ask you to come with us to identify him."

She sat down, staring blankly at the carpet. "My d-daughter. She's at a friend's house. I-I have to call her." Picking up the cell phone beside her, she hit the girl's number. "Is Skye there?"

As she waited for an answer, Emma felt her shoulders shake as a jumble of voices murmured in her ear. "Is Skye there?" she asked again.

"Mom, I'm here. Wake up."

Again, her shoulders shook.

"Devon, she's not waking up," a tearful voice cried.

Emma squeezed her eyes closed tightly. "This isn't real. Please, don't let this be real."

"Emma, hun, come back to us," said another familiar voice. Something warm came to rest against her cheeks. "Come on, sweetheart. I know you can open your eyes."

She slowly opened her heavy-lidded eyes and found herself on the ground in front of a huge audience, the stage lights blinding her. Devon and Skye were kneeling beside her.

Humiliated, she buried her face in his chest. "Get me out of here."

Picking her up, he carried her to the front row and sat her in an empty chair. She leaned against him, his arms wrapping around her while the pastor finished the service.

The calm and relaxing way that his thumb brushed the skin of her shoulder helped her breathe a little easier, and the brick lodged in her stomach slowly dissipated. "Thank you."

Smiling down at her, he kissed the top of her head. "Anytime."

When the pallbearers picked up the casket and carried it down the aisle, she followed behind them. Skye was on her left side, and Devon on her right, with his hand resting on the small of her back. She heard the crowd whispering, but she didn't care. For the first time in three weeks, her world wasn't spinning like a tilt-a-whirl. She looked up at him, giving him half a smile.

Devon smiled back. He felt like he'd won the lotto when she didn't shy away from his touch. And now, as he led her to the car, an even stronger love took over his heart. He knew he had to take it slow, though, and that was okay with him. He'd waited over twenty years, so waiting until she was ready wouldn't kill him. At least he hoped not.

As they approached the cemetery, flashing red and blue lights caught Emma's attention. She couldn't believe they had the audacity to show their face at her husband's graveside. And not just one cop. It looked like their entire team was there, lining the walkway to her husband's final resting place.

She climbed out of the car and was about to give them a piece of her mind when Mr. Moore rushed over.

"I know you didn't want them here, but trust me, it looks good for your case. It's an acknowledgement that they messed up."

Global Television news was on site filming. Reporters were talking into the cameras off to the side. Why couldn't she have her privacy? Why did it have to be a big media gong show?

Six decorated officers came over to the hearse to carry his casket to the grave. Her stomach cramped as they reached for it, her eyes burning with tears. She followed behind them as they carried the coffin through the line-up of officers, who saluted her.

As they reached the front, she saw a cop with a full-leg cast sitting in a wheelchair. His face downcast. The young man behind him glared at Emma as he wheeled the cop over to her.

"Madam," the injured man said, "I want to offer you my deepest apologies for your loss. If there is anything we can do to help, please let us know."

Emma stared at him. It wasn't fair that this man survived with only a broken leg while her husband lost his life. "Can you bring him back?" she asked him before turning to look at the row of cops, her hands closing into tight fists. "Can any of you bring him back?"

They all averted their eyes, looking at the ground.

"Damn you. Damn all of you," she cried.

Devon put his arm around her and coaxed her toward her husband's grave. "Ignore them. We'll get through this together."

"I want to hit them so bad," she said, flexing her fingers.

"I'll take you to a gym after, and you can picture them on a punching bag."

"Promise?"

"You bet!"

"Actually, I want to get drunk. Stone cold drunk. Forget everything. Just for one night."

"We could do that, too."

The pastor said another word or two as a machine lowered Peter's casket into the waiting grave, but she couldn't focus on the pastor. Her mind wandered back to the day she had met her husband.

She had started a new security job and was working in a parkade in downtown Vancouver. On her first night, her boss told her that a gentleman by the name of Peter would show her the ropes. They had hit it off right away.

How was she going to survive without him? He'd been such a big part of her life for so long. Emma wrapped her arms around herself as a bowling ball took up residence inside her. Much to her surprise, another set of arms closed around her. Leaning back, she rested her head against Devon's chest.

Skye stood next to her, shifting from foot to foot, her fingers resting lightly on Emma's arm. "Can we go, Mom?" she asked.

She knew exactly how her daughter felt. Neither of them wanted to be the center of attention, all eyes focused on them. They wanted to be alone.

"Soon, sweetie."

The afternoon sun beat down on her black veil, making her sweat. She tore off the veil and took a shaky breath, letting it drop to the ground. Could the day get any worse? Emma twisted the wedding ring around her finger. "I, Emma Fraser, take you, Peter Praught, to be my lawfully wedded husband. To have and to hold from this day forward. For better, for worse. For richer, for poorer. In sickness and in health, until death do us part," she whispered to herself. "Until death do us part."

Leaning down, she placed the bouquet of flowers, the few that survived from their garden, near his headstone. Peter had planted and grown them himself. They were his babies, not hers. She couldn't believe she was already a widow at thirty-nine years old. That was not something you could ever prepare for, especially when he had a clean bill of health. He should still be here.

Fiercely turning around, she glared at the cops standing there, and was about to run up to them, but Devon held her back.

"Let me go," she cried. She wanted to hit them. Hurt them like they hurt her.

"It won't help, trust me."

"They deserve it, damn it!"

"Come on. I'll take you home." He took her by the shoulders and steered her through the cops. The officers stepped back, giving her family space to pass by.

Devon helped Emma into the car and reached over to buckle her seatbelt. If given half the chance, he had a feeling she would pounce at the nearest cop. She was livid. Her eyes were shooting darts in every which direction. Thankfully, not at him this time. That was progress. Maybe.

"Can I sleep over at Stephanie's house?" Skye asked as she and her friend huddled in the backseat of Devon's car.

"I'm not sure. I'm not overly comfortable leaving you alone yet."

"I won't be alone," she responded. "Please, Mom. I just want to forget about things for a while, and I can't do that at home."

"Okay. Just for the night, though."

They dropped the girls off at Stephanie's house and then they were back on the road again. As he was driving, he looked over at the woman who had captured his heart. "What do you want to do now?"

Reaching up, Emma undid her ponytail, letting her long hair flow down her back. "I want a drink."

"Where do you want to go?"

"Home."

Swallowing hard, he wiped his suddenly sweaty palms on his pants. He knew what could happen if you mixed alcohol and beds together, and he didn't think she was ready for that step yet. And he didn't think he'd be saint enough to try.

"How about a bar and play a game of pool?"

"No. I want to go home."

Uh oh! He was toast unless he could figure out how to resist the challenges that were coming. But she wanted to go home, so home they would go.

~

"Wow. Slow down, Em." Devon put his hand over hers as she reached for yet another Mike's Hard Root Beer. "You've had three in just over an hour."

Sticking her tongue out at him, she grabbed another. "So have you."

Eyeing her up and down, he smirked. "Ya, but I weigh more than you."

"So what? I meant what I said. I plan on getting absotu, absoluey... absolutely. Eureka!" She pumped her fist in the air at finally figuring the word out. "Absolutely plastered!" For one night, she wanted to forget everything and just be.

"I'd say you're halfway there already," he replied, chuckling.

"Nope!" she said, as she popped the top of the can. "I need more."

"You do realize you're going to feel as sick as hell in the morning, right?"

Taking a long sip of the drink, she looked over the top of the can at him and rolled her eyes. "Yes, Daddy!"

He roared with laughter. "Smart alec."

She leaned back against the couch with a cheeky grin spreading across her face, studying him. His blond hairline had slightly receded over the years, and there were a few more wrinkles around his gray-ish-blue eyes. But it made him look more distinguished, cuter even, than he did as a teen. His eyes locked with hers and the intensity in them almost blew her away.

"It's good to see you, Em."

With her cheeks on fire, she averted her gaze down to the can in her hand and took another large sip. She wasn't sure how she felt about him being there just yet, and she wasn't quite drunk enough to not remember their last two weeks together in high school.

"Uh huh," she murmured into the can, unsure of how to respond.

"I mean it."

"Uh huh."

"You don't believe me?"

She shrugged her shoulders, not trusting her mouth to speak because she knew if she did, she'd ask him again why he broke up with her. And that wasn't something she wanted to care about right now. Her husband had just died. That was all that should matter to her.

"I'm a horrible person," she muttered under her breath.

"What was that?"

"Nothing, Mr. Nosy."

Nothing she wanted to reveal to him anyway. He had barged his way back into her life at the worst possible time. And all the questions she'd ever had about the two of them wanted to come tumbling out of her mouth. They never argued and never quarreled. Yet he still dumped her. And because of that, she moved away and met a creep who stole her innocence. Thanks to Devon, she had lost her moral compass and made choices that had gotten her into that mess to begin with. With that thought, she took another large gulp of her drink, shuddering. She'd been so stupid.

Although she knew that if those things would never have happened, she wouldn't have met Peter and fallen in love with him. Never would have had her daughter, Skye. But she couldn't help but have bitter-sweet memories of her past. And rightly so.

"What are you thinking so hard about?" Devon asked, tilting his head as he looked at her. Not that he had to ask that question. He could see the conflict in her eyes and chose to keep his distance, not wanting to spook her.

She quickly shook her head. "Nothing."

Getting information out of her was harder than finding a needle in a haystack. Maybe he should be the one to broach the topic. After all, she had asked him a question when he first arrived. Leaning forward, he grabbed his drink off the large redwood burl coffee table.

"Did Peter make this?" That wasn't the question he was going to ask, but it seemed safer. The last thing he wanted to do was push too hard and have her shut him out completely.

"No, my dad did."

"How are your parents?" He could still remember them, even though he hadn't seen them in ages. Her mother was this short and sweet brown-haired woman, and her dad was this tall and intimidating dark-haired giant. Her parents always kept a close eye on them whenever they hung out in the basement. They didn't want him to deflower their daughter.

"They wanted to be out here today, but my dad is still recovering from his last hospital stay."

"Ah, I remember you mentioning that," Devon said, giving her a sympathetic glance. He was glad he was able to come down since they couldn't. He hated the idea of her going through this alone. "Kidney infection, wasn't it?"

She nodded her head as she took another drink. Before long, she pulled it away from her lips and peered into the hole in the top of the can. "Empty."

"Man, girl, you sure can guzzle those drinks."

"I've learned a thing or two since I drank that Tropi...um..." She paused for a moment before continuing. "Tropikiwi."

"Oh, god, I still remember that. You and Claire called us, saying you were drinking."

A light smile played on Emma's lips as she nodded. "And you guys were like, *we're coming over*."

"Your parents were away that weekend, too."

Her cheeks turned bright red as she reached for her fifth can. "Yep."

The look on her face told him she remembered the day just as well as he did. In his teen mind, he had gone over there to get lucky, but all they really did was make out. Once they were together on the couch in her basement, he couldn't quite find the heart to go all the way as much as he had wanted to. She was his sweet little angel, and he didn't want to be the one responsible for changing her.

"I swear we could be in the Guinness Book of World Records as being the first teen couple to not have sex while unsupervised," she said, giggling.

That was when he knew the drinks had finally caught up to her with a bang. He tried to reach for the can in her hand, but she leaned backward, pushing her bare feet against his chest.

Looking at him over the rim of the can, she said, "Mine."

The challenge in Emma's eyes was evident, and Devon was never one to back away from a good dare. Maybe it was the alcohol in his own system, but he grabbed her foot and tickled it. He could remember every ticklish spot on her delectable body.

"Stop," she shrieked with laughter, trying to pull her foot away from him, but he kept a firm hold on it.

"What if I do this?" He reached further up her leg and brushed his fingers against the back of her knee, earning him another round of giggles. Oh, how he missed her laugh. Missed everything about her.

Before he realized it, she was holding the can above his head, pouring it on him. Devon licked the liquid as it rolled down his face and across his lips. "I thought you said it was yours, not mine," he commented, as he shook himself like a dog, flicking droplets of the drink in her direction.

Her lips curled into a breathtaking, mischievous grin. "Looks so much better on you."

It caught him off-guard. He loved seeing her smile and looking free as opposed to being weighed down by the world. And it made him feel good that she was smiling in his direction, instead of the frown that she had been sporting since he showed up at her door.

"Cheers." Emma tilted her head back and drank remaining contents of the can, giving him a glimpse of her long slender neck.

His whole body hummed with desire. *Hot damn.* She was going to be the death of him. There was no one in the world he wanted more than her. Never has been and never will be. It took every ounce of his strength not to pick her up and carry her into bed, finishing what they had started back in high school.

Devon unknowingly tightened the hold he had on his own can, crushing it. Liquid squirted out the top and hit him square in the face, making him jump. The rest landed on the crotch of his pants.

Emma doubled over in laughter. "Looks like your dam burst."

He looked so cute sitting there, soaked in liquor, giving her his signature lop-sided grin. "Still plenty in the reserve tank."

"Oh, gosh," she said, as another round of giggles bubbled up inside her. She'd forgotten how much fun he was to be around. They could spend hours together and not get bored.

Using his shirt, he wiped the alcohol off his face and then pulled it up over his head, giving her an unbridled view of his sculpted upper body. She licked her lips as her eyes wandered over his chest, following it down to his toned abs. No beer belly in sight, except for the liquor that colored his skin a darker brown.

Butterflies fluttered in her stomach, and heat pooled between her legs, making her underwear damp. *Hot tamale.* She fanned herself with her hand. He was sexier than she remembered. This wasn't the young boy she knew. This...this was a man.

She desperately needed another drink. Standing up far too quickly, she held out her hands to steady herself as the walls spun around her. "Umm, the walls are moving."

"It's called being drunk, sweetheart," he said, pulling her back down onto the couch. "Tell me what you want, and I'll get it for you."

You, naked on a beach. Her eyes widened, and she slapped a hand over her mouth as another giggle overtook her vocal cords. Emma prayed that she hadn't said that out loud. "Drink. Another drink," she croaked, her face burning.

He grinned. "I'm not so sure you need another one."

"I'm going to get one, even if I have to crawl."

Sliding off the couch onto her knees, she crawled toward the kitchen. Her butt high in the air. He groaned and mumbled something under his breath. She only got a few feet ahead when his strong arms wrapped around her waist. He picked her up and tossed her back on the couch. Emma giggled as she bounced on the cushion.

"You're going to kill me, woman!" Devon growled. "I'll get you the god damn drink."

Her cute butt was utterly tantalizing, and it took all his strength not to lean forward and smack it. It was right there in front of him, the perfect target, making his mouth water. Things were heating up far too quickly for his liking. Well, he liked it and didn't like it at the same time. Devon walked into the kitchen, shaking his head in near defeat. He didn't know how much longer he could restrain himself, but he knew for her sake he had to.

What made it even more difficult was she knew exactly what she was doing, too. He saw the knowledge in her eyes when he put her back on the couch. All proud of how she played him. Shaking his head, he opened the door of the fridge and grabbed another can. He thought about grabbing another for himself but chose against it. If he drank anymore, he would find himself in her bed, and he had far too much respect for her to take advantage of her vulnerability. One day, he hoped to find himself in it, but only when she made the choice by her own sober volition. And that would be a day he would treasure forever.

"Did you get lost in my fridge?" she yelled from the living room.

"I'm coming."

"Already? I'm not even touching you," her sultry voice replied.

Oh hell. He was in trouble.

When he returned, Devon handed her the drink, and Emma made herself right at home by placing her feet on his lap, smiling. "I haven't felt this good in weeks."

Drinking wasn't a strong pastime for her, but now she understood why some people got as carried away as they did. She knew she would pay for it in the morning. But right now, she felt as light as a feather. The strangest part of the day was sitting next to her smoking-hot ex and still feeling the pull that shouldn't be there anymore.

Shamelessly, she watched him, itching to reach out and run her hand over his bare chest. "Forty-one years old, eh? You're an old fuddy duddy now," she said, giggling.

Holy cow. She was a bubbly teenager again.

He grabbed her ankle and grinned at her, wiggling the fingers of his other hand. "Say fuddy duddy one more time. I dare ya."

Her skin warmed under his touch, and it sent a tingling sensation up her calf, traveling to her throbbing core. Her drunk-hazy mind made her feel like she was traveling down a foggy road, only able to see what was directly in front of her.

She didn't care about anything that was in, or beyond, the fog. Emma could see the shadows lurking and hiding, but they were nothing compared to what was right in front of her—the sweetheart from her youth. A bright, intense halo danced around him. His aura, or whatever you call it, beckoned her to play with him.

Oh, god. She desperately wanted to play with the man who made her body sing, 'take me now.' It was like her lady bits wanted to eat him for dinner and swallow his man parts whole. Emma let her eyes roam down his body, stopping at the zipper of his pants, and she wondered what it would be like to run her tongue along his length, like her own personal popsicle.

Giggling, she lifted her gaze to meet his. When she opened her mouth, she had every intention of saying fuddy duddy, but what came out surprised her. "What do you taste like?"

While part of her spirit was mortified by the question, the far more drunk side of her was reveling in it, cheering on her newfound boldness like a cheerleader. It was telling her to test the theory and find out whether he tasted as sweet and as spicy as he looked.

A crooked, oh-so-cute grin spread across his face. "Do you want to find out?"

Devon knew his question was a dangerous one, but the enticing look in her eyes kept drawing him like a moth to a flame. He wasn't anywhere near as drunk as she was. But, god, he wanted her. When their drinking session started, she was wearing a thick blue housecoat, but now he wasn't so lucky. After the third drink, she threw it on the floor, revealing pink shorts and a matching tank top, which were covered in tiny hearts.

Now, she was asking what he tasted like, causing all the blood in his body to flood his groin, making his pants extremely uncomfortable. The limited alcohol in his system was not helping him stay as cool as he had hoped.

She shifted beside him, pulling her legs underneath her body so that she was kneeling instead. Her breasts bounced as she moved, and he ached to reach out and touch them.

Her response to his question was a sexy growl of approval, which didn't help his painful erection any. He knew coming back to her house was going to be difficult, but he had no idea how intoxicating she would be. Her presence heightened every nerve in his body, singing to him like a siren.

There was nothing about her he didn't like, even the cute little heart-shaped mole on her left foot. She sat back on her haunches, her eyes filling with a come-to-me-now look. If he was a gentleman, he would have helped her back into the housecoat, instead of desiring to rip the cute jammies off her body.

"Well, are you going to kiss me or what?" she asked.

There was only one other time her feisty tigress persona came out to play, and that was during their Tropikiwi night. He still didn't know how he remained a virgin by the end of it. And here she was, as sexy as ever, her pink lips parting slightly. All ready to be kissed.

If their lips touched, he knew there would be no going back. His body was already beyond prepared to take her. It was itching to break free and become one with her for the first time.

As he sat there deliberating with himself on the right thing to do versus what he wanted to do, she leaned forward and pressed her soft, moist lips against his.

Chapter Four

The bright light pouring in from the window aroused Emma from her sleep. As soon as she opened her eyes, a monster jab of pain spread across her forehead, forcing her to close them again.

In a desperate attempt to turn away from the light, she rolled over, but her body brushed up against something warm and hard. She froze, her eyes springing open. Lifting her head, her gaze came to rest on Devon's arm draped across her stomach.

She didn't have much time to contemplate the situation before her stomach started rolling, reminding her that drinking was never a good idea. Emma shoved his arm away and stumbled out of bed. Darting toward the washroom, she threw back the toilet seat just in time to toss the drinks from the night before. Tears burned in her eyes as the acid from her stomach rubbed her throat raw. It definitely didn't taste as good coming out as it did going in.

She wasn't sure how long she remained in the bathroom for, but when she opened the door and carefully peeked her squinting eyes around the corner, she noticed that the room was empty. And she hoped like heck that he hadn't seen her run butt-naked to the bathroom.

Had she imagined him there? With her head pounding, she pulled down the blinds and collapsed on the bed, burying her face in the pillows. The whole thing was a freaking nightmare.

"Hmm, love the view."

Shrieking, Emma grabbed the sheets and covered herself. "What the hay!"

Devon was standing in the middle of the doorway with a glass in his hand, wearing only his tight black and blue boxers.

As he approached the bed, she held her hands out in front of her. "Stop!"

He stopped mid-stride, holding the glass a little higher. "Hangover cure and some Advil."

Eyeing him warily, she asked, "Why am I naked? Did we...uh...you know?" *Please, say no. Please, say no.* The very thought of it made her stomach twist, and she covered her mouth as a rancid burp escaped.

"Don't worry. If we ever do, I'm going to make sure you're conscious enough to remember it."

He went to take another step toward her, but she held her hand out again. "Don't. Can you please put the glass on the dresser and give me some space?"

"I promise you, nothing happened."

She wasn't sure if he was telling the truth or not. If they hadn't done anything, why was she naked? Why was he only wearing his boxers? "That would be so much easier to believe if I were dressed."

"I was the perfect gentleman," he said with a grin. "Despite how hard you tried."

Emma pulled the sheets up to her chin, her cheeks heating something fierce. "I would never try to have sex with you."

His stupid, cocky grin widened. "Whatever you say, hun. I'm going to go make some breakfast. Feel free to make an appearance when you're ready."

Picking up a pillow, she hurled it at him. "Forget breakfast. You've done your duty. Just go home already!"

"I don't start work again until Tuesday, so I'm not in a rush."

Groaning, she covered her head with the sheets and waited until she heard the click of the door before coming out from underneath. It felt strange to have him in her house, especially after not seeing him for so long. How did he track her down anyway? The only person in their group who knew where she lived was Nicole.

Picking up her phone, she found her friend's name.

>Did you give Devon my address?

As she waited for a reply, she got up and grabbed the glass off the dresser, quickly swallowing the Advil. Her phone vibrated on the bed. Glancing at the screen, she clicked on her friend's message.

>I wasn't going to, but he looked horrible.

>You should have asked first.

Nicole replied instantly.

>You'd have said no.

Emma couldn't argue with that. If she had wanted Devon to know where she lived, she would have told him.

>He won't leave my house.

Grabbing some clothes out of her dresser, she got dressed as her phone dinged again.

>You should use that to your advantage. Show him what he's been missing all these years.

"He's already seen it," she mumbled. How was she supposed to walk out of her room and face him, knowing he'd seen everything? Her face was going to resemble a cherry tomato.

She shouldn't have let him come back to the house with her. Alone. And she shouldn't have chugged back a hundred cans of alcohol. Sitting on the side of the bed, she buried her pounding head in her hands.

Realizing that she was sitting on the side of the bed that Devon had slept on, she quickly got up and yanked the sheets off the bed. Collapsing to the floor with the sheets on her lap, tears streamed down Emma's cheeks. How could she have slept in bed with another man? If she had really offered herself to Devon last night, she was a whore. A cheater. Everything she despised. "Oh, god."

Three knocks sounded on her bedroom door. "Breakfast is ready, Em."

Despite her nose being plugged, she could smell the aroma of bacon, which caused her stomach to growl and roll at the same time. "I don't want anything."

"Did you have the drink yet?"

"It's gross."

"It'll help."

She sarcastically repeated his words under her breath and then stuck her tongue out at the closed door. He didn't seem to know he wasn't welcome in her home. She couldn't get that point across to him.

Standing up, she plugged her nose and swallowed the rest of the liquid in the glass. He had better be right about the stuff because it was disgusting. It tasted like the ocean with a hint of lemon.

Emma cautiously opened the door and made sure the coast was clear before heading to the laundry room with the bed sheets. By the time she'd thrown the sheets in the wash, her headache was already subsiding as was her acrobatic stomach.

When she was done, she moved down the hallway to the kitchen and stopped as soon as she reached the entryway. A shirtless Devon was standing in front of the sink washing dishes. To his credit, though, he had slipped on a pair of pants while she was hiding in her room.

She swallowed hard as the muscles in his back rippled as he worked. His body bore the proof of a man who made his living out in the sun. His arms were a light red color, and his back had the outline of a muscle shirt.

Clearing her throat, she asked, "Don't you ever wear sunscreen?"

"Yes, but it gets pretty brutal out there sometimes."

"Whereabouts do you work in Alberta?"

"The head office is in Edmonton, but I work in Sylvan Lake. A small town a few hours south of there."

Picking up her plate off the counter, Emma sat down at the table. "How long have you been working there for?"

"A few years now."

"Do you like it?" she asked, biting into a slice of bacon.

"Mostly. It's good money. Are you sure I can't persuade you to come out for a visit? There would be lots of space for you both."

No space would be large enough if he was in it. "Thanks, but no. I don't think that would be a good idea."

"Why not?"

"How can you not know the answer to that?"

Devon stuffed some scrambled eggs into his mouth and then wiped his lips with the pad of his thumb. "Are you saying you don't want to get away from everything for a bit?"

"We couldn't impose," she replied, especially not after she'd apparently thrown herself at him.

"Look. My apartment has two bedrooms and is big enough for all of us. If I promise to give you space, will you come?"

Pushing her chair back from the table, Emma stood up. "While I appreciate your support, I'm not your responsibility."

After saying that, she spun around and left the room. Just as she disappeared around the corner, the sound of glass breaking made Devon jump out of his chair, sailing in Emma's direction.

"Emma?" he called, his heart racing.

"In here," came her strangled reply.

He entered the living room and found her frozen in place, staring at a broken window. At her feet was a rock, with a note attached. She leaned down to pick it up.

Devon grabbed her arm. "Don't touch it. You don't want to tamper with a crime scene."

"What should I do?"

Pulling out his phone, he said, "I'll call the cops."

"Great, just who I want to deal with." Emma looked at her watch.

It was ten-thirty in the morning. "I told Skye that I'd pick her up at noon."

"Call and see if she can stay later."

She picked up her phone and called her daughter, keeping her call brief. The look on her terrified face killed him inside. He watched as she rocked back and forth on her heels, her eyes scanning the room. He wanted to take her in his arms and comfort her, but he doubted she would let him. Instead, he called the cops on her behalf.

Hopefully, this would make her change her mind and come to Alberta with him. Devon didn't feel comfortable going back home alone after this.

"Do you know why anyone would want to do this to you?"

"If I could read the note, it might give me a clue," she snapped. Squeezing her eyes closed, she sighed. "I'm sorry. This has never happened to me before."

Coming up behind her, he placed his hand on her shoulder, giving it a gentle squeeze. "Don't worry. We'll figure this out." He expected her to pull away, but she did the opposite and leaned against him, allowing him to wrap his arms around her.

"Why is all this happening to me?" she asked, her voice barely above a whisper.

Guiding her over to the couch, he helped her sit down and then disappeared into the kitchen to grab a Mike's Hard Root beer and his shirt, which he had discarded on the chair the night before. Slipping on his shirt, he returned to the living room. She was sitting in the exact place he had left her, dazed and horrified, shaking like a leaf.

Devon sat down and held the drink out to her. "Drink this. It'll help."

Her face paled, and Emma shoved it away. "No, thank you. I just got my head out of the toilet."

"A few sips won't have that effect on you, and it will help calm your nerves."

Succumbing to his persuasion, she wrapped her dainty fingers around the can. As their fingertips brushed, it sent a shock up his arm and down to his crotch. Emma shivered, causing the can to shake. The liquid sloshed dangerously close to the newly opened hole in the top.

"Wow," she whispered.

Devon's sentiments exactly. It was nice to know the chemistry between them hadn't diminished over the years, which gave him a slight edge over winning her back. She was stubborn, though, and he knew she would make him grovel on his hands and knees before she willingly opened her heart to him again. That couldn't be his main focus right now, though. Someone threw a rock through her window and that typically wasn't an accident. He wasn't an investigator, but it didn't take a genius to figure out that her life could be in danger. He was going to do everything in his power to keep her safe.

After they sat there for another fifteen minutes in silence, there was a knock on the front door. Emma stood up and stiffly walked across the room to answer it.

"Hi, Emma, I'm Constable McGregor."

She scowled at him, but stepped aside to let him in. Would she ever get the police out of her life? Emma resented them intensely, and even those words did little to explain how she felt about them.

"We heard that someone threw a rock through your window?"

"Incredible. Give the man a prize," she said sarcastically, folding her arms across her chest.

"It's over there, Constable." Devon pointed toward the broken window. "There's a note attached."

Donning the latex gloves that had been hanging out of his back pocket, the officer picked up the rock and removed the note. His eyes moved over the words on the page, and his forehead creased as he frowned. "Did either of you see who threw it?"

"No," Devon answered. "What does it say?"

McGregor turned it around so he could read it. Devon's body stiffened, and his hands closed into tight fists. Emma saw the vein in his neck pulsate from where she stood.

"Shit," Devon mumbled.

"What does it say?" she asked.

When the constable went to walk over to her, Devon stepped in the way, shaking his head. "She doesn't need to see it. She's been through enough already."

Shoving her ex-boyfriend aside, Emma tried to rip the note from the officer's hand, but he held it away from her. "Can't touch it without gloves."

"Let *me* see it," she demanded, enunciating her syllables clearly.

Sighing heavily, the officer showed her the note, and she wished with all her heart she could unsee the words. It read:

'Your husband deserved to die. You're next, bitch.'

Gasping for air, Emma pulled at the collar of her shirt, trying to open her airway. Sharp pains radiated in her upper chest, robbing her of the ability to breathe. With the world spinning around her, she leaned over and rested her hands on her knees.

"Stubborn woman," Devon said softly, as he rubbed her back.

"Who...what...why," she asked between shallow breaths.

"You forgot where and when," he said in a lousy attempt to lighten the mood, earning him a glare. "Sorry."

"We'll take both pieces of evidence down to forensics," Constable McGregor said, "and see if we can pull off any prints. In the meantime, I'll have a patrol car come by as often as possible to help keep an eye on things."

Emma sat on the couch and nodded her head. Her body numb. She couldn't get the words out of her head. Why would anyone think her husband deserved to die? He didn't do anything wrong. And why would they want her dead? What did she have to do with anything? The whole situation left her baffled, confused, and downright scared.

Devon walked with the cop to the door and spoke with him briefly outside. She heard them mumbling but couldn't make out what they were saying. In a way, she didn't mind her ex-boyfriend's help. Yet at the same time, she wished he'd disappear back into their virtual world. She was fine with their only contact being on the internet. Physical contact was a whole other matter. Her emotions were a wreck, and she knew if he stuck around, she'd grow to rely on him and then hate herself for being so weak.

The pains in her chest were finally beginning to subside, but she couldn't stop shaking. It was like her body had become her own personal vibrator and not in a good way either. Emma stared at the Mike's Hard Root beer on the coffee table and decided that drinking the rest of it wouldn't do any harm. If it stopped the dreadful feeling coursing through her system, then it was worth it. As she picked up the can, Devon walked through the door and closed it behind him.

"Is he gone?" she asked.

"Yep. Are you okay?"

She shrugged her shoulders and wrapped her arms around herself, rubbing her hands up and down her arms, trying to ease the cold chill passing through her body. She didn't want to speak, afraid that she'd start crying like a baby.

Devon sat on the couch beside her and wrapped his arm around her shoulder, pulling her close. "I'm here for you."

She stayed in his arms for a moment, relishing in his comfort, but it wasn't his place to offer it to her. They weren't together anymore, which brought all her emotions full circle again.

Pulling away, she put some distance between them. "You should probably go."

He grabbed her arm, effectively stopping her. "There is no way I'm leaving you alone after that," he said, raising his voice.

She attempted to pull away from him, but to no avail. "You made that choice once before. I'm sure you can do it again."

"If you think I could leave after a death threat, you don't know me too well."

"That's right. I don't," she said, with a hint of ice in her voice. "You're like a stranger to me."

Pain flashed through his eyes as he released her, shoving his hands into the pockets of his pants. "Okay, I deserved that."

"You deserve that and much more. You broke my heart, Devon. You threw me away like trash and didn't even have the decency to tell me to my face. Now, you show up during the worst time of my life and expect me to welcome you back? I just lost my husband, and unlike you, I don't plan on moving on so quickly."

"I—"

She cut him off. "No, save it. I don't want to hear it. I just want you to leave," she said, her chin wobbling. If she didn't run out of the room now, she was going to bawl her eyes out. She turned to leave, but he grabbed her arm again. Looking up at him, she intended to tell him to shove it where the sun don't shine, but the tears forming in his eyes made her bite her tongue.

He wiped the tears with his sleeve, but his eyes quickly filled again. "You were so beautiful, so innocent, and I treated you like shit." He reached out and ran his thumb across her cheek. "I've regretted it every day of my life. I'm so sorry."

"Why'd you do it?"

"It doesn't matter now."

"It does to me. Why?" she asked again.

He motioned toward the couch, and they both sat down. Devon took her hands in his, lazily running his index finger across her palm. "I don't even know how to explain it. You were almost too perfect, like an angel sent from heaven, and the feelings I had were anything but angel-like. I got scared of corrupting you and ran."

"Let me see if I understand this correctly. You dumped me because you thought I was too perfect?" Emma pulled her hand away and moved to the recliner next to the couch. She couldn't think with him holding her hand.

"I know, I know. It's a stupid reason."

She didn't know whether to believe his pathetic excuse. "That doesn't explain why you refused to make a move on our last date. You had time to think about it by then."

"I didn't feel like I deserved someone like you, especially after the way I treated you."

"Someone like me?"

"Ya, you were this church-going, undefiled, sweet, beautiful girl."

"So, in other words, you got bored of me, and that's why you went after the girl at your restaurant instead." When he gave her a blank look, she continued, "Your brother told me you liked a girl at work."

Understanding dawned in his eyes. "He must have been trying to come up with an excuse."

"Why didn't you talk to me yourself? You owed me that much."

"I couldn't bear to see the hurt in your eyes."

"Yet you decided to come back and make me relive it after all this time. How's that any different?"

"I'm not the same person I was back then. I lived without you for twenty years, and it was the worst decision of my life." He got up off the couch and kneeled in front of her, taking her hands in his, his eyes still damp with tears. "I want you back."

Emma's rosy cheeks paled, and she froze, her eyes widening. Less than a second later, she was scrambling over the arm of the chair, putting sufficient distance between them.

"No. No. No," she mumbled, shaking her head vigorously. "We can't. I can't."

She reminded Devon of a deer caught in the headlights. He knew he had to take this slow and was doing a lousy job. She wasn't ready for another relationship. Being her friend was all that would work for now.

"I'm not talking about right now, sweetheart."

Fire swam in her hazel eyes as she walked up to him, poking him in the chest. "Don't call me sweetheart! Do you really think you can waltz back into my life and pick up where we left off?"

That's exactly what he had been hoping, but he kept his mouth shut and let her rant, knowing it's what she needed to do.

"Let me repeat myself. I just lost my husband. *My wonderful, amazing husband.* Just in case you didn't hear me the first time. All I care about is him. What the friggin' heck is wrong with you?" She pounded her fists against his chest, crying, "You tore my heart out in high school, and you think I'm magically going to fall into your arms again? I left town because of you. Damn it. Damn you."

He wrapped his arms around her, trapping her arms against his chest to prevent her from continuing to hit him. "I was stupid to let you go," he said softly.

For the first time, he saw the depth of her turmoil and the longing that existed in her eyes before she buried her face against his chest, her shoulders shaking. How had he missed seeing it before? Was it always there, and he was just too clueless to see it?

"I'm sorry." The words didn't do her situation justice, but it was all he had. "I'm sorry for hurting you, for leaving you. And I'm sorry for your loss," he said huskily, his throat quickly clogging as more tears fell down his cheeks.

"I loved you—him." Emma shoved herself away from Devon's embrace. Confusion written all over her face. "Him. I loved him." Turning, she fled down the hall and into her room.

He didn't follow her. Instead, he plopped his ass back on the couch and ran his hands down his face. He'd let the cat out of the bag sooner than he planned. His damn impatience may have ruined his one and only chance to get back in her good graces. The only sliver of hope he had left was that she hadn't kicked him out of her house yet.

"Slow down, dickhead," Devon muttered.

Emma had every right not to let him back into her life again. He should be thankful she allowed him to get this far. But what if she didn't want to be anything more than friends? Could he be satisfied with that? The thought created an empty feeling deep inside his gut, making him nauseous. Picking up the controller, he turned on the television, hoping to entertain himself while he waited for her appearance.

Chapter Five

Emma paced back and forth across her room, her bosom burning. "Of all the nerve!" She knew from the minute he had shown up on her porch that he had more on his agenda than he had let on. It was so like him to hide things from her.

Given all that had happened in the last twenty-four hours, she should have realized it. Heck, they had woken up together in bed. His intentions couldn't have been any clearer. Glancing at her unmade bed, her cheeks reddened. A picture of it in the dumpster flashed across her mind.

"That might not be a bad idea," she mumbled.

What was her drunk self thinking, letting Devon sleep in her marriage bed? Had she forgotten her husband so quickly? Emma sat down on the edge of the bed and twisted the wedding ring on her left hand. Why couldn't her life be as simple as the gold band on her finger?

Was that part of her life really over? She still couldn't wrap her head around it all. How could Peter really be gone? She'd given him nineteen years of her life. It felt like someone had rolled over her with a bulldozer. Nothing made sense anymore. And now, Devon has magically shown up after twenty-odd years. She half expected the 'Hidden Camera' television show to jump out and surprise her by bringing her husband back, and then finding out that Devon was in on the gag somehow.

She knew that was wishful thinking. She had watched them close the coffin that contained her husband before lowering it into the ground. He looked like he was sleeping, except his chest wasn't rhythmically moving up and down, and he wasn't snoring.

Emma rubbed at the ache growing inside her, which was getting stronger with each passing second. Laying down on the bed, she wrapped her arms around a pillow and hugged it against her chest.

"Please let this all be a bad dream," she whispered to the invisible ghosts in the room. Sometimes she hoped it was her in a coma and that she'd wake up one day and Peter would be perfectly fine. That was a reoccurring dream she had, except everything remained the same when she woke up in the real world, and reality stung every time.

Exhausted and tired, she closed her eyes.

Startled awake by a knock on her bedroom door, Emma bolted upright.

"I'm ordering pizza," Devon said through the door. "What kind do you like?"

She and Skye usually ordered cheese pizza. But Emma knew that wasn't typically a guy's favorite, and since it was just going to be the two of them, she said, "Order whatever you want."

Her thoughts drifted to her baby girl. Skye was the reason Emma got out of bed every morning and the driving force that got her through the day. Reaching over, she grabbed the phone off the side table and dialed Stephanie's home number. She wanted to make sure her daughter knew why she had to stay another night.

When a woman answered the phone, Emma asked, "Is Skye there?"

"Just a moment," the woman replied. In the background, Emma heard people talking and laughing and instantly missed the carefree life she used to have. Now, worry, fear, and every other crappy emotion one could think of filled her heart.

"Are you sure it's okay if she stays another night?" Emma asked Stephanie's mom.

"It's no problem at all. She's a delightful girl."

It wasn't long before her daughter's heavy footsteps echoed through the phone.

"Here's Skye," the woman said.

"Mom?"

The relief that filled her soul when she heard her daughter's voice surprised Emma.

"Hi, sweetheart. How's everything going?" Emma asked.

"Okay, I guess," she said, then paused a moment before continuing, "Why can't I come home?"

Unsure of exactly how much to say, she kept it simple. "Someone broke the window, and it's a big—"

Multiple loud bangs, like firecrackers, interrupted their phone call, making her jump. Not more than a quarter of a second later, the window beside her shattered into a thousand pieces, followed by another set of rapid bangs. Screaming, she rolled off the bed and ducked for cover.

Emma curled in a ball, making herself as small as possible. Her daughter yelled for her through the phone, which had ended up on the floor by the door. Crawling over, she picked it up.

"Mom, are you..."

A car outside screeched its tires as it sped away, drowning out Skye's voice.

"I'm fine, sweetheart. I want you to stay inside. Don't go out anywhere tonight. Do you understand?"

"Why? What happened?"

"I'm not sure, but please listen to me, okay?"

"I want to come home," her daughter begged, crying.

"Tell me you understand."

"Yes, but—"

"No buts. I'll be by as soon as I can to pick you up. Love you, sweetheart."

It wasn't long before she heard feet running down the hallway.

"Emma!" Devon yelled, pounding on the door. "Emma, answer me."

"Hang on," she said to him as she crawled over to the door, staying low. After she opened it, she joined him in the hallway. Standing up, she pressed her back against the wall. "What the heck was that?"

"Gunshots. Were you hit?" he asked.

"Holy shit!" She wrapped her arms tightly around her waist and slid down the wall, her butt hitting the floor. "Someone wants me dead. Oh, my god. Someone actually wants me dead."

Emma's face was ashen white, her body shaking. Devon kneeled in front of her, checking for wounds. Satisfied that she was unhurt, he cradled her clammy cheeks in his palms. "I won't let anything happen to you. I promise."

"Someone...someone shot at my house. At me. Wh-what if he finds Skye?" she asked. "What if—"

He placed a finger against her lips. "We're going to pick her up, but I have to make sure the coast is clear. I want you to lock yourself in the bathroom and call 911, okay?"

"Don't leave me!" she cried, grabbing onto his arm with a death grip.

"I'll be back for you. I won't leave you this time."

"Promise?"

Leaning forward, he kissed her hard. "I promise," he murmured against her cool lips. It wasn't easy pulling away from her. He wanted to gather her in his arms and never let go, but that had to wait until they were safe. "Now go."

"Be careful."

"I always am."

When she was safely in the bathroom, he turned toward the living room. Rage built up inside him as he neared the front door. The creep had better hope the police find him first because Devon wouldn't show him any mercy. He wanted to strangle the guy with his bare hands for threatening Emma's life.

She hadn't really told him what happened to her husband, but he knew she was the last person in the world who deserved to be treated this way. He cautiously approached the broken window beside the front door and peeked outside.

The coast appeared clear. He didn't understand why the asshole didn't break into the house and kill them if they really wanted her dead. Was the guy just playing with them? Whatever the case, Devon was going to make sure they didn't have another chance to mess with her life. She was coming to Alberta with him, one way or another. If he had to, he'd carry her to his car. It didn't take long before sirens filled the air.

When the first cruiser pulled up to the front of the house, he went back to get Emma. The minute he knocked on the door, she barreled out of the bathroom and into his arms, knocking the wind out of him.

"You're okay!" she cried breathlessly.

"Told you I wasn't going anywhere."

"Shut up," she said with a relieved smile that removed any animosity from the words themselves.

"Come on. The cops are here." He took her hand, her fingers trembling as they curled around his.

They watched as three more cop cars came to a stop in front of her place. One car had dogs in the back. A group of them approached the house with guns in their hands as they surveyed the area.

"He's gone," Devon told them.

The same constable from earlier approached them, asking, "What happened?"

"Someone shot out her bedroom window."

"Did you see anything suspicious in the area after I left?"

She and Devon shook their heads. They'd been too distracted by their conversation to keep watch, which is what they should have been doing after the rock went sailing through her living room window.

"We heard tires squeal, but that's it," Devon told Constable McGregor.

"Can we come inside and look around?" the man asked.

Begrudgingly, Emma stepped aside to let them in. Why was all this happening to her? She just wanted to be left alone and not keep having the cops barge into her home. If she could do without them, she would. But in a case like this, she had no choice but to let them do their job. Her life had been thoroughly invaded, and she was struggling to keep up. Dirty footprints littered her carpet as officers wandered around taking pictures and gathering evidence.

Constable McGregor watched his crew work as he stood beside Devon. "Are you sure you didn't see anything?"

Devon shook his head again. "I was more interested in making sure Emma was okay."

"Do you have a security system installed, Emma?" McGregor asked.

"Yes, but no cameras."

"We'll speak with the owners across the street and see if they have any cameras." McGregor motioned for one of his men to come over. "Once my guys are done, I suggest getting those windows fixed as soon as possible."

"No duh, Sherlock," she snapped.

Devon placed a hand on her shoulder, giving it a gentle squeeze. "Easy, Em. They're just trying to help."

"I'm tired of needing their help."

"Hang in there. We'll get through this," he said.

She wanted to say there was no *we* but couldn't bring herself to say the words and nodded instead. He was trying so hard to be help-ful, and she was being downright horrible to him.

Her phone vibrated in her hand. Her daughter was calling. How was she supposed to bring Skye back to the house with a crazy psycho on the loose?

Emma answered the call. "Hey, Skye."

"What happened?" her daughter asked, her voice shaking slightly.

She wondered how much to tell her fourteen-year-old kid. The last thing she wanted to do was frighten her. "Some people thought it would be amusing to break another window."

Devon grunted and pulled the cell phone out of her hand. "We're coming to get you. You guys can stay with me," he blurted as she fought to get the phone back.

Skye squealed with excitement. "Can we, Mom, please?"

Emma had to hold the phone away from her ear. "That was low, Devon," she said in a hushed tone, sticking her tongue out at him.

A grin spread across that annoyingly cute face of his, and he hooked his thumbs through the belt loops on his pants as if to say, *there's no way you can say no now.* She hated that he put her on the spot.

"Can I call you back, Skye?"

"Mom, please say yes. Please, please, pleeease!" Skye pleaded.

"Don't you know any other word in the English dictionary?" Emma complained.

"Want to hear me say the longest word again? Pneumonoultra—"

"Oh, shush." She pinched the bridge of her nose in frustration, knowing she was fighting a losing battle. "All right, we'll go." Looking over at Devon, she mouthed, "I'm going to get you for this."

Chapter Six

After a few phone calls and an hour or two of waiting, a window repair man arrived and fixed both windows in a relatively short period of time, which worked well for Devon. He wanted to be on the road as soon as possible. It was dark already.

"You haven't slept all day. It's not safe to drive," she warned as they continued packing the car. "Let's sleep tonight and leave in the morning."

"And give you time to change your mind?" He picked up the last piece of luggage, tossing it in the trunk. "Hell, no."

"I don't know why you're insisting that we take your car."

"Whoever is targeting you knows your car, so you might as well leave it behind."

"That means we're stuck until you decide to bring us back."

"You'll be fine, I promise."

She studied him, confusion wrinkling her cute forehead. "I find it odd. None of this started until you showed up."

"Maybe it's another jealous boyfriend who wants you back."

"Ya sure, like I had plenty of those," she said, rolling her eyes. "I'm serious, Devon."

Taking her hand, he led her to the stairs by the door outside. He wanted to be mad at her for making that assumption, but after all she's been through, he couldn't blame her.

Devon cupped her chin and gently made her look up at him, their eyes meeting. "Look at me and tell me what you see."

Studying his eyes under the dim porch light, Emma found fear. Good to honest fear and genuine compassion lurking in their depths. One other emotion fluttered through them, but she couldn't name it, or maybe she didn't want to. She glanced away, uncomfortable with their close proximity.

"Fine." She stood up and wiped the dust off the seat of her pants. "Let's do this."

Her house wasn't exactly in the shape she wanted it. The dirt-covered carpet had seen better days. Glass was still on the floor by the windows, but at least the dishes were in the dishwasher and the windows had been repaired. She wouldn't win the June Cleaver Award or Mother of the Month, but oh well. She and her daughter would be safe for now.

Although she wasn't exactly sure how safe her heart would be. Devon may not be the one out to kill her, but he still might be the one who caused her heart to stop beating if she allowed him to have power over it. Emma knew he would try relentlessly, and she had every intention of fighting back with a big fat no.

Climbing into the passenger seat, she put on her seatbelt and watched him out of the corner of her eye, trying not to be overly obvious. How did she wind up agreeing to go with him?

Oh, right.

Devon opened his mouth and offered the trip he knew her daughter wanted. Skye had wanted the opportunity to get away from everything and everyone.

"Underhanded weasel," she muttered under her breath.

She was a little nervous about calling Mrs. Jackson in the morning. The woman was anything but forgiving and would likely fire her for taking off again. But she couldn't say the thought of being fired bothered her as much now as it did before she spoke to Mr. Moore. The settlement that was bound to come from her husband's accident would give her a little breathing room.

Currently, she worked as a Freight Coordinator. Not exactly the most glamorous job, and it was beyond stressful to boot, but it paid the bills. There was a time when she liked the position, but lately, her heart wasn't in it. If she was honest with herself, she didn't want to do it anymore.

"What was that?" Devon asked.

"What was what?"

"You said something."

"Oh, I called you an underhanded weasel."

Devon shook his head and laughed as he signaled to pull out onto the road. "You're just finding that out?"

"Maybe I should change my mind."

"Too late. We're on the move now."

Brain fog descended over her, making her tipsy as though she'd had a drink or two. Everything had an unrealistic feel to it, like a dream. Her life was barely recognizable anymore.

Devon reached over and gave her knee a squeeze. "It'll work out, you'll see."

Emma gave him a guarded smile and then removed his hand from her knee, which tingled under his touch. She knew exactly how he wanted things to work out, but it wasn't on her agenda. They'd had their time under the sun, and he had conveniently decided she wasn't the one for him.

She'd made partial peace with that a long time ago, and if her marriage taught her anything, it was that loss was inevitable. Everyone she loved would eventually leave, whether it be walking away or death, and she wasn't a glutton for that type of punishment. All she needed or wanted was Skye.

"Can we set some rules, please?" she asked.

"Like what?"

"Like keeping your hands to yourself, for starters."

"What if I don't want to?"

"Then just turn around and take me home."

He tightened his grip on the steering wheel. "That's not an option, and you know it."

She knew it and totally despised the current predicament she found herself in. Crossing her arms, she turned and stared out the window at the houses passing by. This was her home. They'd built a life here. Now, it felt like a stranger's world.

"Any other rules?" he asked.

"If I think of anymore, I'll let you know."

The chances of him following her no touching rule were probably next to none. One part of her wanted him to test the rules, but the other wanted him to keep his distance. Being under the same roof with him would not be easy.

Heaven help her.

Around six in the morning, Devon's eyes grew heavy. They were still another four hours away from their destination. He pulled into a rest stop and laid his chair back, deciding to rest his eyes for an hour or two. The previous day had made him more exhausted than he realized, packing quite the wallop on his all senses.

He couldn't believe someone attacked Emma. Not only did she have to face losing her husband, but now she had a crazy psycho after her. He didn't know exactly what happened, but it had been his understanding that her husband was innocent in the whole ordeal. He was going to do everything in his power to keep her safe and hidden from the madman until he was caught. Hopefully, during that time, he'd earn her love again. Truthfully, she had every right to refuse his advances.

He glanced at her. Her seat was reclined, and she was half on her side, with her hair falling over her face, sound asleep. Reaching over, he brushed the stray hairs behind her ear, giving him a good look at her beautiful, innocent face.

No matter how long he lived, she would always be the one. There was no one like his sweet, angelic Emma. She wasn't the teenage sweetheart he'd left behind anymore, but the essence of who she was would never change. Her heart was still as sweet as honey and as pure as gold. That's what made her stand out from the rest.

He always liked how she didn't listen to what the magazines had to say about how a woman should look. Her room wasn't cluttered with make-up or all the other things that women believed they needed to be beautiful. And she didn't spend hours getting ready to go anywhere. Yet she still had an untouched exquisiteness about her.

Maybe it was because she didn't try so hard to be someone she wasn't. She was real and true to herself. Nothing fake about her. That quality appealed to him more than any other.

Turning, he glanced at Skye in the backseat, and a pit lodged in his throat. She should have been their daughter. She looked like a spitting image of Emma's younger self, albeit Skye's hair color was lighter than her mom's, and she wasn't as short.

Devon knew their chance of having kids was coming to an end, and it pained him that they may never share that opportunity due to his immature idiot self. They weren't spring chickens anymore. She was turning forty this year and had probably already taken measures to prevent anymore kids. But whether or not they had that opportunity, he wanted to spend the rest of his life with her.

Closing his eyes, he drifted off to sleep, slipping into a world where dreams could become reality. Where everything under the stars was his for the taking, including the woman of his dreams. His toes sank in the white sand of a beach that went on for miles. The sun was low over the horizon and an array of pink and purple hues filled the sky, creating a photographer's dream. He wasn't looking at the sky, though.

Emma stood in front of him wearing a silk see-through shawl overtop of a short, figure-hugging red dress, her hair fluttering in the breeze. Her eyes sparkled like the ocean beside her, and an enchanting smile played across her lips as she walked toward him. Her beauty masked the spectacular sunset.

As she neared him, Emma reached for her shawl, letting it fall to the ground. He wanted to move toward her, but he couldn't make his legs move. His body wouldn't listen to his brain's command. It was frozen like a statue. He wanted to touch her and hold her in his arms. She stopped just out of his reach, but close enough for her delicate sweet scent to wrap around him, making him ache to taste her.

"Come closer," he begged.

Instead of listening, she tilted her head and sent Devon a hot, sultry look. He felt like he was staring at a magazine centerfold, one you could look at but couldn't touch. He wanted to hold her so badly his hands were tingling, and that wasn't the only thing responding to the sight before him. Desire had all his blood flowing in one direction, right to his groin.

He tried to reach out to her, but she shook her head, her smile widening as she ran her hands through her hair and slowly down her body. His eyes followed her hands. When she reached for the spot between her thighs, he moaned in frustration.

She raised the backside of her dress and hooked her thumbs into her black lace panties, sliding them down. Once it was in her hand, she twirled it around her finger and then tossed the panties his way, smacking him square in the face.

He caught a slight whiff of her womanly smell. "Oh, god." Damn it. He still couldn't move. Why wasn't he in control of his own body? Instead, he was merely a spectator in her game.

Emma giggled. She knew exactly what she was doing to him as she stayed out of his reach, walking behind him. He couldn't even turn around. The only thing moving was his cock straining against his shorts. He expected her to touch him, but she didn't, and it irritated him to no end. He couldn't see what she was doing. Pushing against the invisible force holding him, he tried to move. Anything to get out of the jail he was in, but it was useless.

A second later, her sexy red dress went flying over his head, falling to the ground in front of him. Her black bra quickly followed, which she dangled over his shoulder before dropping it.

"Unleash your hold on me, woman," he groaned. Knowing she was naked behind him made his shorts increasingly uncomfortable. He couldn't even adjust himself.

Pressing herself up against him, she let her fingers run along his hips until they reached the button of his shorts, her hardened nipples flush against his back. His skin heated under her touch.

She undid his belt and slipped her hand inside, letting her fingers wrap around his pulsating erection as she ran her thumb across the sensitized head. Bringing her lips close to his ear, she said huskily, "And to think you were foolish enough to let me go."

By the time she said the last three words, her voice was barely a whisper, and her touch was fading like the morning mist. The clothes on the ground sunk into the sand by his feet. The invisible ropes that prevented him from moving released him, and he spun around. Her appearance was that of a spirit, see-through and ghostly, and then she was gone.

"Emma," he yelled.

"I'm here."

Closing his eyes, he shook his head. When he opened them, he wasn't on the beach anymore. He was in his car, and Emma was looking at him curiously, her eyes drifting down to his pants.

"You might want to cover up," she said.

Chapter Seven

Devon's face turned crimson as he reached between the seats for his jacket, giving Emma a cheeky grin. "It's called a morning woody, darling."

"I don't need a lesson in men's anatomy, especially not now." Emma glanced over her shoulders to make sure Skye was still sleeping. "My daughter is in the backseat, remember?"

"We'll continue the lesson later," he said, winking.

"Absolutely not."

"It could be fun."

Emma crossed her legs, attempting to ease the ache caused by his tent pole. He was obviously well-endowed in that department, but she was determined not to make a fool of herself again. "No, thanks."

"You know you want me."

"In your dreams."

"Even there you're stubborn," he grumbled.

She coughed as laughter bubbled inside her. "Good to know." Emma almost kept a reign on her emotions but ended up bursting out laughing.

"What's so funny?" Skye asked, yawning.

"I was just telling your mom—"

Emma decked him in the shoulder.

"Ouch," he said, feigning hurt by rubbing his shoulder. "You shouldn't bite the hand driving you."

If she had her way, she would have driven herself. At least then she'd have a means of escape, but chances were high that the perpetrator knew her car.

Wait a darn minute.

Wouldn't the shooter know Devon's car, too? He was the one who drove her to the funeral, graveside, and back again.

"I guess we should get on the road," he said, glancing at the clock on the dash. He turned the engine on and pulled out of his parking spot.

Sneaky twerp. And the annoying thing was he knew it, and he appeared to enjoy being a manipulative son of a gun. He would have done anything to get her to go with him. She almost felt like she was being taken hostage, and yet her body hummed with the excitement of what was to come. She couldn't seem to do anything to stop her needs, her wants. And her body still wanted the man who dumped her, and she couldn't understand why.

She wished she could go back in time and tell herself to ignore his initial text message. Her husband deserved her loyalty and not whatever was happening here. Again, she slugged Devon in the shoulder and not a light tap either. She grew up with two brothers and knew how to punch.

Grabbing her hand, he brought it to rest on his right leg. "Hey, what was that for?"

"For good measure." Emma tried to pull her hand away, but he held it securely.

"Nope, I think I'll just hold it a while," he said. "I don't recall you being quite this feisty before."

"I can be a lot more than feisty if you don't let go of my hand."

"You wouldn't try anything," he said, grinning. "I'm driving."

"That doesn't mean I won't wipe that smirk off your face when we stop," she replied, glaring at him.

"I look forward to it." He gave her hand an intimate squeeze.

"I could yell out the window, you know."

"But you won't."

Growling, Emma said, "You make me crazy."

Devon laughed. "You sounded exactly like Marge Simpson."

"Shut up."

"You really did, Mom." Skye said, piping up from the backseat.

"I liked it better when you were sleeping," Emma said, trying hard to glare at her daughter but failing miserably. She knew she sounded like Marge.

"How much longer?" her daughter asked.

"Around four hours, depending on construction," Devon said.

That was four hours too long to be cooped up with Mr. Annoying Butt. She couldn't believe she actually took her clothes off in front of him. That was something she had never done in high school. Weren't you supposed to have more control over your hormones with age? She was going in the opposite direction with a man who shouldn't even be on her radar. Someone was screwing with her senses and having a heyday with it. She wasn't ready, and she didn't think she ever would be.

Peter had been her world. Her life. A hollow feeling settled deep within her heart, and she felt a familiar lump clawing its way up her throat as tears filled her eyes. *No.* She didn't want to start bawling, especially not with Devon sitting beside her.

"What are you thinking about?" he asked.

"About how I want you to let go of my hand," she said, her voice slightly trembling.

"I let go a few minutes ago."

Looking down, she found her hand still resting on his leg. Totally free. Both of Devon's hands were on the steering wheel. Releasing him like a hot potato, she stuffed her hand between her crossed legs, her face burning.

"I think I like that position better," he said, looking down at her legs.

Red as a fire hydrant, Emma crossed her arms instead, unconsciously pushing up her breasts. His eyes, filled with a look of appreciation, drifted to her chest.

"Eyes on the road, buster. Geez Louise!"

Shrugging his shoulders, he said, "I'm a man. What can I say?"

"Sit up, Skye," Emma ordered.

"Why?"

Unhooking her seatbelt, she said, "I'm joining you back there."

"But, Mom, I want to sleep."

"You can sleep when we get there."

Leaving no room for argument, Emma climbed into the backseat with the car on the move. Devon slapped her butt on the way by.

"Sorry, it was the perfect target." He looked at her through the rear-view mirror, smirking.

She gave him her best 'I'm going to get you look' before averting her eyes. Didn't the man know the meaning of the word boundaries? Her body wasn't his to touch, and she would make that abundantly clear before the day was out.

Just not while her daughter was in earshot.

Devon drove into Sylvan Lake and wished he could keep on driving. Emma had refused to look directly at him for the rest of the trip, evading his eyes. Mostly, she pretended to be asleep, but he knew better. He would catch her peeking at him now and then. He was pretty certain she either wanted to kill him or kiss him.

The look in her eyes mystified him enough that he didn't want to find out. He was stuck between being a coward that hides his tail between his legs, and being the adventurer, who was willing to go through perilous trials trying to get up the mountain. But right now, she appeared as daunting as Mount Everest. He spent about thirty minutes driving through town, avoiding his driveway like the plague.

"How come you're driving in circles?" Emma asked him.

Crap. He'd been found out. Clearing his throat, he said, "You guys looked so peaceful back there. I didn't want to disturb you."

"If it's all the same as you, I feel like a sardine in here."

"You could always join me in the front."

"Just park the darn car."

"As you wish, mi'lady," Devon said, giving her a salute. After he drove a few more blocks, he pulled into the parking lot of his three-story building. Looking into the backseat, he saw both their eyes on him. "We're here."

It was an older nineteen-seventies apartment with brown wooden paneling that desperately needed loving care or at the very least a good pressure washing. The second and third-floor apartments had balconies that jutted out from the front of the building, with matching brown railings. The railing panels were close enough together that kids couldn't fall through, which was exactly what he was looking for at the time.

He knew it wasn't the Ritz Carlton, but it served its purpose. Rent was good, and he had more than enough space for his kids. He missed them like crazy and couldn't wait to see them. Two more weeks and Emma could meet them.

Walking around to the trunk of the car, he opened it and grabbed their luggage. Devon was shocked at how lightly Emma packed. Most women he knew would take their entire closet with them. But then again, she wasn't *most women.*

That's probably why he was drawn to her. She was in a league all her own, not afraid to be her own person. He was thrilled that she wouldn't spend all morning in his bathroom, following a strict make-up ritual.

Emma reached for her suitcase, but he rolled it away from her. "I'm not an invalid. I can take my own bag."

"I got it." He closed the trunk and turned to walk toward the building.

They trailed behind him into the building, through the hallway, and up the stairs to his apartment on the second floor. A light Febreeze smell replaced the usual stale air. It was a pleasant surprise as they walked through the brightly lit hallways.

Devon stopped in front of his place. "This is it."

Emma couldn't help but wonder what it looked like behind the door, given it was a bachelor's cave. She held her breath as he opened it, half expecting to find naked woman magazines all over the place.

To her surprise, the place was spotless. There were a few men magazines on the table. And yes, one with scantily clad women, but nothing was out of place or particularly objectionable. "A man does live here, right?" she asked.

"Part of the time, anyway. I'm away a lot."

"When do you head out next?"

"I work again on Tuesday, but I'll try to stay close to home while you're here."

"Don't change things on my account." If he was gone, she'd be able to gain some control over the waterfall of emotions coursing through her. She felt completely out of her element. Nothing in her life was normal. Yet being with him had an old familiarity to it that she missed more than she realized. She despised him for barging his way back into her world and reminding her of what was and what could have been.

The last thing she wanted was for him to change his routine and stay home. She'd rather have time by herself to process everything. He was like this big question mark in her life. Did she even want him in her life? She was fine with the Facebook thing, but actually staying with him she wasn't sure about.

Pushing open a door, he led them inside a bedroom. "You guys can stay in here,"

Emma examined the door handle and groaned. The door had no

lock. Nothing to keep him out. "Does the other bedroom have a lock?"

"Yes."

"Can we stay in there instead?"

"You want to sleep in bed with me?" He laughed when her face turned red. "I love making you blush."

"Other you room." She smacked her forehead. *Idiot.* "I mean, you can take this room, and we'll sleep in yours. Wipe that smug look off your face, darn it," she snapped, stomping her foot.

"What look?" he asked, grinning. The 'you want me, and you know it' look grew more apparent in his features.

She pointed at him. "That one right there. Stop it!"

Skye stood there, watching the two of them interact with an unsure look on her face. "Can I go exploring?"

"I don't know," Emma said hesitantly. Without her daughter there, there was no saying what the man would try.

"Let her go," he encouraged, holding out his key to Sky. "Here's my key to get back in."

"Thanks." Without waiting for her mom's response, Skye took off out the door.

"Hey, wait," Emma yelled, but she was two seconds too late. Why couldn't her daughter move that fast in the morning when it was time to go to school? Putting her hands on her hips, she turned to face enemy number one. "She's my daughter, not yours. Do you understand? I make the decisions, not you."

He shrugged his shoulders and then walked away. She followed him, hot on his heels, as he moved through the living room and into the walk-through kitchen.

"Did you hear what I said?"

"Want a drink?"

"Answer the darn question."

"Fine, I'll have one," he said, taking a bottle of whisky from the fridge. For a moment the room was quiet, until he spoke again. "Do you ever wonder what it would have been like if we had kids together?"

Emma pushed away the yearning that threatened to surface. It was a topic she'd pondered many times in the past, even during her marriage, which made her feel like a lousy wife. "Devon, let's not go there, please."

"Why not?"

"You keep trying to discuss our non-existent relationship."

"Doesn't feel so non-existent to me," he said, locking eyes with her.

Every emotion under the sun flew back and forth in her eyes. Hatred. Anger. Love. Lust.

"I still love you," he said softly.

"Damn it," she cried, plugging her ears. "Stop it. Just flipping stop it."

Devon came around the island and stood in front of her. "And I think a small part of you still loves me, too."

Clenching her jaw, she looked up at him. "That means noth—"

Leaning in, he kissed her words into oblivion. Emma shoved him away immediately and wiped her lips.

"Can't you give me room to breathe!" she cried, her voice catching as she struggled to keep control. "This isn't some darn romance movie. I'm not going to fall into your arms just because you kiss me and tell me you love me."

He backed off and held up his hands. "Sorry."

"Don't you get it? I just lost my husband. I don't want another relationship, with you or with anyone right now." Walking to the couch, she sat down and buried her face in her hands, crying. Devon sat down beside her and tried to console her, but she shied away from him. "I've had enough loss to last a lifetime."

"I'm being an insensitive jackass. I'm sorry," he said softly.

Emma looked up at him, knowing she looked horrible with red eyes and all. "I need a friend. Can you handle that?"

"Anything for you, hun."

The words flowed so easily off his lips that she wanted desperately to believe him, but she knew better. If he didn't eventually get what he wanted, he'd give up and walk away, like he did before. She wasn't stupid enough to think the lines he gave her were the real reason they broke up. Almost too perfect for him? All right. Okay. Did he think she was born yesterday?

Standing up, she took a few steps away before turning to face him. "Anything for me, eh? What about my no touching rule?"

"Sorry, but your butt was so tempting."

Wagging her finger at him, she said, "My butt, mister, is my butt."

Devon locked eyes with her, and the corner of his mouth curled into that sexy grin that always made her heart flutter. "Hence why I like it so much."

"Stop that!"

The other side of his mouth joined in the grin, and he shot her a hot, spicy look. "Stop what?"

"That!"

"You gotta be a little bit more specific."

"That I want to eat you look."

"You've got the same look in your eyes."

"I not do." Darn it, not again. "I do not!"

He got up and approached her. "You are so cute when you're flustered."

"Stay," she said, holding her hands out to ward him off.

"Woof," he replied, continuing to walk toward her.

She took a step backward as her pulse kicked up a notch. "A good dog would have listened."

"Who said I was good?"

Emma pulled at the collar of her shirt as she took another step backward, sweat pooling under her armpits. It didn't take long before she found herself backed up against a wall as he continued to advance on her.

"I tried playing by the rules once, didn't like it too much," he said huskily, resting his hands against the wall, encasing her in between.

She slipped under his arms and darted across the room, feeling very much like a mouse being pursued by the cat. Crossing her arms protectively across her body, she made sure she placed the couch between them. It was so easy to ignore everything and joke around with him as though life was peachy keen.

Life wasn't okay. It would never be okay. She'd never hold Peter in her arms again, never hear his sweet voice say I love you. He'd never see their daughter grow up. Wouldn't be there to walk her down the aisle and give her away. A heavy knot gripped her chest, and her eyes burned with the pain of all her husband's unfulfilled dreams. They wouldn't grow old together, didn't even have time to celebrate their upcoming twentieth anniversary.

Her stomach cramped, and she fell to her knees, taking in sharp, short breaths. It was over. He was gone. "I can't..." she gasped as she tried to breathe. Her throat tight. "I can't do this."

She didn't want to live without Peter, didn't want to figure out how to get through the pain of losing him. She had never been on her own before. They had gotten together shortly after she left her hometown. It was a whirlwind romance. Why did this happen to her? She tried to live a good life, a perfect life. Bad things weren't supposed to happen to good people. Touching the ring on her left hand, she cried, "Why God? Why him? Wasn't I good enough for you?"

"Oh, sweetheart. I'm so sorry." Devon picked her up off the floor, cradling her in his arms. He expected her to fight him, but she wrapped her arms around his neck and buried her face in his shoulder as she wept. There wasn't much he could do or say. He knew the battle was hers to fight, but he'd be damned if he would let her do it alone. She needed someone to take care of her, and that was exactly what he was going to do.

When he sat on the couch with her, she raised her head and looked at him with sorrow-filled eyes. "Why would God let this happen?"

"I wish I had the answer," he said, brushing his lips against her forehead.

Bad things happened all the time but watching her go through this made him want to thump the cop's ass that brought all this down on her life. Not that it would do her any good if he wound up in jail. Devon should have let her have her way with the cops instead of stopping her.

He felt helpless and holding her didn't seem to do the situation much justice. If only he could take some of her pain and make the journey easier for her. But, as hard as it was, he knew Emma had to find her own way out of the darkness. He just hoped that when she found her way through, she'd see he was there for her.

"Everybody I love leaves me," she said quietly, her voice so broken that his throat clogged. "I don't know how to live without him."

"We'll figure it out together."

When she looked at him, her eyes were weary and filled with an uncertainty he knew no words from him could ever quell. She didn't quite trust him yet, so he didn't even try. Instead, he wrapped his arms around her tightly, hoping his actions spoke louder than any words ever could.

"How?"

"The only way possible," he said, running his hand soothingly over her back. "One day at a time."

Leaning her head against his chest, she sighed heavily. The sound wrapped itself around his heart, pulling him in even deeper. He rested his chin on top of her head as he held her close. No matter what happened, he was going to stick around this time. That was a promise.

Chapter Eight

"I'm so going to beat you guys," Skye said, sitting on the carpet beside the coffee table and tucking her monopoly money under the edge of the board.

"I was the monopoly king back in my day," Devon said, his lips curling into a grin.

"Mom, tell him that I whip your butt every time."

Emma was a little ashamed to admit it, but her daughter was right. She really sucked when it came to board games. But family game time allowed her and Devon to keep their conversation civil and not have it drift into the steamy realms where it usually liked to go. She glanced at him. He was wearing jeans and a muscle shirt with his arms bare. His muscles rippled as he leaned forward, resting his hands on his knees. This was a man who still had the physique of a twenty-year-old, and she was keenly aware of that fact as he sat next to her.

While he was looking better than ever, she had a jelly belly and wasn't keen on showing it to the guy who previously saw her rock-solid abs. Well, caught a glimpse of them anyway whenever they went swimming. Now, she was a woman of age with extra pounds to boot, not her tiny one hundred and three pound self anymore.

Emma pulled her cardigan across her body and protectively covered her stomach, cautiously aware that his humor-filled eyes never strayed too far from hers, even when he took the dice from Skye.

He knew what was going on in her mind as much as she knew what was on his. And it didn't sit well with her. She wished she could pack up and go home. But that meant putting Skye in danger, and she had no intention of doing that.

Leaning forward, Emma took the dice from her Devon and rolled it on the table. Just like with most things, her luck was already off to a rotten start. She rolled the lowest number, and Devon the highest, so he got to go first.

"See? I'm already on a roll," he said, grinning as he tossed the dice. His grin slipped a little while counting five spaces. He had to pay income tax.

Skye picked up the dice off the board, tossing him a teasing grin. "One step closer to losing, Mr. King."

Emma shook her head and took a moment to sort her money while Skye moved her piece to the first of the railroad properties, Reading Railroad. "I'll take it," she said.

Grabbing the money, Emma handed the card to her daughter. Somehow, she had a feeling she'd be the one losing, and both Skye and Devon would joke about it all night. Taking her turn, she landed on the lowly Mediterranean Avenue.

She groaned. Luck and Monopoly are two words that never joined together on her side. But at least that was better than paying taxes. Her daughter often struck it rich every time they played. Skye was this good luck magnet, so it was going to be interesting to see how this played out.

Little by little, they bantered around the game board, vying for the best properties the game could provide. But like she figured, her luck was as dry as ever; Skye and Devon were duking it out with each other. One had Boardwalk, the other had Park Place, and neither was willing to give the other up.

And that was fine by her. She didn't want houses or hotels on those properties. If she was going to land on something, it would most certainly be those. There was only one property left, and they kept skipping it every time.

"Momsey, I want hotels on my red property," Skye grinned, handing her more money. They'd all been landing on it, so it came as no surprise.

Her daughter was quickly becoming the queen of the empire. She was even giving Devon a run for his money, but they both seemed bent on backing Emma into a corner. She was down to her last few dollars, and most of her properties had already folded to pay rent.

But it brought a smile to Skye's face, and that meant more to Emma than winning a silly game. Devon was also doing his best to make them both comfortable in his apartment, including giving up his own room, so they could have the room with the lock on the door.

As aggressive as he was in pursuing her, he really appeared to care for her and her daughter. He didn't attempt to butter her baby girl up to get closer to Emma, and she respected that greatly. But she still wished she was at home. She needed something familiar. Something comforting. And she didn't want that *thing* to be him. And it was hard not to be drawn to him in his own personal space. Everything breathed Devon...Devon...Devon.

So did her body. He'd wrapped himself all around her five senses. Even sitting there beside him and playing an innocent game had his pheromones permeating her senses. The more she battled them, the stronger they became.

"Mom?"

Shaking herself from her line of thinking, she turned to face Skye. "Ya?"

"You had that zombie-ish look on your face again."

Emma's face heated. "Zombie-ish? Maybe we should have you doing some homework?"

Devon slapped his leg, laughing. "Night of the Living Emma."

"Oh, shut up," she said, smacking his knee. Picking up the dice, Emma rolled them onto the game board. The dice knocked over the thimble and rolled into her row of houses on Connecticut.

"A literal housing market crash," Devon said, laughing even harder. Skye fell back onto the floor, giggling.

Emma crossed her arms over her chest. "I think you guys are overtired."

It didn't take long before the infectious laughter made her smile. She hadn't heard Skye laugh that hard in a long time. Emma didn't think it was particularly funny, but if it brought joy to her daughter's heart, then she could live with it.

"Well, guys, as much fun as this is, I'm out. It's getting late, and I'm tired."

"Aw, don't be a party pooper, Mom. We have to finish the game."

She held up her two one-dollar bills. "You guys both have three times as much cash as me, so you win, I fold. I want to go have a shower."

Devon's hand froze as he went to roll the dice, and he locked eyes with her. The same fire coursing through her body swam in his eyes. She should have learned by now never to mention the word shower in his presence. It conjured up images of steamy bodies entangled until the hot spray.

"No. Just no," she said, shaking her finger at him. "Just finish the game with Skye."

"Yep. She's being a party pooper." He smirked as he looked at Skye, who thankfully appeared to be oblivious as she typed sorted her cards.

Turning, Emma quickly left the room, but his eyes bore into her back, heating her core. He needed to come with warning label. She stepped into the bathroom and securely locked the door, leaning back against it. The thought of staying here for much longer was enough to make her body go ballistic. Thankfully, she had Skye sleeping in the queen bed with her at night; otherwise, she had a sneaky suspicion he'd try to join her.

Emma was going to honor her husband if it was the last thing she did, and he deserved more than her wayward, confused heart. No more men for her. Peter was it. He was to be her one and only for the rest of her life. They were supposed to have a long, happy life as man and wife. They had even made plans to travel the world together after he retired.

He always talked of these grandeur plans, like winning the lottery, buying a sailboard, and cruising the world. Now, instead of cruising the world, he was cruising the heavens. Emma slid down the wall. The ever-present ache rose in her chest, her eyes zoning out as they filled with tears.

"I feel so lost," she cried softly, rubbing her arms as she tried to get rid of the chill that filled the room. "And confused."

Was this her punishment for not loving Peter enough? Lifting her hand, Emma held her wedding ring close to her heart. It wasn't worth much. They'd bought it at the pawnshop, but to her, it meant more than almost anything she had ever owned. It meant forever.

She had to refuse Devon's advances, or it would be like her heart never belonged to Peter to begin with. A cry bubbled up inside her, and she slapped the ground with her hand. "God! I don't want these feelings."

But no amount of crying or thumping the floor changed the feelings inside her. They were flooding over her like a tidal wave. Peter. Devon. Devon. Peter. She hated feeling like she was the rope in an unseen tug-o-war.

Standing up, she turned the shower on as hot as she could stand it. Maybe she could wash the confusion away. Emma stepped into the shower and pulled the curtain closed, allowing the water to cascade down her back.

Leaning down, she picked up Devon's shampoo bottle and popped open the lid. It smelled uniquely of him, making her nether region come to life. She let it slide from her fingers and hit the floor of the tub.

Tears mingled with the water as they dripped down her cheeks. One of these days, she was going to become a woman who could no longer cry. Realizing she had no other choice but to use the shampoo, she picked it up and quickly did her business with it before shoving it into the corner of the bath.

The last thing she needed was to wrap herself with Devon's scent as she went to bed. That would not help her situation any. She wanted to be grateful for his help, but his help was sullied by the fact he desired more from her, and damn it, her body was full on ready for it.

"I'll never be ready for it. Do you hear me?" she cried to whatever unseen force was hiding in the bathroom with her. "Never!"

But even as she said the words, the tingle between her legs defied them. She felt like her body was splitting in two down the middle. Picking up the soap, she scrubbed her body, trying to wash away her feelings for Devon.

Again, she made a verbal promise to whomever was listening. "I'm never going to be his! Do you hear me?" she said, stomping her foot as though that could scare fate away.

She belonged to one man—Peter—and whether he was in the grave or not, she was still his. Always would be. That would never change, not if she had any say about it. And that's the promise she made again as she climbed into bed, mumbling the word 'never' as she closed her eyes.

Within two weeks, Skye had made friends with one of the teens next door, and Emma found herself alone with Devon more than she wanted to be. When her daughter was there, she had a safeguard, but even then, he'd try to say things to her inconspicuously. She felt like the honey in Winnie-the-Pooh's honey jar. He was always finding ways to touch her.

And as annoying as it was fending him off, her body liked the attention, even craved it. It was driving her insane. She didn't want to like it, didn't want to feel the need building inside her. Things felt as wrong as they did right, and it was confusing.

Her body's desire for her ex-boyfriend disgusted her. There was nothing she could do to turn it off. Finding her underwear wet all the time made her resort to wearing pads so she wouldn't embarrass herself.

And it made her feel even worse, because in the months before Peter's death, she'd had a hard time getting aroused. He always seemed to be mad at something, and it put a serious damper on her hormones. All Devon had to do was be in the same room, and her vagina turned into Niagara Falls. Where was a dam when you wanted one?

At least when Skye was around, she had something else to focus on instead of him. And he knew it, too. He always upped his game whenever they were alone. Tonight, unfortunately, was one of those nights. He came home with groceries, a plan for supper, and a bottle of champagne already chilling on ice.

"Please, don't go to any trouble for me," she begged.

Reaching high into the cupboards, he produced two wine glasses. "You've cooked every night this week. It's my turn. I want to spoil you before my kids come tomorrow."

When he went to pour her a glass, she shook her head. "None for me, thanks." Drinking made her guard go down, and she needed every ounce of sobriety to keep her wits about her.

"One glass won't hurt."

Crossing her arms, she said, "So you keep telling me. Yet every time I have a drink, I wind up making out with you on the couch."

"That happened once." When she raised her eyebrows at him, he said, "Okay, three times, but the first time doesn't count."

"How so? The first time we drank together you ended up in my bed."

"I was the perfect gentleman, so you can't use that against me."

"Champagne tells a woman you're trying to seduce her."

"It also says I'm making a fancy dinner, so humor me and have a drink." He filled the glass and slid it across the kitchen island toward her.

Emma reluctantly took it and swirled around the contents, breathing in deeply. The freshly baked bread aroma, mixed with a hint of apple sauce, tickled her nose. She wasn't much of a wine drinker, but this one smelled delicious.

"You can mix it with pop if it's too strong."

If she mixed it, she was liable to drink more than she should, and it would definitely increase the chances of her doing something stupid. "I'm good, thank you. What did you buy?" she asked, trying to look in the bag.

"Crab, sweet potatoes, and corn on the cob."

"Now I know you're trying to seduce me."

"Is it working?"

Desire opened her lower flood gates again, causing Emma to cross her legs. "You wish."

The cocky grin spreading across his face told her he knew the truth. "I guess I'll have to try harder than." Reaching into the bag, he pulled out a box and put it in the fridge, without letting her see what it was. "These are for dessert."

Curious, she put her glass down and went to check it out, but he stepped in the way. "Not till after dinner."

"I just want a peek," Emma said, trying to go around him.

Devon leaned over and picked her up, tossing her over his shoulder.

"Hey, put me down!" she shrieked. His face was dangerously close to her behind, and she hated to think he might be able to smell how much she wanted him. Hanging over his back, his woody-earthy scent from working outdoors all day made her want him even more.

He walked over to the couch and plunked her down on the cushion. "Stay."

"Woof," she said, mimicking him as she made another beeline for the fridge. His arm wrapped around her waist, pulling her against him, her back to his front. The bulge in his pants pressed against her lower back, making her all too aware of his own longing.

"Let me go," she said breathlessly, not wanting to spark the raging fire growing within her.

"Are you going to listen?"

The warm breath on her neck sent a tremor through her body. *Holy Hannah.* She was like a marshmallow held over a campfire, slowly being roasted until it was all gooey and ready to eat. Feeling him pressed against the small of her back made her crave him, like a smoker craves cigarettes. She wanted him inside her, wanted to know what it would feel like as he guided himself home. Do what they'd never done before.

Shut up, Emma.

"Yes, I'll listen," she muttered, trying to pull away from him.

"You should let the naughty girl come out and play," he said, brushing his lips against the side of her neck before releasing her.

"The naughty girl needs to take a trip to the Sahara Desert and never come back."

Devon chuckled as he wandered back to the kitchen to prepare supper. She stayed where she was, trying to get control of her runaway hormones as she listened to him mess with the pots and pans.

After a few minutes, he reappeared in the living room with her wine. "You forgot your drink."

Forgetting about her hesitancy to drink, she snatched the flute and downed the contents, relishing in the warmth as it slid down her throat.

"And here I thought you didn't want it."

Emma stared at the empty glass and shrugged her shoulders. With alcohol came danger. They both knew it. He didn't seem to mind the idea, but she didn't exactly want to throw herself at him and give him the wrong idea about their relationship.

"That's it for me." To prove her point, she made her way into the kitchen and placed the glass in the sink.

Walking up behind her, Devon let his hands come to rest on her waist. "You sure I can't convince you to have another?"

"Don't forget about the no touching rule," she reminded him.

He turned her to face him. "I haven't forgotten."

"I hate to state the obvious, but you're still touching me," she said, trying to extricate herself from his hold.

"I know." He tightened his grip, backing her up against the counter, so she had nowhere to go.

"Do..." She looked up at him and the heat in his eyes made her words trail off into the setting sun. He wanted to kiss her. It was written all over his handsome face.

"...I want to make love to you?" he said, pretending like he was finishing her sentence. "Yes."

She rested her forehead against his chest, avoiding his hunger-filled eyes as she tried to catch her breath. But it was virtually impossible with the grip he had on her, his fingers lazily caressing the skin under the hem of her shirt. She ached to feel the touch of his hand between her legs.

"I'm not ready," she whispered.

"Your body is, though." As if to prove his words, he slid his hand into the waist of her spandex pants, and he cupped her mound, letting a finger slip beneath her underwear. "Swollen and moist already."

She clenched her legs together, trapping his hand. "No fair," she moaned as his fingers played between her folds, dipping inside, exploring her most intimate spot. "Oh, good gracious."

Emma's legs buckled, and she grabbed onto his shoulders for support. How was she supposed to fight him off when his fingers knew how to do the tango? "Devon, you gotta stop," she begged.

"Why?" He pressed his palm firmly against her clit and slid his finger inside her as deep as it could go.

"Dinner. You have to make dinner," she gasped, trying to hold on to her sanity as her body rushed toward the ever-explosive climax.

"Come for me, just this once."

"I already did the other d…" Her words turned into a husky moan when he hit the perfect spot. Her fingers closed tightly around his shirt, desperately holding on for the ride. "Oh, god."

He chuckled. "You like that, do you?"

"Mhmm," was all she could manage as his finger moved in a come-hither motion. His heavenly hands worked miracles in ways she had only imagined in her dreams.

"I can feel your muscles clenching. You're so close," Devon said. "Look at me. I want to see the look in your eyes when you come."

Emma raised her head, but her eyes refused to focus on his face. They wanted to roll with the pleasure swimming through her blood. "We—oh my." Talking was almost next to impossible. Every nerve in her body felt like it was on drugs.

Her toys didn't even come close to the effect of his fingers inside her. Suddenly, she felt a familiar sensation. "Stop," she moaned. "I have to pee."

"No, you don't."

"Yes. Yes, I do."

"Just let go. Come on, just for me." His fingers moved even more quickly inside her.

"Let me…oh crap," she cried as her muscles clenched. He slid his fingers out and gave all his attention to her clit instead. She rocked against his hand as wave after intense wave rocked through her body, liquid spilling on his hand and down her leg. "Oh, god." Her legs shook, turning to mush.

He picked her up, and she wrapped her jelly-filled legs around him. Still dazed by the orgasmic high running through her body, she held on as he walked them over to the couch. Her pants were cool against her legs, wet from her release. Did she pee? Oh, god. What if she did?

"I-I need to go to the washroom," she muttered breathlessly.

"Later." He laid her on the couch and tried to remove her pants. She tried to move away from him, but her limbs wouldn't obey her commands. He slid them down her legs and tossed them to the floor, her underwear quickly following.

"No," she said, as her chin wobbled, her eyes filling with tears quickly. "I have to go. Now."

The abrupt change in her demeanor made Devon pull back. "What's wrong?"

She shook her head and scrambled off to the bathroom, picking up her pants along the way.

Chapter Nine

Baffled, he returned to the kitchen and did what he had planned to do all along—cook a good supper that left her craving for other things afterwards. Somehow, after what they just did, he had a feeling she would keep her distance for the rest of the night.

Supper was nearly ready when she emerged from the bathroom. Her hair was damp, and she had on a different pair of pants. He loved how her hair looked when it was wet. It took on a wavy style. But what he couldn't get over was the look on her face. Her eyes were dark, and a deep sadness lurked in their depths. He knew she had enjoyed it, so he wasn't sure what the problem was.

Stopping at the entrance to the kitchen, Emma fiddled with the ring on her finger, spinning it around, over and over, as a tear slipped out of her eye. He watched the teardrop trace a path down her cheek.

"Take me home," she ordered.

Devon couldn't say her words surprised him. He had pushed his luck a little tonight, and it was to be expected. Given the orgasm she'd just had, it was bound to play with her sensibilities.

"Was that your first g-spot orgasm?"

"What business is that of yours?" Emma folded her arms and glared at him. "I want you to take me home."

He picked up the corn on the cob pot and drained it over the sink. "Impossible." There was no way in hell he was taking her back to that crazy city.

"No, it's not. We get in your car, and you drive us home."

Carefully putting the pot back on the stove, he said, "It's not that simple and you know it."

"Then take me to a darn hotel."

"Like hell I will. I have a perfectly good bedroom here." Turning, he pulled some plates out of the cupboard and set them on the counter.

She was running scared, but the last thing he was going to allow was more distance between them. Here she was safe, and he could go to work without worrying about her.

"I appreciate the offer, but I don't think it's working out very well."

He grinned. "I think it's working perfectly."

Emma rolled her eyes. "Why doesn't that surprise me?"

He loved having her at his place and having her back in his arms felt like the most amazing thing in the world. But apparently, she didn't think so yet. "Why don't you make yourself useful and melt some butter for my crab sauce?"

She stomped over to the fridge and threw open the door. "After dinner, I'm booking us into a motel."

"Sounds good to me. I could use a break from my apartment," he said, deliberately misunderstanding her.

A deep-throated growl emanated from her as she slammed the butter container on the counter. "You are so frustrating!"

"I've changed my mind," he said out of the blue.

She scooped up a spoonful of butter and rested the handle on the side of the container, staring at him curiously.

"I thought you were cute when you were flustered. But anger makes you downright gorge—"

Splat.

The butter hit him between the eyes. Smacking her hands over her mouth, Emma's eyes sparkled as they widened in shock. The butter slid down his nose, landing on the floor with a distinct *plop*.

He should have seen that one coming. Leaning over, he picked some up off the ground as a crooked grin spread across his face.

"Don't you dare," she said, shielding her face with her hands.

Moving quickly, he squished it like an egg on top of her head. "All's fair in love and greasy hair."

"You!" Emma swatted his shoulder. "It's going to take me a week to get it out of my hair."

"So, you are a girl, after all."

Reaching up, she ran her hands through the greasy mess, and then pressed her palm against his face, adding to the mess that was already there. He could feel his arteries clogging as he licked his lips. Butter really did taste better on crab.

He thought about suggesting that the two of them take a shower, but given the spirited glare in her eyes, he had a feeling she'd dump the rest of the butter container on his head if he so much as hinted at it. Opting for a safer conversation, he said, "You can have first dibs on the shower after dinner."

Emma's stomach gurgled at the mention of dinner. She was hungry, but she wasn't exactly looking forward to sitting at the table with him. Their conversations always took a weird turn. Whether it was her fault or his, she had no idea. "I'll have a shower at the hotel, thank you."

After making the sauce, he started dishing out their food. "Don't you think you should stay off the radar?"

"What do you mean?"

"If you use your credit card or your name at the hotel, you could be traced."

Sitting down at the table, Emma stared at the food on her plate, avoiding his eyes. She hadn't thought of that. But what were the odds that someone was trying to track her down?

"You're just trying to scare me, so I change my mind."

"You have Skye's safety to think about."

Poop. He was right. She could always send Skye off to visit her parents on the East Coast, but then she'd be left to fend off Devon's advances on her own, and he'd likely follow her home like a stray puppy. Her daughter, at least, acted as a buffer against her runaway emotional freight train. It was easier to remember that she was supposed to be mad at him when someone else was around.

Refusing to look at him, she focused on her meal. If anything, the man was a decadent chef. The crab melted in her mouth, making her moan in delight. She couldn't help but think he missed his calling.

"Why did you stop being a cook? This is delicious."

"It's just the way things worked out," he said, shrugging his shoulders as he dipped another piece of crab in the sauce.

They lapsed back into silence, occasionally sneaking a peek at each other. Her heart skipped a beat each time their gaze crossed paths. He was a totally open book and appeared to take great pleasure in making her uncomfortable.

As she sucked her thumb clean of the sauce, their eyes met across the simple pinewood table. Fires of lust burned in the depths of his grayish-blue eyes as they followed the movement of her thumb. Sexual energy emanated from him and zipped around the room like lightning on a stormy night, electrifying every inch of her body.

"Why me?" she mumbled under her breath. This wasn't supposed to happen. They were supposed to be over. She didn't want him, didn't want to desire him. Being aroused by another man—one from her past—made her feel filthy and horrible, almost like she was soiling her husband's memory. It wasn't normal. All she could really do was chalk it up to being vulnerable.

She needed to make it through this without him. Didn't the police have a witness protection program? They could give them new names and identities until the suspect was caught.

Keeping the idea to herself, she fumbled her way through the rest of their dinner. After she stuffed the last morsel of food into her mouth, she jumped up from the table. In the process, her feet got tangled in the legs, and before she knew it, she was falling backward with the chair. Emma landed flat on her back with a loud *oomph*, her legs still hanging over the horizontal chair. Devon smacked his hand on the table, roaring with laughter.

"Gee, thanks, Mr. Knight in Shining Armor," she said as she scrambled to get up, her cheeks heating like a furnace.

"Anytime, Ms. Sea Turtle."

"Do you have a smart alec answer for everything?"

"Life's no fun without," he said with his signature lopsided grin. One she wanted to wipe off his face with a magic eraser.

Rolling her eyes, she turned and stormed away from him. Emma entered the bathroom and massaged her aching shoulders. Knowing that Devon would likely try to barge his way into the room, she locked the door. She needed a chance to breathe and to escape from his irritatingly charming personality. The man could charm a cobra into sleeping with him.

But she refused to fall into bed with a man just because he wanted to sleep with her. In high school, she had refused to let anyone consider her to be easy pickings, and she wasn't going to start now, even if the man tickled her insides with the feather of desire.

She had resisted him before, and she could do it again. Mind you, having been a virgin in high school and absolutely clueless about sex had made it a little easier to avoid certain situations with boys. Now she knew exactly how hot and spicy things could get when two people were the perfect complement to each other, like her and Peter used to be. Well, somewhat. He was older than her, so their desires hadn't always meshed. She had to play by his timetable instead of her body's, which made it a little irritating.

Truthfully, everything in their life had been based on him and his choices. She had worked for the same companies he did. If he left, she had to leave, even if she liked it. Finally, she had enough and chose to do her own thing. That's what led her to the Freight job. She didn't exactly like it any better, but it was a choice she made, not him.

Shaking her head, she pushed away all the bad thoughts. Her husband had barely been in the grave for six weeks, and she was already dissing him. He didn't deserve it. He only did what he thought was best for their lives. She gave a hard laugh. Best for him anyway.

No!

She wasn't going to traduce a man who couldn't defend himself. They were together for over nineteen years. He deserved more from her. Resting her hands on the edge of the sink, she closed her eyes and sighed.

"Sorry, Peter," she whispered.

Devon was making her think about all the things that had gone wrong in her marriage. Things she had always pushed to the back of her mind. She had been determined to keep her vows, focusing less on herself and more on Peter. Now, with him gone, she was seeing all the things that could have been better in their relationship, and it was driving her a little batty.

She belonged in a straitjacket, tucked away in the corner of a funny farm. Staying with an ex-boyfriend was the first sign of her going crazy. They'd barely had any contact over the years. He was practically a stranger in every way. Yet their relationship carried on as if they had never been apart. That made her uncomfortable because she and Peter never had that type of connection. Even when they sat together on the couch, it felt like Peter was in a separate universe.

Emma stared at herself in the mirror, her cheeks flushed, and her eyes had this *come-hither* appearance. "No. This can't happen." She didn't want it to happen.

Liar

"Shut up, brain," she growled.

"Did you say something?" Devon asked from the other side of the door.

Emma jumped at the intrusion of his voice. "No," she snapped.

The sooner she got out of his clutches, the better. Each day she stayed with him, the closer she came to doing what shouldn't be done, and she didn't want a do-over. The past was best left in the past, lest history repeat itself.

The police protection program seemed to be her only option, not that she had any confidence in their ability to protect her. They hadn't done her husband any good, but what else could she do?

Come tomorrow, she was going to call them and get it organized. For now, she had to get herself into her bedroom without falling into the arms of the man on the other side of the door.

"Wish me luck," she groaned to no one in particular.

Chapter Ten

Getting to her bedroom proved much harder than expected. When she opened the door, Devon was standing outside with a box of chocolate-covered strawberries. He was in mid-bite, with melted chocolate resting on his lips like lipstick. She wanted to walk over to him and lick them clean.

Emma's stomach growled as she ran her tongue across her untouched lips. "You are so mean."

"Do you want one?"

If she gave in, the man was going to think she was a pushover. Is that how she wanted to be remembered when he finally walked away? And he would walk away. She knew it in her gut, but she couldn't ignore the sweet succulent strawberries dipped in chocolate. Walking toward him, she reached for a strawberry. When her fingers were about to close over the stem, he moved the box away, holding it high over his head.

"If you want one, we're going to sit on the couch and watch a movie."

Emma crossed her arms. "You do realize that your crotch is in perfect striking distance, right?"

"You wouldn't."

Tilting her head, she smirked and tapped her foot on the ground. "Wouldn't I?"

Devon stared at her as if attempting to gauge her threat levels. She had no intention of actually doing it and fought to keep a serious look on her face, biting her cheeks to prevent a smile.

Second guessing his decision, he lowered the box. "Remind me never to play poker with you."

As she bit into the mouth-watering strawberry, she cast him a sidelong glance. Her head held high. "Beaten by a woman," she said, her voice garbled by the remains of the strawberry.

"Didn't your parents ever teach you not to talk with your mouth full?"

Shrugging her shoulders, she grabbed a few more strawberries and then meandered her way toward the bedroom, her hips swaying purposely. "Good thing you aren't my dad."

When Devon swept her up in his arms, she shrieked. Her hands were full of strawberries, so she couldn't defend herself without dropping them.

"I agree. My thoughts are anything but daddy like."

"I don't want to know your thoughts," she said, pushing against his chest with the base of her palms.

"Are you sure? They're juicy."

Emma stuffed another strawberry in her mouth, emptying her left hand. "Yes...I'm...sure," she replied between bites. "I should have kicked you in the nuts when I had the chance."

A deep laughter rumbled in his chest, making her insides squirm. She enjoyed hearing him laugh, missed it even. It was strange what her mind could remember after all this time. The way his eyes lit up when he was happy. The way her body felt when he so much as looked her way in class.

They had an unusual relationship back in the day. Neither had asked the other out. It kind of just happened. It only made sense it kind of unhappened, too. Together, then suddenly, they weren't.

Things had never felt finished between them. It lingered in the dark recesses of her mind, never fully disappearing.

Stuffing the other strawberry in her mouth and freeing up both hands, Emma tried to untangle herself from his hold. "Put me down."

"I quite like the feel of you in my arms," he said, as he walked over and sat them both on the couch, letting his hands roam down her back. "Besides, I want to watch a movie with you."

Emma shivered under his touch and tried to scramble off his lap. "Stop manhandling me, Mr. Hercules."

He held her firmly in his grasp. "Please, watch a movie with me?"

She knew what that meant. Their previous movie nights had always played out the same way. They'd be all chummy watching a movie, and then he'd pull out a drink, and before she knew it, they'd be making out. It was so easy to get lost in the touch of his hand and the feel of his lips caressing the length of her neck.

When that happened, the movie was soon forgotten in the throes of passion, until he would try to remove her clothes, and then it was like someone tossed a bucket of ice on her. She knew if it happened again, she wouldn't have the strength to pull away. Each time they touched, it chipped away at the wall surrounding her heart. "I've watched enough movies this week. I want to go to bed."

"I thought we might watch *The Notebook*."

She pulled at his fingers, trying to untangle herself from his hold. "You wanna watch a romance? Do you think it's going to change my mind or something?" The last two movies had been full of action—ones she had enjoyed herself. If she had to sit through couples kissing and having sex, she'd be liable to do something stupid. Her lady parts turned into a slip and slide whenever he was within reaching distance.

"You're welcome to watch it. I'm going to turn in early tonight. I'm tired."

"No, you're not. You're running."

"Hardly," she said with a quick uneasy chuckle.

Devon ran his finger along her arm. "Prove it." The minute the words left his mouth, fire flared in her eyes. He loved egging her on.

She pulled her arm away and rubbed it with her hand. "I don't need to prove it."

Letting her go, he allowed her to get up, and when she was halfway toward her bedroom, he said, "I didn't take you for a chicken."

Emma spun around, hands on her hips. "Chicken? Are you really going to go there? Last I recall, you were the one who ran away first. And you didn't even have the decency to tell me the real reason why."

"I told you."

"You said you left because you thought I was too perfect for you. That's a lame-ass reason and you know it. You can't expect me to believe that."

"It's the truth. I wasn't ready for what you wanted, and it wasn't fair to hold you back."

"Oh, and now you are?"

"Yes."

"Why can't you just say it?"

"Say what?"

"That you left because I wouldn't have sex with you."

Devon shoved his hands in his back pockets and stared at her bare toes, not a speck of nail polish on them. She was still the same girl he'd left behind, but he wasn't the same man. He desperately wanted her to see that.

At the time, he never wanted to get married. Not after watching his parents go through a bitter divorce. He never even knew that they were having problems. What if despite the perfect relationship he had with Emma, she chose to leave him, too? The thought of getting married and going through the same thing had freaked him out. He couldn't bare the thought of hurting Emma that way. Yes, he'd been a coward, leaving her first before they got any closer. He knew he had acted pathetically and would spend the rest of his life kicking himself in the butt.

"That was all I had to offer back then."

"So, it's true?" she asked.

"Not in the way you think. I was nineteen, sex was all I was ready for, and you deserved more than that. You were a girl meant for marriage and babies. I knew you wanted more than I had to give. And with how we felt about each other, I knew we would do something eventually, and you would hate me for it. I did what I thought was best."

"You had no right to decide for me."

"Are you saying you would have been happy with just sex? Hell, you were this cute little church girl. If we would have had sex back then, you would have ran the other way." He knew he'd hit the nail on the head when she stayed silent and wouldn't even look at him. "I wanted to keep your virtue intact and not waste it on someone like me."

"And that's supposed to make me feel better?"

Devon stood up and raked a hand through his hair. "Maybe this will. After we broke up, I did a lot of bad things, Em. Things I'm not proud of because I couldn't handle letting you go. I try to live without regrets, but after everything I've been through, after everything I've done, my one regret was hurting you."

When she finally looked at him, her eyes were brimming with tears. She wiped them away viciously with her sleeve. "I'm going to do what you never had the courtesy to do. I'm not ready for what *you* want. I'll be leaving in the morning."

His heart dropped into a hellish pit in his stomach, surrounded by a hundred demons chomping away on it. "Emma, please."

"No, Dev. You had your chance and you let it go."

She turned away from him and took a step toward her room. He grabbed her arm. "It's not safe for you to leave."

"It is safer out there than in here with you. I'd rather have my body break than my heart again."

Desperate, he said, "Think about your daughter."

The glare she shot him could have won a world record for the world's deepest and darkest glare. Her eyes darkened like the depths of the Mariana Trench.

"You don't need to concern yourself with my daughter. I've been taking care of her since she was born."

"Don't be stupid."

"I don't plan to be. We're going under police protection."

With that, she turned around and stomped her way to the bedroom, slamming the door behind her. He knew it would be useless to go and speak with her. There was nothing he could do but wait for her to come around. But he'd be damned if he was going to let her take off to God knows where, for God knows how long, without him.

He still had an ace or two up his sleeve, and he planned to use them all. He wasn't going to let her walk out of his life. Not if he could help it.

Chapter Eleven

"I'm not sure I heard you correctly," Emma said into the phone, her mind spinning. "You want us to what?"

"Get married. You wouldn't really be married, but you'd pretend while under the witness protection program. You'd be given new names and a place to stay. Essentially, a whole new life until the perpetrator is caught," Constable McGregor said.

"How long could that take?"

"Hard to say."

Emma pressed her palm against her forehead, shaking her head. This was not going the way she had hoped. "Can't he marry someone else, hide somewhere else?"

"It's best if you guys remain together. That way, it's easier for us to keep an eye on you both."

"Did he put you up to this?"

The man remained silent for a second. "What do you mean?"

"What are you hiding, Constable? I may not be a social psychologist, but as a mother and a w-wife..." She stumbled over the word, but quickly regained her composure. "I've gotten pretty good at recognizing a lie."

"I'll be the first to admit that we usually only do things like this for witnesses of illegal activities that need protecting."

"But he's not a witness of anything and has nothing to do with any of this."

"Look, you are the wife of a man who died, and now for some bizarre reason, you have someone who wants you dead. We believe the two are connected somehow, but so far haven't found any leads. And Devon was with you when the threats started, so he needs as much protection as you."

"Has anything else happened at my house?" She'd rather go home than get stuck somewhere else with Devon, let alone pretend to be married to him. He would milk the game for all it's worth.

"No, it's been quiet."

"Maybe we could go back home, then?" she asked with a touch of wistful hope in her voice.

"Unadvisable."

"Isn't it my decision?"

"Yes, it is, but we can't let your daughter be put in harm's way."

"Damn it!" Emma thumped her fist on the kitchen table. "Why can't you people just leave my daughter out of this?"

"I know it's not what you want to hear, but you need to think about her safety."

"I could send her to stay with my parents," she said. At least, then, Emma could go back home and return to work. Her job wasn't going to wait around forever and certainly not if she went into hiding for who knows how long.

"Not a good idea. Whoever it is may know where your parents live."

"Then why aren't you moving them, too?"

"We do not believe they are in any immediate danger."

"Good, then they can take Skye."

"That might put them in danger, as the killer might try to take her to get close to you."

"He could do the same with my parents. I'm not stupid, Constable."

"The least amount of people involved the better, and for us, that is the three of you. They are being watched and will be moved at the first sign of trouble."

Leaning forward, Emma rested her forehead against her forearm on the kitchen table. She couldn't seem to find a way out of this mess. There was no doubt in her mind that Devon was involved in it somehow. It reeked of his annoyingly sexy self. If the truth ever came out that he'd organized this, she would never speak to him again.

Upon hearing Devon's bedroom door open, she grabbed an apple out of the white ceramic bowl on the table and tossed it toward his head. He easily scooped it out of the air and took a bite.

"Thanks," he said, holding it up.

She scowled at him before returning to the phone call. "Fine. When should we be ready to go?"

"A car will be swinging by the apartment at noon."

Hanging up the phone, she turned to look at Devon, who was pouring himself a cup of coffee. Pointing at him, she said, "I don't know how, but I'm certain you had something to do with this."

Scratching his head, he asked, "What do you mean?"

"Constable McGregor wants us to go into the witness protection program together as a married couple."

"I like the way the man thinks," he said, his mouth curling upward.

She rolled her eyes, desperately wanting to deck him. "Of course you would. I wouldn't be surprised if you were the one who put him up to this."

"Who, moi?" His eyes widened as he pointed to himself. "I'd love to have that kind of power."

She searched his eyes, hoping it would show if he was involved in the decision, but like her game from earlier, he wore his own poker face. "That isn't an answer."

"Yours wasn't a question."

She let out a puff of exasperation. "Geez Louise! Kill me now."

How the heck was she going to get through this ordeal in one piece? The killer and the man standing in front of her both wanted her body. One to harm it and the other—well, by time this was all over, Devon was bound to harm her in one fashion or another. Either way, she wasn't going to come out of this unscathed.

If it wasn't for Skye, she'd run for the hills by herself and just disappear. Slip on a cruise destined for the other side of the world and leave all her troubles behind. It was times like this she hated her responsibilities and wished for more freedom to do as she pleased. But she loved her daughter and would do anything to keep her safe, even if that meant sticking it out with a man she despised.

Devon walked up to her and wrapped his arm around her waist. "It could be fun."

She shoved him away. "Don't be getting any ideas."

"I hate to disappoint you, my dear, but the ideas are already there."

"Well, keep them to yourself."

"But they are so much more fun to share." He reached out and tucked a stray strand of hair behind her ear.

Emma smacked his hand away. "I'd like to know what writer shoved me into a horribly written romance novel."

"Fate."

"Next, you're going to tell me that we're connected by the red string of fate."

"Don't you find it odd that we reconnected after all this time?"

"You used your fingers to send me a text message. How was that fate?"

"The fact that you answered me, that was fate."

"So just because I decided to be nice, you think it's meant to be?"

"Oh ya."

"Have you taken lessons in frustrating people? Because you're doing a heck of a job. Excuse me." She shoved by him and went to her bedroom to pack. They only had an hour to get ready. Did she even bring enough stuff to last until this was over? Emma had only brought a few changes of clothing, but her daughter virtually packed her whole closet.

She yanked open the drawer, causing it to teeter on the edge of the track. Shoving it back in slightly, Emma began removing the clothes, throwing them on the bed.

How could someone be so infuriating? Were there classes in the art of annoying someone? She could see him being an honor student, passing with flying colors.

She half expected him to follow her and continue their conversation, but he must have gone to get ready. Having a few minutes alone without him allowed her a chance to gather her thoughts.

Not that she could gather them, they were scattered in every which direction. She'd rather hide out on an island with no wi-fi than be trapped with Devon in the witness protection program. Who was going to protect her body and heart from him? Focusing on the task at hand, she disappeared into the bathroom to gather their hygiene products.

"I have to go away for a bit,"

"How come?" Leila asked.

He could always count on his ex-wife to be nosy. Despite them not being together, he knew she cared for him a great deal. He was itching to open his mouth and tell her everything, but that would have to wait until it was all over.

"I'll fill you in after."

"How long are you going to be gone for?"

"Not sure."

Leila huffed into the phone, clearly not liking his answers. "What have you got mixed up in now, Devon?"

"It's not what you think."

"Do you remember the last time you told me that?"

He remembered it all too clearly. Their mutual friend, Jack, suffered the fatal consequences of Devon's stupidity. It was only by helping Leila through her pain and her pushing him to change his life that he found his way out of the darkness that had threatened to overtake him.

They had grown closer and became more than friends. But for him, it was more about his desire to protect her than it was for love. He hadn't known it at the time, though, not until his emotions settled down, and he was thinking with a clear head again. That was when he realized that every minute he stayed with her was one less minute that she had with her true love, her soulmate. He couldn't bear to get in the way of that. She was more than happy to stay with him because of the kids, but he had wanted more for her.

"This is different, I promise," he said as he stuffed some clothes into a dusty old suitcase, one that hadn't seen the light of day in years. Glancing down at his watch, he noticed that the time was quickly ticking by. "Can I talk to the kids?"

"You better be right about that. I don't want to bring you home in a body bag, too."

"You won't." He waited as the phone was passed to his youngest child. "Hi Bri, how's my baby girl?"

"Good. I'm baking. Mommy is helping me make a baking video," his daughter replied, each word bubblier than the next, sounding much like she had downed an energy drink. He'd love to have that much energy again.

"What are you making?" he asked.

"Chocolate chip cookies."

"Hmm, my favorite."

"How come you aren't coming home, Daddy?" she asked in that quiet voice of hers that left his heart aching. How they could flip a switch so quickly from one temperament to another was beyond him.

"I wish I could, but I have to go away for a little while on important business. But I promise when I get back, we'll go to Disneyland, okay?"

"Really?" she asked, her perkiness returning slightly.

"Yes!"

And that was it with his phone call with Brianna. She laid the phone down, screaming her brother's name with excitement.

A few minutes later, his son Jacob spoke into the phone, his voice full of suspicion. "Are we really going to Disneyland?"

"Just as soon as I get back from a business trip."

"How long are you going to be gone for?"

Devon walked into the bathroom and grabbed a few toiletries. "I'm not sure. But if you behave while I'm gone, we'll go as soon as I get back."

"I always behave."

"That's not what Mommy says."

"That's cause Brianna is a poopy..." Jacob giggled at the word before continuing, "...girl who tattle tales."

Devon couldn't help but laugh. Good old kid humor. Bodily functions were all the rage at that age. "Son, I need you to be the man of the house while I'm gone. No more teasing your sister. Can you do that?" he asked, placing the bathroom items in the front pocket of the suitcase.

"She starts it."

"The man of the house needs to be strong and protect our women folk."

"You can count on me, Dad," his seven-year-old replied assuredly.

"Good. Now can you put Mommy back on the phone? I have to go soon."

It pained his heart to not be able to see his kids like he had planned, especially as he had wanted to introduce them to Skye and Emma, but now he didn't know when that would happen. Hopefully soon, their life would be back to normal, and he could resume his weekend visits with his kids.

"Devon, we've talked about this. You can't go promising them a trip. We don't have the money to go to California," Leila said.

"We can swing it at least once in their lifetime, even if I have to do overtime."

He could almost hear her shake her head. She was more practical minded than he was, always finding ways to save a dollar. This trip went against everything she believed in. "You do realize I'm never going to hear the end of this, right? Every day the kids are going to ask when you're coming home."

"Then I guess I better go, so I can get home faster."

"You better come back alive!"

"I don't plan to go six feet under just yet."

There was a moment of silence on her end, and she sighed heavily. "Just come back safe, okay?"

"I plan on it. Love you guys."

"Love you, too," she said softly.

Devon shook his head. They were more like siblings than ex-lovers. Always fighting, yet not fighting in the true sense of the word. He would always love her, but love-love was reserved solely for Emma.

Glancing down at his watch, he saw it was nearing noon. After he tossed the few remaining items into his suitcase, he zipped it closed and opened his bedroom door. Walking over to the sink, he decided to do the dishes and clean up while he waited for their ride to arrive.

How was she supposed to tell Skye that they were leaving yet again and that they had to pretend to be a stinking family with a man her daughter barely knew? Mind you, Skye didn't seem to mind being around Devon. The way they joked together at her expense drove her insane, but it was nice to see her daughter laughing. They hadn't had many reasons to laugh lately. The front door open and closed.

"Mom?" Skye called.

"In here, honey," Emma replied.

"Guess what? Melanie dyed her hair..." Her daughter stopped talking the moment she entered the room. "Wait. What's going on?"

"There has been a change of plans."

Skye plopped down on the bed and crossed her legs as she placed her elbows on her knees, resting her chin in her palms. "Seriously?"

"Sorry, sweetheart. I know you were just beginning to make friends here."

"What if I don't want to go?"

Emma sat next to Skye and wrapped her arm around her shoulders. "I don't want to go either, but we're kind of stuck with no choice."

"Can't I stay with Melanie?

"Afraid not. We have to stick together."

"Where are we going?"

"We'll find out when the cops pick us up. We're going into the witness protection program."

Intrigue filled her daughter's eyes. "Like the movies?"

Her life had turned into a very cheesy Rated-B movie. She'd have to write a book when all this was over. No one was ever going to believe how crazy things were turning out. Back in high school, she was voted as the one most likely to still be living with her parents when she turned thirty. No one thought she'd get married. Let alone live a life that felt unreal.

She felt like she was having an out-of-body experience, watching herself go through the motions. Yet not really being a part of it. Now, a time portal had opened, pushing her back through time and into the arms of a man she once loved. She had wanted to spend her life with him, but he left her. She was dreaming of forever while he was dreaming of someone else. Emma slammed the suitcase closed.

"You okay, Mom?"

"I'm just peachy," she snapped, tugging on the zipper that was stuck to the interior lining. "Life is just great. We have to pretend to be a family."

"But we are a family?"

"Not you and me, us and"—she turned to face the door and threw both hands toward it in exasperation—"him!"

"You're not making any sense."

"We have to pretend that he's your dad and my husband."

Skye stayed silent. Her eyes downcast at the mention of the word 'dad.' The plan was preposterous. Surely there was a better idea than to stuff a pretend husband and father on a family who had just lost theirs. She had every intention of continuing to fight this decision as soon as the briefing started. It wasn't fair that she had no say in the matter.

A loud knock on the front door echoed its way toward them.

Devon appeared in the bedroom doorway. "Our ride is here."

Chapter Twelve

"Wait. Aren't we going to the police station?" Emma asked.

The cop in plain clothes, who was driving, shook his head. "No, we're going to a drop point. They'll brief you there."

"But I wanted to discuss the situation first." She didn't want to go through with the cockamamie idea and had hoped to reason with the commanding officer. "Can I refuse to go along with this?"

"We can't force you to go, but I really think it is in your best interest."

"Ya, seems a lot of people think they know what's best for me." She slouched in the backseat, leaning her head against the headrest. Out of the corner of her eye, she could see Devon grinning. She wanted to slug him in the shoulder, but the last thing she needed was an assault charge. Instead, she reached across Skye and pinched his upper arm.

He turned his head, and the heat in his eyes boiled the fluids inside her. If she didn't know any better, she'd almost assume that there was steam rising off her body like smoky tendrils drifting toward the roof. She was a lobster being boiled alive.

Emma turned and stared out the window. Pretending to be

married to Devon, the same man she had wanted to marry in the past, didn't sit right with her, especially when her youthful fantasies had quickly been squelched by a hard-swift kick in the butt by reality. Sometimes she wished she had focused more on a career than the typical white picket fence dream. Maybe then, it wouldn't have hurt so badly being dumped, and she wouldn't have lost herself along the way.

At the time, she had no idea what she wanted to do with her life, beyond being a wife and mother. When she met Peter, and he proposed to her as they sat on the couch, she was ecstatic. She couldn't believe someone actually wanted her.

But in the end, she ended up losing herself even more, getting sucked into whatever company her husband worked for. After living in her husband's shadow for most of their marriage, she finally stumbled into the shipping industry. Peter couldn't understand why she needed to do her own thing and took the change personally. She didn't hear the end of it for days.

Were they going to get new jobs during this pretend charade? She kind of hoped so because she didn't want to be stuck in the house with him. Her heart was having a hard enough time coping already. They had better have separate rooms, too.

"What are you thinking about?" Devon asked, looking at her curiously.

"Nothing."

He leaned in and whispered, "I bet you're thinking about what it will be like to sleep in the same bed."

"No, I'm thinking about how many ways I can fit you into a garbage can." Her deadpan expression would have made him question his safety had it not been for a slight sparkle in her eyes, and the way the corner of her lips twitched as she fought to suppress a smile.

"You're losing your poker face, my dear."

An evil 'Chester the Cat' grin spread across her face. "Are you certain about that?"

"I know you too well. You probably catch spiders and release them outside."

"Shows what you know. Skye does that. Me? I grind them into smithereens with a shoe."

Emma's daughter didn't even acknowledge her name being spoken. She was too busy watching a movie on her phone. Devon glanced between them both. It was hard to believe that Emma was the mother of a teenager. She still looked like one herself.

His kids hadn't even reached the double digits yet, but he knew it wouldn't be long before they were teenagers, too. He was grateful to their mother, who was doing an amazing job raising them. She was a wonderful and understanding woman. People couldn't understand why they broke up when they seemed to get along okay. Leila deserved someone who could be everything he couldn't be. Someone who could give his heart and soul to her. That wasn't him, and they both knew it.

The two of them had gotten married after she got pregnant with Jacob. They had given it a good run, but he wanted something better for her, and it looked like he'd made the right decision. Within a year of breaking up, she had met another guy, Curtis. His kids adored the man. That part irked him a little, but he'd made peace with it. Besides, they were going to adore Emma, too. He knew they would.

Life was bizarre. Who would have thought he and Emma would have a second chance to reconnect? You rarely get do-overs, second chances. She was happy and not happy to see him at the same time, and thus was fighting him every step of the way, but she was already giving in. She just didn't see it yet.

People always talked about finding their soulmates. Something he never believed in until he tried to live without Emma. Even after he realized it, he'd been too stubborn and prideful to beg her to come back. And then it was too late. She was married and off the eligibility table.

But now she was back. And this time, he was not giving up or backing down. He knew he couldn't push her. She had to mourn. He knew that. But he was going to do everything in his power to breathe life back into her eyes. A life they could share together.

"We're here," the cop said as he pulled the car to a stop behind a large, abandoned building. There were two cars parked ahead of them. One was a gray Mazda, and the other a black Ford Escape, which looked a lot like an undercover cop car with the distinguishable radio antenna. Skye waited in the car while the rest of them gathered outside.

A tall man in plain clothes, jeans and a t-shirt, approached them with a sealed bag in his hands. As he neared them, he stuck out his other hand to shake theirs. "Hi, I'm Constable Case."

"Hi, Constable," Emma said. "What are we doing here? I'm confused."

"This is as far as we go. In this bag, you'll find all the details you need to know. Study them carefully before you interact with anyone. As soon as we wrap things up, you'll be able to come home." He handed the bag to Devon. "Don't open it until you get in the car."

"Why not?" she asked.

"There are only a handful of people who know what's in that bag. None of us know either for your own safety. They don't want you opening it and asking us questions about it."

Emma stared at the bag. "But how are you guys supposed to watch out for us if you don't know where we are?"

"Don't worry. Everything has already been arranged."

"I don't think I like this," she said, shaking her head. "Why does it have to be this way?"

"For your own protection, Madam. We wouldn't be doing this otherwise."

"How are you guys supposed to find him if I'm not here to draw him out?"

Devon could hardly believe how astute she was in judging the situations around her. With her ability to assess things, she should have become a detective or something. She surprised him more and more every day.

"You just go get settled in your new place and let us worry about that." The constable handed her ex-boyfriend the car keys and pointed to the gray Mazda. "That is your new ride."

"Come on, Em." He took her by the arm and guided her toward the car. Devon wanted to go before she asked another question or fully decided against the idea. The wheels in her mind never stopped turning.

They settled inside the car, with him in the driver's seat. She didn't object. Her eyes were intently staring at the bag on his lap as if it were a rattler poised to bite.

"Why don't you open it?" he suggested.

Emma went to reach for it, but then pulled her hand back, sucking in a breath. "You do it."

He ripped open the top of the bag, which had been sealed with two staples, and glanced inside. There were three passports, a few other pieces of identification, three phones, and an old-style street map. Most people used an app for directions these days, not the paper ones that took all day to fold right.

Devon pulled out the map and unfolded it. Their current location was circled, and a line was drawn to their destination. By his calculations, it would take them about twelve hours to drive. Why they had them going to Manitoba was a good question, though. There had to be closer places that worked just as well.

"Well?" Emma asked.

"Winnipeg."

"Yikes, that's so far away."

"Here's your identification and Skye's." He handed her several different cards and two cell phones.

"Cool, an Apple iPhone!" Skye gasped, holding it against her chest.

"Be careful with it," Emma warned. "Do you understand?"

Skye nodded and flashed her a Grand Canyon grin. Devon continued to fish out the rest of the contents from the bag, including a letter-sized envelope. It contained information about their jobs, names, and so on.

"So, Mrs. Tara Jackson, now that we're officially husband and wife, we should seal the deal with a kiss," he said, making kissy faces at her.

"In your dreams, sailor," she replied.

"What's my new name?" Skye asked.

"Hailey Jackson," he said.

"I so don't look like a Hailey," her daughter said. "But this is so cool. I can practice my acting."

"You like acting?" Devon asked.

"I want to be an actress, but my mom hasn't been able to get me signed up with an agency yet."

"How come?"

"It's not like I have the time to drive her around when I'm working all day," Emma muttered. She wanted to help her daughter fulfill her dreams, but if she didn't work, they wouldn't have food on the table and a roof over their heads.

"I know someone. I can probably help," he offered.

"Will you stop trying to help!" She slammed her palm on the arm rest. It didn't take long before the ugly feeling of regret took over and her cheeks heated because of her outburst. "Sorry."

"No problem," he said, shrugging his shoulders.

No matter how she acted, Devon never batted an eyelash. Her husband had been the total opposite. He got angry at anything he deemed to be an inconvenience. "Don't you ever get mad?"

"When the situation warrants it," he replied.

The man had the patience of a saint while she was acting like the grumpy ex from hell. She didn't want to be that person, hated being that person. She'd always been able to control herself before and wasn't sure why everything inside her wanted to rip his head off now.

He has been being nothing but kind and sweet to them. She might as well try to make the best of it while they were together. No use making it harder than it needed to be. But that didn't mean she would sleep with him, though. No way. No how.

There had better be two double beds. Otherwise, whether he liked it or not, he'd be sleeping on the floor.

"Are you sure this is the right place?" Emma asked, examining the map again as Devon drove along the driveway. There were flat fields as far as the eye could see. Ahead of them, they could see a wind-break of trees, likely surrounding the house.

"It's the spot circled on the map," Devon replied. He was pretty certain he had followed the directions correctly.

"But it's so far away from everything. How is anyone supposed to help us if there's a problem?"

"I'm sure with all the precautions they've taken, they have something lined up."

With their name changes and moving so far away, he didn't think they had anything to worry about. He liked the idea that he would have her all to himself, without having to worry about someone getting the drop on them.

Entering the poplar windbreak, they spotted a two-story pale-yellow farmhouse, with a wraparound porch, smack dab in the middle of the yard. Devon spotted a wooden patio swing hanging beside the front door. And an image of the two of them sitting there popped in his mind, his arm wrapped around her as she rested her head in the crook of his shoulder. He pulled to a stop in front of the paint-chipped stairs and got out of the car. Emma and Skye climbed out and stood together near the hood of the Mazda.

"What am I supposed to do way out here?" Skye complained.

Emma placed her hand on her daughter's shoulder. "Don't worry, we'll find something to keep ourselves busy,"

"Why did we have to come out here, anyway? Couldn't we have just gone home?"

"Weren't you the one who wanted to get away?" she asked Skye.

"Yes, but this," she said, spreading her arms wide, "is the middle of nowhere."

Devon watched their exchange and was still amazed at how the two looked so much alike. With Emma's youthful appearance, the two could have been sisters, not mother and daughter. It pained him that he'd given up their chance to have kids together. All because his stupid self hadn't known what love was when it stared him in the face.

But it was no use wishing for what could have been. He couldn't change the past, and even if he could, he didn't think he'd be able to. If he did, then Brianna and Jacob wouldn't exist, and they were his world. He couldn't wait for Emma to meet them.

Ducking back into the car, Devon grabbed the bag containing the keys and pulled them out. The keys jingled in his hand as he approached the door. They didn't have much information about the house. But other than it needing a little TLC, it looked decent. After he opened the door, he blocked the entrance as he turned to face the girls.

Emma had a feeling Devon was up to something by the way his eyes lit up when he looked at her. "Whatever you're thinking...don't!"

"We are married now, aren't we?" he asked, taking a step toward her.

She moved backward, away from the predatory gleam that radiated off his body. "Don't you dare."

"What do you think I'm going to do?"

"Geez, give it a rest." Skye zipped by them, disappearing inside. She was obviously tired of their banter.

Distracted by her daughter, Emma didn't see Devon move until it was too late. He scooped her up in his arms again.

"What are you doing?" she cried.

"Carrying you over the threshold," he said with a grin.

Emma rolled her eyes as he carried her through the door. Once inside, he released her legs, allowing her to slide down his full length.

Her crotch brushed against his, causing all her blood to rush to the center of her body, waking her up as quickly as a rooster crowing.

When her feet touched the ground, she mumbled, "You and your bright ideas."

"What can I say?" he said, shrugging his shoulders, his hands resting on her hips. "You should know by now I love holding you."

"I never would have gue..." Her words trailed off when his fingers slipped beneath the hem of her shirt. His eyes darkened with lust. She swallowed hard. "I...uhh..." There were so many reasons they shouldn't be touching, shouldn't be feeling this way, but she couldn't seem to remember a single one.

He watched her reaction as his fingers skimmed over her bare flesh. "You are so beautiful."

Her breath caught in her throat, and her gaze dropped to his mouth before returning to his dreamy, gorgeous eyes. As she rode the tidal wave of her emotions, fighting the growing feelings inside her, he kissed her. The warmth of his lips, ever gentle and ever seeking, sent a shiver down her spine.

She couldn't prevent the moan that escaped from her throat. Taking advantage of the new opening, Devon swept his tongue inside, as though her mouth was his to own and do with as he pleased.

And in that moment, she didn't care. Linking her hands behind his neck, she rose on her tiptoes and pulled him closer to deepen the kiss, giving herself completely and totally to him.

His hands glided over her and cupped her butt, pressing her firmly against him so she could feel his desire. Her nipples stood to attention and her parts, damp and swollen, felt like she'd jumped into a pool full of nothing but lustful intentions.

All rational thought fled her mind. All she could focus on was how her clit was pulsating and aching to the point of not wanting to turn back. "Please," she found herself saying, surprised by her words and the huskiness in her voice.

"Tell me what you want," he murmured against her lips.

"You."

"You've already got that. What else?" Devon didn't want to mistake her invitation.

With a shy smile, Emma slipped a hand between them and pressed it firmly against the bulge in his pants, giving him a squeeze. His cock jumped at her touch. For the first time since he was a teen, he was worried that he'd come before he took his rightful place inside her.

Devon picked her up, and she wrapped her legs around his waist. He fumbled his way through the house, with his lips locked on hers. His knee connected with an end table next to the staircase, and he grunted in pain. She slipped slightly in his hold before his grip tightened around her again, his muscles trembling with need.

"Hurry," she said huskily as her lips roamed, her breath tickling his neck. He wished he could take the steps two at a time, but the added weight forced him to be careful. Her kisses were driving him up the wall, and the friction against his cock made him almost come before he even made it up the stairs.

Temporarily breaking contact, he placed her on her feet and took her by the hand. He pushed open the closest door and pulled them both inside, shutting it behind them. In front of them was a double bed with a floral pattern comforter. Off to the side was an old Victorian dresser, but it mattered not to him. All he could think about was the woman standing in front of him.

Emma's cheeks were rosy, and her eyes laden with desire. She bit her bottom lip as she grabbed the ends of his t-shirt, pulling it over his head. He couldn't believe this was happening. Was he dreaming?

When she reached for her own shirt, he stilled her hands. "Here, let me." He'd waited all this time to undress her. Even in their make-out sessions, they had mostly kept their clothes on, except once when he'd taken her pants off. If anyone was going to take off her clothes, it was going to be him.

Carefully, he removed her shirt, and his gaze dropped to her mouth-watering cleavage. He'd felt her breasts before but seeing them was a whole other matter. She wasn't huge, but anything more than a handful was a waste.

Reaching around, he unclipped her bra and slid the straps off her shoulders. He ran the back of his fingers across her erect nipples. She gasped softly under his touch. It never failed to amaze him how responsive she was. Caressing her breasts, he leaned down and took her in his mouth, lazily circling her nipple with his tongue.

"Devon," Emma moaned as she arched backward, giving him better access. When his mouth closed around her, the ache between her legs intensified a hundred-fold. She wanted this, wanted him to take her. Reaching for his belt, she tried to undo it, but her fingers were shaking too much.

She'd only done it to him in her dreams. And there, she was a confident sexy woman. Here, her fingers were like Jell-O, and her body felt like a vibrator that wouldn't turn off. Stilling her hands, he undid his belt and allowed his pants to fall to the floor, leaving his blue and black boxers on, His hard-on evident behind the stretched material.

Giggling nervously, she reached out to touch him. "Just a little excited, eh?"

He stepped out of his pants and backed her up toward the bed. "A little. Are you crazy, woman? I'm on the verge of bursting."

When she reached for his boxers, he stilled her hand. "I need to keep them on for now. But I wouldn't mind helping you out of yours."

Emma climbed on the bed and laid down on her back, her hair resting like a halo around her head. She reminded Devon of an angel from heaven. But an angel would likely strike him down for what they were about to do. He gave his head a quick shake. He wasn't about to be detoured now. He'd waited twenty years for this moment, and he was going to take it. Come hell or high water, she'd be his before the night was done.

He pulled off her pants and threw them across the room, her damp underwear quickly following. Her scent aroused the animal inside him, but he didn't want to rush it. Pausing, he took a second to breathe and relax.

She deserved everything he could give her and more. No one captured his heart like her. Now here she was, laying naked on a bed, waiting for his next move. And all he could do was stand there amazed.

Seemingly impatient, she jumped up and grabbed him by the shoulders, pulling him onto the bed. Her strength took him by surprise as she climbed on top. "You're taking too long," she said with a giggle.

Flipping her back over, he straddled her. "Easy does it, missy. Lay back and let me spoil you." She reached for the waist of his boxers, but he grabbed both of her hands, placing them on the pillow above her head. "No touching."

Emma pouted, squirming beneath him. "No fair."

"Don't make me tie you up," he said, grinning.

"You wouldn't."

"Wouldn't I?" he replied, wiggling his eyebrows. "I'm sure I have a few ties in my suitcase."

The thought of tying her up and having his wicked way with her made his flesh harden painfully. He fought to contain himself, but his body was running full speed ahead, and he wasn't even sure if he'd have enough strength to pleasure her first.

He reached between her legs and eased his fingers into her warm, wet pussy. She was as ready as he was. Damn it, he wanted to take it slow, but knowing she was aroused drove him up the wall. It didn't help that he hadn't taken matters into his own hands for days.

And with all their playing around, he seriously ached for release. Taking off his boxers, he positioned himself above her. She took hold of him and started to guide him in.

Neither of them noticed the squeak of the door as it swung open beside them.

Chapter Thirteen

"Ew, Mom!" Skye's voice filled the room.

Devon dove off the other side of the bed, taking the floral comforter with him. Emma lay there dumbfounded as her daughter stormed out the door, slamming it behind her. How could she have forgotten to lock the bedroom door?

"Oh geez." She covered her face with her hands, her cheeks flaming like a blazing campfire.

From beside the bed, under the comforter, she heard Devon stifle a chuckle. Reaching down, she gave the blanket a smack. A hand reached up and grabbed hers, pulling her off the bed. He grunted when she landed on top of him.

"Did you have to knee me in the groin," he groaned, still hiding under the blanket.

"Whose bright idea was it to pull me off the bed?" she asked, attempting to climb off him, but he held her firmly. "Let me go."

Instead of listening, he rolled them over, so he was on top again, and she was the one trapped in the blanket this time. "Chase after her later," he said, grinding his erection against her. "We've got unfinished business."

"Devon, get off me," she said, giving him a shove. "Now."

Begrudgingly, he climbed off and stood up, his erection painfully obvious. He made no effort to cover himself. Turning away, she got up and wrapped the comforter around her as she searched for her clothes.

"How could I have been so stupid?" she grumbled. Her daughter must be devastated. "Why are you still standing there naked? Get dressed."

"In case you haven't noticed, I have a major woody here," he said, pointing to himself.

Unable to stop herself, she glanced at it, and her parts throbbed with anticipation. Crossing her legs, she said, "Glad I'm not a guy."

"What am I supposed to do with it?" he complained.

"I heard it goes back into hiding if you take a cold shower." She quickly got dressed before she made any other bad decisions, like joining him in the shower, for example.

"Are you really going to just leave me hanging?"

Walking to the door, she shot him a look over her shoulder. "If it was hanging, I doubt we'd be having this discussion." Without saying another word, she went in search of Skye, leaving him standing in the middle of the room.

Emma found her sitting on the front porch swing. Skye's legs were pulled up against her chest, and her arms were wrapped around them, her chin resting on her knees. Her daughter wouldn't even turn and look at her as she approached.

"How could you, Mom?"

Sighing, Emma sat down and kicked off with her feet, setting the porch swing in motion. "I have no idea, sweetheart."

"Don't you love Daddy anymore?"

The words broke her heart, and she fought to hold her tears back. "Oh, honey, of course. I'll always love him."

"I miss him," Skye cried, burying her face in her mom's shoulder. "I want him back."

No matter the challenges they'd faced in their lives, Peter and

Skye had been Emma's entire world. Now it felt like there was this huge gap in their lives, an emptiness that couldn't be filled. She tried to hold herself together for her daughter's sake, but tears still stained her cheeks.

Pulling Skye close, she said, "Me too, baby girl. Me too."

Nausea bubbled in her queasy stomach. She couldn't believe she had almost given in to her desires. They were on the bed, ready to have sex. He'd been poised above her. A second later and he would have been inside her. Her behavior created a mixed reaction inside her, from pleasure between her legs to utter despair in her heart.

She was a walking contradiction. Her body was more than happy to pick up where they'd left off so long ago. There was no sweeping that under the rug. But she wasn't one to be ruled by her physical feelings, especially not when she was being torn in two over them. Yet that's exactly what she allowed to happen the minute they stepped foot in the new house.

Her marriage was over, and she was a free woman who could do what she wanted. She understood that on an intellectual level, but emotionally, she still belonged to Peter. There was no way she could let another man in, not yet, even if that person still held a piece of her treacherous heart. It wasn't right. Emma reached for Peter's ring on her finger, a cry bubbling up in her throat. At night, she still reached for him and the pain of him not being there was like a massive shock every time.

Her mind would fill with flashbacks of the worst week of her life. Peter was considered DOA—dead on arrival. There was no great goodbye. No last hug. No last kiss. No more *I love yous* or *hug, hug, kiss, kiss* at the end of their phone calls.

"Will it always hurt this bad?" Skye asked.

Emma had asked herself the same question and really had no answer for her. Her pain was as prevalent today as it was on the day she'd heard the news. Death was a part of life, but no one was ever quite ready for it. "I think it will always hurt, but we have each other. We'll learn how to make room for the pain somehow."

"I don't want to keep feeling this way."

Kissing the top of Skye's head, Emma gave her a gentle squeeze. "I wish I could make the pain go away, but we gotta work through it."

"Can you sleep in my room tonight?"

"Of course," she replied.

Later, when the two of them were fast asleep, Devon sat on the swing outside, holding a can of beer. The air had cooled off enough that you could sit comfortably without breaking a sweat. Looking up, he stared at the stars. It was one of the things he liked about country living. You could see so much more in the sky, even the Milky Way.

There was something peaceful about it and he'd hoped that it would bring peace to Emma and her daughter, too. The pain in their voices made Devon wish he had the power to make things right again.

He knew Emma and Peter hadn't had the perfect relationship, based on some vague Facebook posts Emma made every now and again, but it was obvious she loved the man...in the good and in the bad.

He was beginning to see that once she loved someone, she loved them for life. Her heart was more special than he'd realized. You rarely find someone willing to give you their all and stick with you, no matter what. People tend to only think about themselves.

He had left Emma without even considering how she felt about him. In trying to do what he thought was right at the time, he had still screwed things up royally. Even now, he was still messing things up, thinking with the wrong brain.

Hell.

She'd be better off without him. Was he even capable of the love a woman deserved? That she deserved? There was no one in the world as amazing as she was. He wanted her, but she was making it abundantly clear that she wanted nothing to do with him. Smart woman.

What was that in the bedroom then, Mr. Genius?

The most amazing experience of his life, that's what. If Skye wouldn't have walked in, they would have made love. That had to count for something. No woman would have sex with a man she hated, right? But did that mean she loved him?

Her eyes told two different stories, and it was hard to gauge what was going on inside her mind. One minute, her eyes had the ability to melt him into her lustful play toy, and the next, they were telling him to back away before she set fire to his balls. If he wasn't careful, his confused member would throw a mutiny and go into hiding, never to be seen of again. Someday, he was going to have an interesting story to tell their friends.

Glancing up from his lap, a movement of light in the trees caught his attention. Devon squinted, trying to identify it. *Holy hell.* It was a flashlight, which meant someone was moving toward the house. Unease filled him. Had someone found them already?

His heart leaped in his chest. He reached inside the door and grabbed the baseball bat he'd placed there earlier that day. His gun was upstairs buried in the closet, so it would have to do. He wasn't going to even bring his gun with him to Manitoba, but given the circumstances, he knew that it was better to be safe than sorry.

The light was getting brighter by the minute, and he could hear twigs snapping underneath the intruder's feet. Whoever it was wasn't making any effort to stay quiet, and that eased his concern a little. But he still didn't like the fact that someone he didn't know was on their property.

"Hey, you there!" he yelled, closing his fingers around the handle of the bat. "Stop!"

The person froze in their tracks, and Devon raised a hand, shielding his eyes from the blinding flashlight.

"This is security. Identify yourself." a raspy voice ordered. The smell of the man's cigarette filled the night air.

Not wanting to give away any information, he said, "I live here. Who are you?"

"I'm Greg. One of the guards hired to secure the premise." Lowering the flashlight, the man asked, "Are you Trevor?"

Swinging the bat onto his shoulder, Devon studied the man standing in front of him. Greg was a few inches shorter than he was, but that meant nothing in terms of skill. There was a cigarette sticking out of the corner of his mouth, and he wore a hat with the same symbol as those on his jacket.

"Where's your security identification?" Devon asked.

Greg reached into the pocket of his cargo pants and pulled out his wallet. Flipping to the first section, he held it out to Devon. "Here."

Devon gave a nod of his head, letting the guy put his wallet away before holding out his hand. "Yes, I'm Trevor." He hadn't expected to find any security personnel on site. The constable had left out that pertinent piece of information. It would have been nice to know. Idiots.

Greg shook his hand. "We weren't expecting you until tomorrow."

"We drove straight through. How many of you are on duty?"

"Three of us. If you need us, we have a trailer situated at the Northeast corner of the property or you can call us on the phone. Our numbers should already be programmed into your phones."

That caused Devon to raise an eyebrow. "How much do you guys actually know?"

"Not much, only enough to do our jobs. Are you guys like famous or something?" Greg asked, taking a long drag on his cigarette.

Devon laughed. "I wish. Well, I should get back inside."

"It was nice to meet you. If you have any problems, call us."

They gave each other a quick head nod before going in separate directions.

～

It was their first official day as 'man and wife,' and so far, they hadn't been able to celebrate adequately. Devon had just spent the last eight hours at work and was dying to have some time with his new bride. And he knew just what they could do. His new boss was throwing a party and had invited all the newcomers and old employees to join him at his house.

His first workday went okay. The first few times someone tried calling him by the name of Trevor, it went over his head, but by lunch time he'd gotten into the swing of it. Climbing out of the car, he walked up to the house.

"Oh, honey, I'm home," he said after pushing the door open. His senses got assaulted by the aroma of bacon. It smelled like they were having breakfast for dinner. Hopefully, they'd still have enough time to get ready for the party tonight.

Walking through the living room, adorned with age old furniture, he wandered toward the kitchen. If they were going to be living here for any length of time, he'd have to see if he could get permission to get rid of a few things. The interior decorator had failed miserably in keeping up with the times.

The moment he stepped foot in the kitchen, Devon lost all coherent thought. Emma was bent over, messing with something in the oven. Her favorite type of clothing, spandex, shaped her ass perfectly.

The temptation to go over there and smack it arose within him, but he didn't want to risk getting burned by whatever she was cooking. Instead, he leaned back against the wall and watched as she moved her sweet ass in time to some unheard music.

As she stood up and closed the oven, she swayed her hips as she continued to dance. His body tightened in response to her innocent seductive moves. When she tucked her hair behind her ear, he noticed the ear buds. No wonder she hadn't heard him come in.

Reaching up, she grabbed a few plates. Doing a little twirl, she turned to place them on the counter. He moved into her line of sight, and she jumped, her ear buds falling to the ground. "Holy Hannah! You scared me."

"Don't you ever swear?" he asked comically.

Emma pulled her lips to one side and looked up at the ceiling, deep in thought. "Not if I can help it."

"I bet I can get you to say a few naughty words."

"Damn is about as wild as I get."

He walked over to her intently. "I'd love to see how wild I could make you."

Her breathing quickened as she took a step backward, her back hitting the counter. "I'm trying to cook here."

"My body is already cooking from watching you dance."

She blushed and averted her eyes to the ground. "I didn't know you were watching."

He placed a hand on either side of her, closing the distance between them. Leaning down, he whispered in her ear, "Do you know how sexy you are?"

Her cheeks turned a fire engine red. She placed a hand against his chest, likely to push him away, but she stopped when their eyes met. Heat flooded her eyes, pupils dilating. "What are you doing to me?" she asked huskily.

"Same thing you're doing to me."

With that, he crushed his lips against hers, pulling her close so she could feel what she did to him. He'd been living in an almost permanent state of arousal. Last night, he had taken a cold shower, but it didn't help, not when he knew she was just down the hall.

He'd expected her to resist, but she melted in his arms instead. She reached up and locked her hands behind his neck, urging him to deepen the kiss. Their tongues were swept away in a seduction-induced striptease, breaking down every barrier between them.

"I want you so bad," he said, nibbling on her bottom lip as his hands caressed her breasts through her shirt.

"Me too."

Her voice was so quiet he wondered if he had misheard her. "Can you say that again?"

Emma opened her mouth to talk, but another voice beat her to the punch, dousing her with imaginary ice water.

"Mom, seriously?"

Shoving Devon away, Emma placed the island between them. Clearing her throat, she said, "Honey, why don't you go wash up. Supper is almost ready."

"Dad hasn't even been dead for two months, and you're already shacking it up with some guy."

"Go," she ordered, leaving no room for nonsense. When her daughter hesitated, Emma said, "Now."

Skye stomped out of the kitchen, throwing her bag on the sofa as she disappeared upstairs. Emma didn't know what to do. The closer she got to Devon, the further her daughter got away from her. She knew Skye liked Devon, but she couldn't blame her for not being comfortable with their newfound closeness. She wasn't exactly comfortable with it herself.

"Devon, we can't do this."

"She's a kid. She'll come around to the idea sooner or later."

Emma sighed and plopped herself down on a chair at the kitchen table. "Don't you get it? She's right. I can't do this. Not yet."

"Don't let her get in between us. Not now."

"There is a lot more than only her in between us, Devon."

The buzzer for the oven sounded. She got up and removed the food, placing it on top of the stove, suddenly not hungry anymore. The bacon wrapped scallops, as appetizing as they sounded before, just made her stomach roll.

"I think I'm going to go to bed. Good night, Devon."

She went to sneak by him, but he grabbed her arm. "Wait, please. My new boss is having a party tonight, and I was hoping we could go."

"You go. I'm not interested."

"All the other men's wives will be there," he pouted.

Emma couldn't help but give a weary chuckle at Devon's boyish charm. "If they all jumped off a bridge, would you do it, too?"

"Oh ya!" he said with a grin.

Pressing her palm against her forehead, she shook her head. She was fighting a losing battle. "I can't leave Skye by herself."

"Bring her. There will be other teens there, too."

"I have nothing to wear."

"I'm sure Skye has something that would fit you."

Groaning, she said, "Fine!"

Chapter Fourteen

For the fifteenth time, Emma pulled at the pink miniskirt her daughter had coerced her into wearing. She wasn't used to wearing anything above the knees. In fact, she never wore skirts at all. Hence why her shoe rack was full of runners and not high heels.

"You look great, trust me," Devon whispered in her ear. "Every guy in the room is looking at you."

"Gee, that makes me feel so much better."

"I'm the envy of every man here," he said, slinging his arm over her shoulders.

Looking around the room, she spotted at least a half a dozen ladies far more elegantly dressed than she was and more beautiful. The guys were only looking at her because they could see skin. Their expressions made her feel like a piece of meat on display, making her desperately want her jacket back.

"I'm going to go get us a drink," he said, pointing to the bar.

Emma leaned against the wall while she waited for him to come back. About five minutes later, a lady with short, vibrant red hair and a knee-length, hip-hugging green dress approached her, with two wine glasses in hand.

"You must be Tara, Trevor's wife. Our husbands are going to be working together." The lady held out a glass to her, but Emma shook her head.

"Trevor has gone to get us a drink."

"He asked me to bring this to you. My husband, Ted, commandeered him. Something about a tree out back," the woman said. "I'm Sarah by the way."

Reluctantly, she accepted the glass of wine and shook Sarah's hand. "It's nice to meet you."

"So, where did you guys move from?"

Emma had to admit that she hadn't read over the information they'd been given beyond their names, so she gave the safest answer she could think of. "Here, there, and everywhere."

The woman laughed. "Moved around a lot, then?"

"More than I wanted to," she answered honestly. She'd rather be back in her own house, in her own town. Not stuck out here with a pretend husband, acting like they were a family.

"Ted used to cart me everywhere until I said enough was enough. Sometimes you need to put your foot down with these pigheaded men. They like to go where the wind takes them."

"And apparently this wind took them into the backyard," Emma said with a half-smile, glancing around the room for her pretend spouse.

"Come, I want to introduce you to my friends."

When Devon and the other guys came back inside, he found Emma smack dab in the middle of a group of women, their hands on their chests as she spoke to them. Well, *hell*. They had tears in their eyes. The guys quickly retreated back outside, not wanting to get caught up in the tear fest.

"What kind of trouble have you brought us, old man?" one of the younger guys said to Devon.

"Hey, who are you calling old, beanpole? I could whip your butt."

"Challenge accepted."

Before the guy could even blink, Devon had him in a choke hold he couldn't get out of. "See. Told ya."

"Let him go, Trev, before he passes out," Ted said, laughing.

"What do you think the women are talking about in there?" Devon asked.

"Probably not about how loudly they can belch," another guy said, earning him a round of laughter.

And off the young guys went to guzzle their beer, entering a belching contest. He probably would have joined them, but he was pretty curious as to what his new 'wife' was divulging about their life. He turned to head inside before any damage was done, but Ted stopped him. "Let her mingle. Sheesh, you guys are like newlyweds."

"If I had a wife like her, I wouldn't stray too far either," another man said.

Little did the men know, he and Emma were exactly like newly-weds, despite their fake marriage papers which said they'd been married for sixteen years. What would it have been like watching her walk down the aisle in a white wedding gown accompanied by her father?

She had looked amazing in the picture with Peter on her wall at home. A pang of jealousy rippled through him. She was going to belong to him one day, totally and completely. There was no way he'd ever walk away from her again. Only death could keep them apart. And that, he didn't even want to think about. Instead, he was going to persuade her to dance.

Walking inside, he stopped next to her and held out his hand. "May I?"

"I don't want to dance," Emma replied, planting her feet firmly on the ground so he couldn't lead her onto the dance floor. She always lost her head when he held her, and that wasn't something she wanted to do in a room full of strangers.

"We have to put on a good show. Come on."

"They aren't going to think any differently if we don't dance." She also didn't want her daughter seeing them close again. Skye had already experienced enough trauma in her life, and Emma's heart didn't know what to think or feel either. Her body did, but she'd be a shallow person if she only did what her body wanted.

"Please?" Leaning forward, he whispered, "I promise to behave."

His warm breath on her neck sent an intoxicating shiver through her system, goose bumps appearing on her skin.

Stop it, traitor.

"I'd rather not," she said. But even as she spoke, he took her hand and guided her onto the dance floor. It seemed she had no control over her own actions.

He pulled her into his arms, but she was determined to keep some distance between them, so she put a hand on his shoulder and took his other hand in hers, typical waltz style. He smirked at her attempt. Holding their conjoined hands against his chest, he pulled her close.

"Dev—Trevor," she warned as she stepped back, but he followed by stepping forward. Emma growled under her breath, and that made his smirk widen.

"It might be better if you smile, instead of looking like you need to take a dump. We're supposed to look like a couple in love, remember?"

"Then dance with one of the other ladies ogling you," she said, breaking away from him. "Excuse me. I'm going to go find Skye." With the whole room watching, she stomped away from him.

"She isn't feeling well," he said to them, trudging after her.

All she wanted was to be left alone, but he insisted on following her. Emma turned down a hallway and as soon as she passed someone, she asked, "Excuse me, do you know where the bathroom is?"

The woman nodded. "Turn left up ahead. The bathroom is the first door on the right."

"Thank you." Emma took a step forward before stopping and looking at her again. "Do you know where the kids are hiding?"

"I think they're in the basement playing games."

"Where's the stairs?"

"At the end of the hallway," the lady said, pointing ahead of them.

With Devon hot on her heels, she had to decide between an audience with the teens or hiding out in the bathroom until he went back to the other room. With his determination, though, he'd likely sit outside the door and wait for her, unless...

"Bingo," she cried as she entered the bathroom, slamming the door behind her. Quickly, she turned the lock and went over to the window. Closing the lid to the toilet, she climbed up and pushed the window open. There wasn't a lot of room, but she should be able to squeeze through, and there was only a four-foot drop.

Contorting herself, she stuck one leg out the window and then the other. After she had slid half of her body through the opening, she came to an abrupt halt.

"Uh oh."

A faint sound of distress came from inside the washroom before she went silent again. Devon couldn't tell if it was a cry of anguish or a grunt from a dirty deed she might be doing.

"Emma, are you okay?"

"I'm fine," she snapped breathlessly. "Go away."

"You don't sound fine."

Ted rounded the corner with a huge grin on his face and tears in his eyes. "You gotta come see this. I've never seen anything so funny."

Hopefully, the man hadn't heard him call Emma by her real name. "I would, but I need to get into the bathroom. I think something is wrong with my wife," he said, pounding on the door again. "Tara, let me in."

"She's fine, in a manner of speaking." Ted grabbed Devon's shirt and gave it a pull. "Come on. I'll show you."

Reluctantly, he followed the man down the hall and out the back door. People were gathered off to the side of the house, laughing. And his new friend was taking him in that direction. He wasn't even sure he wanted to know what they found so hilarious. For some reason, he had a feeling it was going to embarrass them both.

And sure enough, he was right.

As they turned the corner, he saw half of Emma's body sticking out the window, her legs flailing as she tried to dislodge herself. Her pink mini skirt had hiked up in the process, giving them a glimpse of a tan thong underneath. Devon smacked his forehead. Of all the times for her to turn flighty, it had to be at his boss's party.

One of the kids near the back of the group was filming her. "This is so going on YouTube."

"Please turn that off," Devon said to the boy. If the kid posted it, then it could blow their cover.

"It's a free country, pops," the boy replied.

A man came up behind the kid and took the phone out of his hands. "Jared, turn it off. Hasn't your mom taught you any manners?"

"Dad, come on. You know it's funny," the young kid complained. He couldn't have been more than thirteen years old.

Devon walked over to Emma and grabbed her legs, pushing her back in through the bathroom window. He wasn't sure whether he should chuckle or be enraged at her escape attempt. What was the point of it? It wasn't like she could go anywhere. He had the keys to the car.

"Stay in the bathroom. I'm coming inside," he yelled into the open window.

But by the time he arrived, she'd already fled. This was getting a little tiresome. He understood her apprehension about coming, about everything they were going through. But hell, they were supposed to stay under the radar, and she could have just blown the entire thing.

Moving down the hall, he heard a noise in the room off to his left. He poked his head in and saw her hiding behind the door. After he entered the room, he slammed the door and crossed his arms, glaring at her. "Why?"

"So, Mr. Matthews does get angry."

"When you go and nearly blow our cover, you damn well better believe I'm angry."

"I wanted some fresh air, and you weren't giving it to me."

"So, you decide to get stuck in a window and draw suspicion to our relationship?"

"I didn't decide—you know what, never mind," Emma said, throwing her hands up in the air. "You wouldn't understand."

"Try me."

"Forget it. Let's just go home," she said as she tried to get by him.

Instead of letting her go, he picked her up and plopped her butt on the hardwood desk. "Talk, then we'll go."

"It's not like it will make a difference. Please let me go," she begged, her eyes filling with tears as her bottom lip trembled.

"Hey, it's me," he said softly, placing his hand under her chin to get her to look at him.

Emma shied away from his touch. "That's the problem."

How was she supposed to keep pretending to be his wife when she couldn't even get through one stinking party? Maybe she'd become a house hermit, squirrel herself away until this was all over, and she'd never have to see him again.

"Please talk to me."

"This is all still too raw for me." She didn't want to pretend to be what they weren't, not when everything still bubbled too close to the surface. Despite having been married to Peter, she had thought a lot about Devon and what her life would have been like with him instead. And it made her feel horrible because she couldn't let it go.

Emma had spent a lifetime missing the passion the two of them had shared. After he broke up with her, she thought maybe she had imagined it all. But having him in her life again, and seeing all the passion still sizzling between them, made her so stinking confused. She didn't know what to believe anymore.

The last thing she wanted to do was open her heart to him, but her body was fighting her every step of the way, and now her heart was trying to get in on the action. She hated that her body and her heart were betraying Peter, and as hard as she fought against it, it seemed like she was fighting a losing battle.

Emma wrapped her arms around her churning stomach, fighting the tumultuous wave of emotion rushing through her. She had wanted to have fun tonight, but standing there chatting with the girls, hearing them gush over her fake husband made her want to run and hide.

"How do you mean?" he asked.

"I can't pretend to be married to you."

"Why not?"

"Because it makes me feel like a liar and a fraud."

"It's only a fraud if what we feel for each other isn't real."

"Don't you get it? I don't want to feel anything for you. It's wrong. It's not right."

"It feels very right to me," he said, running his finger down her arm.

She shoved his hand away and said, "You're doing it again, not giving me room to breathe. That's why I was trying to get outside. It's too much for me right now. You're crowding me."

"You didn't seem to mind me crowding you yesterday."

Growling, she threw her hands up in the air. "You're impossible."

"That's what you love about me."

"Why here? Why now? Why couldn't you have been this persistent before?"

Devon didn't respond right away. Instead, he picked up a photo sitting on the desk. It was of a couple standing on the beach, looking very much in love and full of passion—so much so, they weren't even paying attention to the person with the camera.

"I shou—" His voice broke, raw emotion blatant in his face. Clearing his throat, he tried again. "I should have been."

"Shoulda, coulda, woulda," she murmured sadly, unable to tear her eyes away from the picture. It had always been her dream to have a beach wedding, but Peter hadn't been too fond of the water and refused to be talked into it. In the end, they had a small backyard wedding at his parents' place.

"I'm sorry I hurt you, Em."

"We could have been good together," she said softly.

"We still can be."

"No. Don't you see? We weren't meant to be together, and sooner or later, you'll realize that like I do, and you'll find the woman you were meant to be with."

"I'm not going anywhere," he said, placing his hand on her knee. "Not this time."

Her heart leaped at his words, but her spirit was conflicted as she stared down at her feet dangling off the desk. His words shouldn't mean anything. All that should matter was the promise she made to Peter to always be faithful and being faithful meant not letting herself fall into Devon's arms. What would people say if she took another lover so quickly?

Hopping off the table, she turned her back on him, hoping it would bring her spirit back in alignment with Peter. They had nineteen years together. That should mean something. She and Devon barely had a year together. Why did it feel like the other way around?

"My daughter isn't ready for another man in her life."

"Now who's using their daughter as an excuse?" he said wryly.

"Oh, shut up," she said, spinning around and hitting him on the shoulder with the back of her hand. "Can we just go, please?" The last thing she wanted was to have a deep conversation with him that tugged at her heart strings. He could charm a snake if he tried, and she wasn't about to let him use his tricks on her.

"Let me say goodbye to the team, and then I'll meet you and Skye at the car."

They both walked into the hallway and then went in two separate directions as she went on the hunt for Skye. After finding her downstairs, they made their way through the house, heading toward the main entrance.

They passed by an open door. Two of the ladies were in there, but she couldn't remember their names.

"Did you notice how their daughter looks nothing like him?"

"Do you think Tara cheated on him?"

Emma's eyes narrowed as a dark ball of anger grew inside her. Reaching out, she went to push the door open.

Skye grabbed her arm. "It's not worth it, Mom. Let's just go."

Red hot tears burned in her eyes as she walked out of the house. Why did people have to be so cruel? Living in a small town, she knew that any hot new gossip would spread quickly. And she didn't relish the looks that people would soon be giving her. And the worst part was, she couldn't tell them the truth. Yet one look in her eyes and they would know she was hiding something.

Life was about to become a barrel of laughs.

"Not!" she mumbled to herself as she climbed into the car. All she wanted to do in that moment was hide in a cave and never come out. Her thought of becoming a house hermit was sounding pretty good. If Devon wanted to take her anywhere, he'd have to hogtie her. She wasn't going to budge an inch until this was over.

Chapter Fifteen

"You can't hide away forever, Emma," Devon said as he put the finishing touches on a Black Velvet cake. He was determined to get her outside, one way or another. Two weeks had passed since the day of the party, and the only time she had gone outside was to go to the mailbox.

Placing her drink on the counter, she swiped her finger along the edge of the bowl of icing. "If you keep baking like this, I'll have no reason to go out."

He tapped her hand with the spatula. "Leave some of that for the cake."

"But it's so good," she said, attempting to take another swipe of the sweet chocolate topping.

Putting the spatula down, he hoisted her over his shoulder and lugged her toward the couch like a sack of potatoes, slapping her on the ass. "That's for stealing my icing."

She shrieked with laughter. "Hey, that's my butt you're touching, mister."

"And that's my icing."

Plopping her on the couch, he returned to his duty of icing the cake. Since it was his day off, he was doing the cooking. He didn't mind in the slightest. Cooking was his thing back in the day.

Emma sat watching him, sipping away on a rum and coke. Her usual drink of choice. Devon wished she was this light-hearted all the time. A few drinks did wonders for the woman. When she was sober, there was more pain in her eyes, and likewise in his, knowing he put some of it there.

The reservations she had about the two of them were never too far from the surface. He could only hope that after spending more time with him, she'd see that he had changed and was in it for the long haul.

He didn't want to replace Peter. Emma and her husband had been together for a long time, but he hoped that she'd make room for him, and they could finally have a life together, too. Maybe, if she didn't take too long deciding, they could still have a baby together.

Wow, slow down. His mind was off galloping, and it was time to pull in the reins. First, he had to convince her they belonged together. She was still miles away from the idea.

Emma sauntered her way back into the kitchen and dipped her finger into his icing again, earning her a second tap on the hand.

"Don't make me tie you up, woman!" he warned, his lips curling into a grin.

"Ha! You don't have the guts," she replied, dipping her finger into the dark chocolate goodness a third time.

His cock twitched as she sucked the creamy icing off her finger. Her eyes watched him, daring him to act. He couldn't very well back down from a dare. Untying his apron, he laid it on the counter and rinsed off his hands. The cake would have to wait until he dealt with his unruly food thief.

Leaving her in the kitchen, he jogged up the stairs, two at a time, and ducked into his bedroom. If he remembered correctly, there were a few ties hanging in the closet. Pulling open the doors, a smirk spread across his face.

Bingo!

He was right. Staring back at him was a row of silk-ties. Bondage wasn't something he had contemplated before, but the thrill rocketing through made him wish he'd tried it sooner. Devon chuckled. His life was turning into Fifty Shades of Grey. He grabbed four of them off the rack and went back downstairs.

The kitchen was unsurprisingly empty. The house silent. His little rebel had become a magician and disappeared. He stared at his cake on the counter and then at the ties, torn between the need to finish icing the dessert or following his desire to hunt her down.

As much as he liked eating, having his wicked way with her sounded a lot more enticing. The growing ache in his pants battled with his growling stomach. Food always hit the spot, but the idea of sex hit an entirely different area. Powered by the caveman inside him, he went on the hunt for his missing prey, armed with silk ties—the best in the business.

"Oh, Emma," he catcalled as he wandered through the house, listening as he went. This time, they didn't have to worry about Skye barging in. She was staying at a new friend's house, which meant he could work on spoiling his 'almost' wife tonight. Show her what he could offer if they stayed together.

Searching for her reminded him of playing hide-and-seek as a kid, but the reward was going to be so much better. Even his friend below knew it. He was raring and ready to go. Devon couldn't remember being this horny since God knows when. Hell, not since he was with her in high school. They had a connection he couldn't even begin to explain.

After searching the main floor, he stood in the living room with his hands on his hips, puzzled. There was no way she was up on the second floor. He would have heard her walk up the stairs. Every step creaked and groaned. It would have been hard to miss, but he might as well check anyway. "If you don't come out, I'll eat the cake myself," he yelled.

No response.

After he searched the last room in the house, he stood there scratching his head. Where could she be? He walked back to the living room and looked around, his eyes honing in on the key rack next to the door.

"Bingo."

The car keys were missing. And sure enough, there she was, sitting in the passenger seat with all the doors locked and a huge grin on her face. He walked up to the passenger door, still carrying the ties.

She stuck her tongue out at him.

"Unlock the door, Em," he said.

She shook her head.

"Don't make me come in there."

With a smug look on her face, Emma held up the keys, dangling them in front of him. What a little tease. She had failed to recall one thing. And he was more than happy to rain on her parade.

"Aren't you forgetting something?" he asked.

Emma stared at him blankly. What could she possibly be forgetting? It was hard to concentrate when all she could see were the ties swinging in the light breeze. The army of butterflies in her stomach fluttered wildly, pounding against her organs. He actually wanted to tie her up.

She'd already used up her holy Hannah count for the entire year and couldn't think of anything left to say that suited the situation. Good golly miss molly? Geez Louise. No, she used those too many times, too.

Devon stuck his hand in his pocket and when he pulled it out, the edge of a key chain came into her line of view. "You can't escape, Emma."

Crap!

Emma smacked her forehead. He had his own keys. The locking mechanism clicked open, but she quickly pressed the lock button before he could open the door.

Amusement danced in his eyes. "I'm going to get in eventually and then…" He grabbed one tie with both hands and snapped it tautly, grinning.

"Nu uh," she said, shaking her head.

He clicked the keys again, but she was quick on the trigger, effectively keeping him out for the time being. But being the resourceful twit he was, it wouldn't keep him out for long.

"Careful. The consequence of hitting that lock button will be a smack on that hot, sexy ass of yours."

Her eyes widened, and liquid heat pooled in her core, dampening her underwear again. *Geez.* What she wouldn't give for an off switch. As hard as she tried to suppress her attraction to him, their bodies were intricately connected. In her mind's eye, she could see herself tossed over his knee and her pants pulled down, her bare butt showing.

The grin on his face widened as he let his hand rest on the door handle, hiding the hand with the car keys behind his back. Only the clicking sound of the locking mechanism would alert her to him pushing the button. Anticipation crashed over her like waves against a rock.

They stared each other down through the glass. His grin couldn't get any wider and neither could her eyes. Any wider and she'd pop her eyeballs. Click went the locks and Devon got the door open before she could hit the button again.

Emma squealed and dove into the backseat, attempting to reach the driver's passenger door. But before she could open it, he wrapped his fingers around her ankle.

"Gotcha."

"Let me go," she cried. When he tickled the bottom of her foot, she couldn't stifle a giggle. "Stop!"

Pushing the door open, Emma grabbed the edge of the car and tried to pull herself out headfirst, kicking at him with her legs. But he grabbed both her ankles and tied them together.

Why? Oh, why did I let Skye have a sleepover today?

Devon climbed into the back seat and straddled her back lightly, grabbing her hands.

"Don't you da..." Her voice faded when he pressed his hard length against her backside, her insides turning to mush. The all too familiar fire gathered between her legs. Emma swallowed hard. Her body was conspiring against her.

"Can't run away now," he said.

"Get off me, you big lummox." She tried to pull herself out from underneath him, but she was stuck.

"Since you asked so politely." Devin kissed the back of her head and climbed out of the car, helping Emma to her feet temporarily before tossing her over his shoulder again.

"Jeepers Creepers, put me down," she cried, pounding his back with her fists.

"I would, but your feet are tied, and you can't walk," he said, chuckling. "Besides, I need to work out. I haven't been to the gym in days."

"Then do some push-ups or something. Just put me down."

"I will."

Despite his reply, he made no move to do so. The thrill of what they were about to do sent her body on a roller coaster ride. She wasn't used to being manhandled but found it strangely erotic. At least her body did. Her mind was scrambling for ways to extricate herself from the situation.

"Let me go or I'll—" She gasped when his hand connected with her behind. "Stop smacking my butt!"

"That was for the first time you locked me out. The rest can wait until I have an unbridled view of your cute ass."

Emma laughed and groaned all in one breath. "You are such a guy!"

His chest rumbled as he laughed. "I'm glad you noticed."

Defeated, she rested her arm on his back and her chin in her palm. Their trip was not going as planned. She had been determined to avoid this *situation* between them. Right now, she was a novelty to him. Once he came down off the high, he'd disappear again. It was just who he was. She had no reason to believe otherwise.

But she was rapidly losing her strength to fend him off. She liked him, wanted him...needed him. She didn't want to like it, but she couldn't stop herself from giving in, not when his strong arms flexed against her thighs as he carried her.

"Yoo-hoo, Emma, where'd you disappear off to?" he asked, cutting into her thoughts as he kicked the front door open.

"Last I checked, I'm laying over your shoulder, dumbass," she quipped.

Devon chuckled as he adjusted his grip on her before heading up the stairs. "We haven't even made it to the bed, and you're already chucking words around. I'm better than I thought."

"Did anyone ever tell you that you have a big ego?"

"Yep."

Emma giggled as he flung her down on the bed, bouncing once. Before she had a chance to move, he straddled her and grabbed her hands. Her heart raced and her eyes widened as he untied her wrists. Was he going to let her go?

Nope. He proceeded to tie up her left wrist again and then secured it to the bedpost.

"Wait!" she cried, her nerves kicking up a notch. "What if there's a fire?"

"The only fire is the one about to be set in here," he said, looking down at her, his eyes smoldering.

Mesmerized, she found herself getting lost in the depth of his smoky gaze, taking her back to their time on the trampoline. This was who they were. Who they always would be. He may not be her man anymore, but in some ways, he always would be.

"Then light it," Emma whispered as she surrendered her free wrist to him, giving herself over to the emotions welling inside her. There was no one in the world she wanted more than him in that moment.

A husky growl emanated from within him, his heart thumping

against his ribcage. He swallowed the lump that was growing in his throat as he stared at her delicate wrist. She was giving herself to him freely. It didn't matter how he'd treated her in the past, she was letting him in.

He felt like a king, one that was being given the greatest treasure in the kingdom. And she was letting him tie her up. Life doesn't get much better than this, and his cock definitely agreed as it strained to break free from his clothes. Taking her hand, he lifted it to his lips and placed a gentle kiss on her wrist before securing it with the silk tie.

After he tied her wrists to the bedpost, Emma giggled seductively, glancing down at her body. "You forgot something."

"Have I?" he asked, his lips curling into a mischievous grin as he ran his hand down the front of her shirt.

"Oh, don't you dare. This is my best—"

Grabbing her shirt, Devon ripped it open, buttons flying.

"You!" She yanked on the silk ties binding her wrist. Lust, mixed with anger, filled her eyes.

"Yes, me." He smiled appreciatively at the black lace bra she was wearing, happy that the clasp was in the front. Devon lightly ran the back of his knuckles across the swell of her breasts.

She drew in a quick breath. Her reaction to his touch filled him with a heady sense of power. He didn't think he could ever get his fill of her, not even if he had her for a lifetime. Her soft, silky skin reminded him of a porcelain doll, delicate and fine.

Running his hand down her chest and across her stomach, he stopped at the faded scar on the lower right side of her stomach. His gut twisted at how close he had come to losing her in the past to appendicitis. The infection almost killed her. Leaning down, he kissed her scar. She'd been through so much, and he, in his stubbornness, wasn't there for her. If she had died—

Devon shook his head refusing to think about what could have happened. He needed to stay in the moment. Right here. Right now. They were together, and that was all that mattered. Grabbing the waist of her spandex and her underwear, he slid them both down, tossing them to the corner of the room. Seeing her laying there made him want to take his rightful place on top and make her his, but it wasn't time yet.

He grabbed the two other ties from off the floor and held them up, grinning. "Time for your feet."

He reached for her left foot, but she retracted her leg, pulling her knee close to her chest. When he reached for the other one, she did the same thing. Devon made a 'tsk tsk' sound. "You know you'll have to pay for that, right?"

Crawling up the bed, he went to grab her foot, but she wrapped her legs around him, making him lose his balance. He landed on top of her, his forearms resting on the pillow on either side of her head. Their faces inches apart.

Sexy little vixen.

"Fancy meeting you here," she said, chuckling.

"Did anyone ever tell you that you're trouble with a capital T?" he replied, kissing the tip of her nose as he tried to get up.

Wiggling her nose like a bunny, she kept her legs wrapped securely around him. "I think you're the one with a capital P," Emma said, grinding her hips into the growing bulge in his pants.

"If you don't let me go, Miss Smartass, I'm going to have to take some drastic measures."

"If I have to be stuck, so do you."

He reached in between them and dug his fingers into her sides, tickling her. She shrieked in his ear.

"Not your best singing voice, Em."

"Stop," she cried, laughing so hard tears filled her eyes. His fingers pressed into her skin again, but she still refused to release him.

"I still remember every single ticklish spot so don't think I'm above using them." Proving his point, Devon touched the spot beside her pelvic bone, making her jump. Her legs loosened slightly, and he extricated himself from her grip.

Disappointment flashed across her face. Laughing, he gave her leg a gentle pat before grabbing her ankle. "Don't worry. I'm not going anywhere. I have a job to finish." He wanted to make this a moment she would never forget. He certainly wouldn't, considering he has never tied anyone up before. Was it wrong that he was enjoying it?

Nah.

Chuckling, he secured her ankle. Once finished, he stood up and happily perused her naked body, legs spread wide. He'd never seen anything so enticing and enchanting before. Devon licked his lips as his gaze stopped in the one spot he ached to bury himself into, her neatly trimmed runway.

"You are so beautiful," he said, huskily. Devon loosened his belt and slid his pants off, his erection creating a tent pole in front of his boxers. She stared at his shorts. A look of appreciation fluttered in her eyes.

"See something you like?"

Emma flashed him a cheeky grin. "Not yet."

He yanked off his shorts and stood there in front of her, running his hand over the length of his cock. "How about now?"

She bit her lip as she stared at his hardened flesh. Her gaze followed his hand as it moved up and down, pre-cum already moistening the head. He'd never been so turned on in his life. Other girls didn't arouse him like she could. There was something about her, about who she was, that he couldn't get over.

"Devon!" Emma moaned, struggling against the silk ties that bound her to the bed. She wanted to feel him, to touch him, and run her own hands along his length. Being tied up was oddly arousing but equally frustrating.

Her core was already throbbing, and he hadn't even started yet. It was like her body was creating nerve endings she didn't even know she had. Could she orgasm without being touched? It almost felt like she was going to. Devon kneeled on the bed between her legs and ran his fingers across her thighs, nearing, but not touching, the part of her body that was on fire.

"Don't tease me." She lifted her hips toward him, letting him know exactly where she wanted to be touched.

Laughing, he said, "Hmm, you aren't just trouble. You're also impatient I see."

As he spoke, he slid his fingers into her warm, wet pussy, and she let out a sweet, husky whimper. Emma gripped the silk ties tightly as he hit her g-spot. Oh gosh. How the heck could he find that spot so quickly?

"Stop," she moaned.

"Why?"

"You're going to make me pee again."

"Relax, you aren't going to pee."

"But..." Another moan ate her words as his fingers hit the spot again, making her forget how to talk. Intense waves of pure ecstasy washed over her entire body, all rushing to meet his fingers moving inside her. How? Why him? She wanted to be cold to him, but everything about him invited her in.

"I can feel it swelling," he said, pleasure lacing his voice. He sounded quite pleased with himself.

"You think you're such a hot shot, don't you?" she murmured. "Oh, holy geez." Emma tried to reach out, but her hands were trapped. *Damn it.* Her breathing quickened, and her heart pounded in her chest as her body raced toward a peak as high as the tallest mountain in the world. Not that she could remember the name of it right now.

"Please, Devon, let me go. I wanna touch you."

"All in good time, now be a good girl and let me see you squirt." He moved his fingers harder and faster against her sensitized g-spot.

"I...don't...know...how," she cried between gasps. The sensation was back. She had to pee, needed to pee. "Devon—"

"Yes, you do," he interrupted.

She cried out as her hips bucked off the bed. Every muscle in her body took on a mind of their own, and she gave into the feeling pouring through her body. Sliding his fingers out, a stream of fluid followed, coating his hands.

"Oh, god! Not again," she moaned, still lost in the overwhelmingly deep sensation rocking through her system, an orgasm deeper than any other she'd ever experienced.

As she started her descent from the peak, Devon positioned himself above her, looking all happy and smug.

"Don't be going and getting all cocky now," she said, all out of breath.

"I—"

The door slammed open behind them, and two people barreled into the room, guns pointing directly at them.

"Freeze!"

Chapter Sixteen

"Are you fucking kidding me?" Devon muttered under his breath, leaning his forehead against her chest. Emma screamed and tried to squeeze into a small ball underneath him as best as she could with her limbs tied up.

"Get away from her," one of the men said. "Nice and slow."

Standing up, he held his hands in the air and turned to face them. When he got a good look at them, he dropped his hands. "Seriously, Greg?"

Greg looked at Devon and then at Emma on the bed, his cheeks reddening. "Oh man. We're really sorry. We heard screaming and thought she was in danger."

Emma knew her cheeks were as colorful as Greg's. They felt like a rolling inferno. Never in her life had she been as embarrassed as she was in that moment. She was like a model posing for a nude painting and not by choice. She wanted to disappear, never to be seen of again.

"Impressive knots, man," the other guy said, pointing to Emma's bindings.

"They aren't that hard to master really." Her wanna-be husband grinned, shrugging his shoulders.

Grabbing the pillow under her head, she gave it her best toss, smacking Devon in the back of the head. "Get them out of here."

"Well, you heard the lady." With a flourish, Devon swung his arm toward the door.

The two men turned and walked toward the exit. The unnamed guy left the room, but Greg stopped and turned around one last time. When his mouth opened, she didn't want to hear what he was about to say, but she couldn't plug her ears.

"I don't suppose you can convince my wife to...uh...you know." Greg pointed to Emma.

"Get out of here!" She threw the other pillow at the security guard, but it fell short of the target. Greg quickly left the room, much to her relief. How was she supposed to look that man in the eye again after this? A shiver slithered through her body like a snake. This was not something she wanted to be remembered for.

Devon turned around, chuckling. "Just when you think you have the place all to yourself."

"Get these ties off me," she begged, suddenly not in the mood anymore. She was never drinking again. That's it. No amount of pleading or begging would make her reach for the sex inducing beverage again.

He kneeled on the bed between her legs, running his hands up her inner thighs. The shock of his touch was like the euphoria you get from a drug-induced high, leaving her almost incapable of rational thought. As she moved her wrist, her ring snagged on the tie, making her cringe. *I'm sorry, Peter.*

"Devon, please, I want to stop."

"Damn it, Emma. This game you're playing is getting annoying." Devon frowned as he yanked at the tie that bound her left wrist.

She winced, tears forming in her eyes. Why did it always have to be about sex with guys? You'd think his hormone levels would have dipped by now. He wasn't a teenager anymore. She didn't think that the talk her brother had given her as a teen about *boys being pigs* included adult men, too.

"I'm not playing a game." She hated how her chin wobbled as she spoke. *Be strong, don't cry.* Reaching over, she undid her other wrist.

"Why don't you let me get you another drink?"

"I don't want another one."

"Well, you're a helluva lot more fun with a drink."

That stung, like a hundred bees jabbing at her heart. "I'm not here to have fun. All I want is to stop hurting and get on with my life. I want the bad guy caught, and I want to go home."

His eyes softened, and he took her face in his hands. "I'm sorry, Em. I'm an ass sometimes. He's going to be caught. I promise."

"You make a lot of promises," she whispered.

"If they don't find him, I know some people who can track down that son of a bitch," he said, his voice cool and certain.

There was a lot about this man that had changed and yet a lot remained the same. And as much as she hated it, everything about him intrigued her. She had a hard time keeping her hands to herself. They itched to reach out and touch his bare chest, his sculpted stomach, and his erection. Her body started aching all over again.

Clearing her throat, she said, "I can't believe I'm saying this, but we should let the police do their job." It would be great for it all to be over and done with, but she didn't want to see him get into trouble or his friends.

"Well, the offer is there. You just have to say the word." Devon couldn't believe he was offering to help find the shithead. In a way, he didn't want the asshole to be found because that would put an end to their time together. And she'd boot him out of her life quicker than he could bat an eyelash.

"Thanks." Emma finished untying her ankles and wrapped the sheet around her body. As she went to walk away from him, he got up and stepped on the sheet, preventing her from moving away.

"You do realize this is going to happen eventually, right?" he said, with a twinkle in his eyes. The sexual tension between them was so thick you could cut it with a knife. They never failed to wind up in bed after she had a drink, and he couldn't help but laugh. She reminded him of a female version of Raj from The Big Bang Theory, except she didn't have the caramel-colored skin, and she had all the right female body parts.

One day, they'd have sex, and it would be when she didn't need a drink to open up to him. He was going to wait for that day. No more stealing moments when she wasn't sober. He'd let her make the first move. And when she did, he'd make sure their time together was something she'd never forget.

The knowledge of their inevitable meeting was blatant in her eyes as she pulled away from him. She wanted it as much as he did. That was easy to see. Emma was an open book when it came to her emotions and maybe that was why it frustrated him a little.

Nodding her head at his question, she pulled away and quickly left the room, leaving him sitting on the bed, naked and in desperate need of release. He could have pushed her a little more, and she probably would have caved, but that's not how he wanted their first time to be. Their time would come, and it was going to be hot, as hot as he could make it. Looking down, he stroked himself, wishing he could be inside her. *Patience, boy, patience.* They'd have their time under the sun, but it wasn't happening tonight.

The unfinished cake crossed his mind, making his stomach growl. Having a shower and then devouring the cake sounded like a pretty good second choice, as long as his little minx didn't eat all the icing before he got back downstairs.

Was there anything to the proverbial phrase, you can't have your cake and eat it, too? Would she let him have both? Her friendship and her love? She wanted to keep him in the friend zone, but he wanted more. A lot more, but would he have the time to get there?

Why the hell did he even offer to contact his friends? If they solved the mystery, she'd pull herself away, and he'd never have another chance to get close. He was lucky that McGregor was willing to go along with his ploy, but things were moving a little more slowly in the relationship department than he was hoping.

"Please, let me have enough time to change her mind," he prayed, hoping that God would hear his plea. The big man probably wouldn't have approved of his little scheme. But he knew if God did exist, he'd understand what it meant to love someone enough that you'd do anything for them.

Standing up, he walked into the bathroom to drown his sorrows in the shower. At this point, he would give up almost everything to be with her. But he had no idea what it would take to change her mind.

"Life! Why can't it ever be easy?"

"Mom, seriously! I haven't been able to stay at anyone's house for two weeks. Why are you treating me like I'm grounded?" Skye complained, following Emma around the house.

"I need you here," she replied, as she dusted the bookshelf.

"Why?"

"Because I do." Emma tried to continue down the hallway, but Skye stepped in front of her. Given that her daughter was as stubborn as she was, this conversation would not end well.

"It's not fair to put me under house arrest. I didn't do anything."

"You aren't under house arrest."

"What do you call not letting me go anywhere? It's just one night, please."

"Why don't you invite them over here? You haven't had anyone over yet," Emma suggested.

"That's because I don't want to."

"Why not?"

Her daughter raised her eyebrows. "You guys are embarrassing." In a high pitch flirty voice, Skye said, "Oh, Devon, stop that. Tee hee hee."

Emma cringed. "I do not sound like that."

"Yes, you do and it's gross," Skye replied, her eyes taking on a despondent look. "You were never like that with Daddy. It's like you love Devon more."

Emma took her daughter by the hand and guided her to the couch. "Your daddy and I had our flirty time, too. Maybe not as much in the end, but it was still there. I loved him so much and always will."

"Then why are you even flirting with Devon?"

"Boy this is hard." Emma sighed as she laid her head back against the couch, closing her eyes for a moment before looking back at Skye. "Have you ever heard of the phrase, the one that got away?"

"Yes."

"Devon was my first love. I fell head over heels for him, so much so I was planning our wedding in my head. When he dumped me, a part of my heart went with him. I didn't realize exactly how much until he showed up at our door and all my old feelings resurfaced."

"Why do you even still like a guy that dumped you?"

"That's a mystery for the ages, sweetheart. Beats the heck out of me." She would probably never know the answer to that one and wondered if the idea was enough to label her insane. What sane person would set themselves up to be let down again?

"You should put laxatives in his coffee. You know, pay back."

Emma stifled a chuckle. "We're going to do no such thing. Now scoot. It's your turn to do the dishes."

"If I do the dishes, then can I go to Julie's house? I promise I'll be back bright and early tomorrow morning."

Something about letting her go to her friend's house didn't sit right in Emma's spirit. "I haven't met Julie or her parents."

"You didn't meet Tammy's parents either, but you let me stay there. Besides, Julie isn't allowed to come over, her older brother is visiting."

"If they already have company, they might not want another mouth to feed."

"Her parents said it was okay."

Groaning inwardly, Emma pushed herself off the couch. As

much as she wanted Skye to stay, she knew she couldn't hold her hostage forever. People would start questioning her parenting ability.

That meant she'd have another evening alone with Devon and after the heart to heart with Skye, she was a little too vulnerable to handle his advances. She hated that she still cared for him, and yet, she loved the giddy feeling. It was addicting and frustrating.

"Fine. If you do every single dirty dish in the house, you can go."

Skye squealed and hugged her mom. "Thank you, thank you."

As her daughter took off toward the kitchen, Emma yelled, "Don't forget the utensils this time."

Often, Skye would only do half the dishes, leaving the other half on the counter. And when Emma inquired about them, her daughter would say they weren't there when she was doing the dishes. Seriously, could kids really not see what was sitting right in front of them?

"I won't," her daughter yelled from the kitchen.

Considering she wanted Skye to stay home tonight, it would probably be the one night that her daughter actually did them all. It wouldn't surprise her in the slightest. Placing the duster back in the closet, she turned to go up the stairs when the front door opened.

Knowing it would be Devon, she ducked into the computer room, her heart pounding. She wasn't ready to spend time alone with him again. Maybe she should stay with Skye over at Julie's. Emma smirked. That would totally cramp her kid's style.

Her daughter was lucky she wasn't that mean. It was too bad she didn't have any girlfriends to go out with. But she didn't want to get close to anyone and risk them finding out her secret. She hated keeping secrets and sucked at it.

"Emma?" His voice rang like a symphony through the house.

She desperately looked around the room for something, anything she could hide behind. Okay, so maybe that was childish. But, heck, he made her feel seventeen again. If she could hide the rest of the night, she might get through the evening without making a fool of herself. She was the queen of fools where he was concerned.

"Emma?" he called again. "I know you're here."

The sound of his footsteps echoed down the hallway. Emma raced to the closet and dove inside, pulling the door closed behind her just as he entered the room. Holding her breath, she could hear Devon's footsteps closing in on the closet. Did he hear the click of the door?

Please don't come in. Please don't come in.

There was no way she was going to be able to avoid him all night, but hopefully he'd make plans with his buddies and leave her alone at home. Or maybe she could take the car and go to a movie or something.

Soon, silence filled the room again as his footsteps faded down the hall. Emma peeked her head out of the closet to make sure the coast was clear. "This is so silly," she muttered to herself. She was a grown woman who was capable of handling a man.

Ha!

Who was she kidding? The only man in the world she couldn't handle was Mr. bonehead. He was...he was...heck, she didn't even know what he was, or how he had so much power over her. One would think that twenty years would have been enough time to distance herself from him. The hurt, the pain, even the love should have died already.

Emma plopped herself down in the large rocking chair and leaned her head back against the seat. Would he always have this whirlwind effect on her? She had the feeling that no matter how much time passed between them, she'd always have feelings for him. Her body and her heart took to him like a fly on a sticky trap. Stuck like glue no matter how hard it tried to get away.

It was harder to fight him than to let herself give in. But she owed it to Peter to fight. She didn't want to dishonor him by sleeping with the first guy who showed interest in her. And, of course, it had to be Devon. She couldn't seem to stop herself from climbing into bed with him. If it wouldn't have been for her daughter or the security guards, they would have had sex by now, of that she was certain. And what made it worse was that she desperately wanted to hold him and touch him.

But she couldn't escape the nagging feeling it wouldn't last for them. That it wasn't meant to. She'd already lost one man she had loved, and that was enough. If she let Devon in and lost him, she'd lose her strength to keep going.

Why did things have to be so hard? Some people never had to face a single hard time in their life. And then, there was her. Resting her elbow on the armrest, she leaned her forehead against her palm, rocking the chair gently back and forth. It was like her life was doomed to be a tough ride.

Maybe she should warn Devon to stay away from her, so he didn't somehow get hurt, too. She was the one that got him wrapped up in her mess by responding to him in the first place.

"Idiot," she muttered, smacking her forehead.

Standing up, she walked toward the door and out into the hall-way. Emma screamed when hands came out of nowhere, sweeping her feet off the floor.

Chapter Seventeen

"Damn you, Devon." She smacked his chest as he held her like a baby. "Stop freaking me out."

Skye came running around the corner, and when she saw the two of them, she placed her hands on her hips. "Can't you guys wait until I'm gone?" she said in a huff.

"Let me go," Emma whispered.

He let her legs go, and her feet touched the ground. She'd have to discuss relationship boundaries with him again. They desperately needed some ground rules. Not that Devon would ever follow them, though.

Turning to her daughter, Emma asked, "Are the dishes done, Skye?"

"I was working on the last dish when I heard you scream." Spinning around, Skye went back to the kitchen, leaving the two of them alone.

"You really have to stop doing that when my daughter is around. She doesn't like us flirting."

"So." He wrapped his arms around her again. "She'll have to get used to it."

Pulling away, she said, "It doesn't quite work like that. She's had a rough enough time already. I'm not going to do anything that makes it any worse for her right now. It's hard enough that she has to pretend you're her dad."

"Maybe it will get her used to the idea before I pop the question."

Emma plugged her ears, afraid of what he had in mind. "No popping."

"It's gonna pop someday."

Knowing he wanted to ask her *the question* made her insides tingle viciously. "Pop it elsewhere." She turned and walked away with her hands still over her ears.

Devon grabbed her hands as he wrapped his arms around her. Her back to his front. "You're going to marry me someday."

His breath on her neck and the confidence in his voice made her heart skip a beat as an electric shock raced through her body. His lips gently brushed the side of her neck. She drew in a sharp breath.

"I'm going to drop on one knee and say, Emma Praught, will you marry me?"

Her heart leaped into her throat. He wouldn't? He couldn't.

"And you're going to say yes."

"No," she whispered in a strangled voice.

"Yes."

"No."

"Emma, I could do this all day."

Emma pushed away from him, her tearful eyes blazing. He'd never seen her flip so quickly from quiet to full on angry.

"Don't you get it? I don't want to marry you."

When she whirled around to storm away, he grabbed her arm. "Why?"

"Gee, I wonder why, genius. You have commitment issues, and you don't even realize it. You left me for a stupid reason. You left your wife, the mother of your kids, for whatever reason. I'm not going to give you a chance to do that again. I've lost too much already." She yanked her arm free from his clutches and turned to walk away.

That stung more than he wanted it to, but in one way, she was right. He had left her for a stupid reason. And as for why he left his ex-wife, it was finally time to reveal the truth on that too.

"I left her because I was still in love with you." Emma paused mid-step, not saying a word. But he knew she was listening, so he continued, "It wasn't fair to keep her tied to a relationship when my heart belonged to another."

She made a low-pitched sound of distress before bolting down the hallway, leaving him there, scratching his head. Now what? He had thought telling her would help his cause, but it clearly had the opposite effect.

Throwing his hands up in the air, Devon turned and walked the other way. "Women!"

"Are you sure you don't want to come in for a bit?" Julie's mom, Karen, asked.

"I don't want to impose," Emma replied, stuffing her hands in the pockets of her windbreaker.

"Not in the slightest. The boys have gone out for the evening, so it would be nice to have someone to chat with for a bit."

Reluctantly, she followed the tall, elegant brunette inside the modest two-story brownstone house. Like the woman walking in front of her, nothing in the house was out of place, not a speck of dust to be seen. She wondered how people found the time to keep up with their housework. When Peter was off work, he would help occasionally, but Emma always found herself falling behind.

When they neared the kitchen, the woman knocked three times on the entrance way before turning the light on. She went to reach for the light switch again, but quickly glanced at Emma and appeared to decide against it.

"Would you like tea or coffee?"

"Just a glass of water would be fine, thank you." The woman gave her a questioning glance, so Emma continued, "I've never been one for tea or coffee."

"A glance of orange juice, then?"

Emma nodded.

"I was so thrilled when Julie said Hailey could sleep over. She hasn't had a friend stay over for a very long time," the woman said, her smile fading. "Partly my fault, I suppose."

"How come?"

Karen pulled three glasses out of the cupboard and proceeded to pour juice into the glasses. As she tilted the juice container over the third glass, she glanced up at Emma and quickly put the container down.

"I guess you could say I have some silly habits that embarrass her." Putting the juice back in the fridge, Karen stared at the remaining empty glass, her fingers curling around the edge of the counter.

"Kids will always find something to be embarrassed about. They'll outgrow it eventually," Emma said softly.

"I hope so," Karen replied, wiping her hands on her skirt. "So, Julie says you guys are from British Columbia?"

"We've been all over the place, really."

"We used to live close to Vancouver ages ago. My brother still lives there. Same with my oldest son."

Emma's eyes widened, and her heart skipped a beat. Swallowing hard, she placed her drink back on the counter.

"Are you okay?" Karen asked.

"Do you have a bathroom?"

"Yes, down the hall. Second door on the left."

Disappearing quickly into the bathroom, she locked the door and leaned against it, desperately trying to get her heart to beat rhythmically again. Vancouver was a big place. The odds of Karen's family knowing her were slim to none. However, the slim chance was more than enough for her chest to ache.

Emma shoved her hands into her hair, gripping it tightly as she slid down the door. What was she supposed to do now? She couldn't force Skye to come home, and if she tried to stay, her daughter would flip out.

Closing her eyes, she let her hands fall to her lap and took a deep breath. As she breathed out, she listened to the sound of the air passing between her lips. It was not like they came from a small town where everyone knew each other.

"You're overreacting, Emma," she muttered.

A second later, an unexpected knock on the door made her jump. "You okay, dear?" Karen asked.

"Yes," she said, her voice cracking. "I'll be out in a minute."

Emma reached into her pocket and pulled out her cell phone. Devon would know what to do.

Devon leaned down and lit the final candle in the living room, and then stepped back to examine his romantic set-up. He'd already warned the security guards not to interrupt them. He wasn't going to woo her into bed, but he did want quality time alone with her.

Glancing down at his watch, he noticed an hour had passed since the girls left. Emma should be back shortly. The chocolates and roses were sitting on the coffee table, and the champagne was chilling on ice.

He'd already changed out of his work clothes and had a shower. There wasn't much else for him to do now but wait. The cell phone buzzed in his pocket. Pulling it out, he noticed it was Emma calling.

"Hey, Em, everything okay?"

"Vancouver...parents...Julie." She spoke so quickly that he only caught every other word.

"Wow. Slow down. Take a deep breath and try again."

Emma gave an exasperated sigh, but he heard her take a few deep breaths before trying again. "Julie's mom said that her brother lives in Vancouver. Her son lives there, too. The same son that just so happens to be staying at their place tonight with a friend."

"Vancouver is a big place. I'm sure they won't know who you are," Devon said calmly.

"My face was all over the news. Of course, they'll know. Then that creep will know. And...and—" she cried, panic lacing her every word.

"I'm sure everything will be okay," he interrupted. "I'm sure McGregor knows everyone in town. He wouldn't have sent us here if he thought we'd be in danger."

"But—"

"No buts. Now come home, I'll take your mind off everything." He sat down on the sofa and crossed his legs, his ankle resting just above his knee.

"I don't think I should leave her here alone."

"If it will make you feel better, I'll call McGregor."

"Thanks, Dev. Call me after you speak with him."

Before he said another word, he heard the click of the phone. Letting out a sigh of his own, he pulled the phone away from his ear and searched for the man's number. She was not going to let this one rest until he'd crossed all the T's and dotted all the I's.

Dialing his number, he waited for the cop to answer.

"Constable McGregor."

"Hey, it's Devon. You left out a pertinent detail in our discussion."

"What's that?"

"That your sister, Karen, has a son living in Vancouver."

Emma wanted to stay safely behind the locked bathroom door until Devon called her back, but she didn't want to leave Skye alone.

Cautiously, she stepped into the hallway and went in search of her daughter.

The girls were in the den playing 'Just Dance,' sweating up a blue streak and giggling as they competed against each other. She sat down on the couch quietly and watched them. Julie didn't give any indication that she knew them and neither did her mom, but still the idea didn't sit well with her.

She opened her mouth to tell Skye that they might have to leave after all, but she closed it quickly when her daughter looked at her with laughter twinkling in her eyes. Her face didn't light up very often, and Emma didn't want to be the one to spoil it for her.

"Mom, what's wrong?"

"Don't worry about me." Emma waved off Skye's look of concern. "Dance away, girls." Her insides twisted with fear, but she forced a smile on her face, nodding toward the television.

Chances were slim that something was going to happen, but she couldn't help the anxiety that weaved its way intricately through every nerve in her body. It was so bad that even the slightest temperature change in the room brought out goose bumps on her skin.

Her phone vibrated in her hand a mere second before it rang, making Emma jump. The phone slipped out of her hand, falling on the hardwood floor. "Geez Louise." She leaned over the edge of the couch and picked it up.

The girls turned and looked at her. She chuckled nervously and shrugged her shoulders as she answered the call. "Well?"

"McGregor says not to worry. He knows the family and says that we can trust them."

She waited for peace to flood her soul, but it stayed hidden from her grasp. Trusting a cop didn't come easy for her, and rightly so. "I'm not sure what to do."

"I do. Let your daughter have fun with her friend. She'll be safe, I promise."

As she watched her daughter twirl around, Emma's heart twisted painfully. She walked up to Skye and gave her a big hug. Her daughter grunted in frustration as her inability to move thwarted her winning streak.

Julie's fist pumped in the air, and she shouted with joy.

"Aw, Mom," Skye complained, but still she wrapped her own arms around Emma.

"Love you, baby girl."

"Love you, too."

As Emma neared the door, she turned back one last time to look at her precious jewel. Her daughter meant more to her than anything in the entire world. *Please don't let anything happen to my baby.*

When Emma entered the living room, Karen looked up from her book. "Is she all settled?"

"Yes," Emma said, with a hint of uncertainty lining her voice.

"But not you. Right, Momma?" the woman asked, chuckling.

"I'm sorry. I don't mean to be rude."

"Don't apologize. I'd be the same way if I left my daughter with someone I barely knew. I'll take good care of her, I promise." Standing up, Karen walked over to her and handed her a piece of paper. "Call me anytime."

"Thank you." She folded the paper and put it in her pocket, and then gave the lady her number as well. "Please call me if there is a problem."

It took a huge amount of courage to step out the front door and slide into the driver's seat of her car. Her stomach churned as the engine rumbled to life. She felt like she was leaving her daughter forever, despite it only being for a night.

Putting her foot on the gas, Emma slowly drove down the long, winding driveway. As she turned the final corner before the main road, she saw headlights coming toward her. The car passed her, and she saw a shadowed face turn and look at her from the driver's seat, his eyes taking on a hollow look. A dreadful darkness fell upon her spirit, munching on what remained of her sanity.

She wanted to stop the car and go back, but they would view her as a crazy person. Somehow, she had a feeling sleep wasn't going to come easily tonight. Emma groaned nervously. Devon probably wouldn't let her rest either. Maybe she should stay near Karen's house and sleep in her car, in case anything happened.

"Suck it up, chicken," she said, berating herself. Listening to her own advice, she pulled out onto the road and headed home.

Chapter Eighteen

Devon stared at his watch and poked his head around the curtain once again, peering into the darkness. Three hours had passed since he'd spoken with Emma, and he was getting anxious. He tried ringing her phone, but it went directly to voicemail, which meant either her phone was dead, or it was off. Something that had never happened before.

Flexing his fingers, he tried to breathe through the growing frustration. He wanted to lash out and hit something. Not knowing where she was was killing him. Tapping her name on his phone, he tried calling her again.

"I'm sorry. I'm unable to answer your call at this time. Please leave a message."

His grip on the phone tightened as he contemplated throwing it against the wall. "Where the hell are you?" he yelled at her picture on his screen.

She looked back at him with that damn cute smile and a twinkle in her eye.

"Why won't you answer the damn phone?" he growled, knowing full well a picture couldn't talk back.

If he could walk to the girl's place, he would, but it was too far on foot. He was beginning to regret being so far out of town. Julie and her family lived on the outskirts of town, too, but on the opposite side.

He wasn't sure if he was being paranoid, or if something had actually happened to her. The odds were as likely as winning the lottery, but not completely out of the realm of probability. Dialing another number, he tapped on the windowsill as he waited for his friend to answer.

"Ted, I need your help," Devon said, not waiting for the man to say hello.

"Sounds urgent. What's up?" Ted asked.

He gripped his neck as images of her body, crumpled in a ditch, filled his mind. "My wife dropped Hailey off at Julie's house a few hours ago and hasn't made it back to the house yet."

"She's probably gabbing with Karen. That woman likes to talk your ear off. Want me to call them?"

"I'd actually like to call myself. Do you have their number?"

"Yes." Ted rattled off a number to Devon.

"Thanks."

"Call me back if you need any help."

"I might need you to drive me over there."

"No problem."

He hung up the phone and dialed the number his friend had given him.

"Harriot residence, Karen speaking."

"Hi Karen, it's Trevor. Did Tara leave already?" he asked, peeking out the window again. Nothing was out there. He smacked his palm on the window frame.

"She left a few hours ago."

Devon ran a hand through his hair, anxiety rising within him. "Damn," he muttered. "Did she say whether she was going anywhere?"

"Isn't she home yet?"

"No."

"Let me check with Hailey. Maybe she knows." He heard the woman yell into the background. "Girls, come here, please."

There were muffled sounds on the other end of the line, as though she had placed her hand over the receiver. The woman came back on the line, saying, "It sounded like she was going straight home."

Something didn't sit right with him. "Can I talk to Hailey?"

"Julie says she's in the washroom at the moment."

Alarm bells went off in his head. "Can you go see if she's okay?"

"Julie, can you go check for us?" Karen asked.

"Actually, I'd rather you do it." Devon wasn't sure whether he could trust Julie to tell the truth as he didn't know the girl, or her mother really. But he'd rather hear it from Karen. Another adult.

Keeping him on the line, Karen wandered down to the bathroom, and he heard her knock on the door. Relief rushed through him when he heard Skye's higher pitched voice in the background.

"Did your mom say anything about stopping anywhere on her way home?" Karen asked her.

"No," Skye replied.

His stomach cramped at her response. There was no reason for Emma to be late. "Thanks, Karen." Devon hung up the phone and quickly dialed Ted back.

"Hey, man, did you find her?" his friend asked.

"No. I need your car."

"I'll be right over."

Devon stayed glued to the window and barreled out the door as soon as he saw the headlights coming up the driveway. He had hoped it was Emma, but it was just Ted's truck.

"Did you see anything?" he asked as he climbed in the passenger seat.

"Nothing on this side of town so far," Ted said, as he peeled rubber, doing a U-turn to get back out onto the road.

Devon's throat tightened. He couldn't lose her. Not now. If anything happened to her, he wouldn't forgive himself for letting her go out alone. From now on, he wasn't going to let her go anywhere without him, not until their lives returned to normal.

After they had driven for ten minutes, Ted pointed ahead of them. "Hey, look up there."

Devon squinted. In the dark, he could make out a car sitting on the side of the road, but the four-way flashers weren't going. *Please don't let it be her.* They climbed out of the vehicle and approached the car. His heart skipped a beat. It was their gray Mazda, and it appeared to be unoccupied.

"Shit." He banged on the frame of the vehicle.

"Wow, Trevor. Are you okay?" Ted asked?

He paced up and down the road, hands on his head, saying every swear word that came to his mind before turning back to his friend. "I'm going to tell you something, but you have to swear not to tell anyone, or I'll beat you to a pulp, got it?"

"Sounds serious."

It took a few minutes, but he brought Ted up to speed on their situation, from the time of Emma's husband's death until now.

"Boy, that explains some of the rumors going around."

"Rumors?"

"Ya, the womenfolk think that Tara—I mean, Emma—cheated on you."

Any other time, Devon would have chuckled at the accusations, since Emma didn't have a single deceptive bone in her body, but he was too scared to even come up with a rebuttal. He walked back to the car and searched the contents, hoping to find something that might lead to her whereabouts.

He pulled his keys out of his pocket and stuck them in the ignition. The car did nothing more than sputter when he turned the keys, refusing to start. Had Emma wandered off because the car died? What were the odds that her cell phone and the car would die at the same time?

"Does anyone live nearby?" Devon asked.

"Genevieve and her husband, Johnathan. They are a retired couple that moved here a few years ago."

"Do you have their number?"

"No, but I can drive you there. Just give me a second, and I'll call Chris from Plower Towing. He'll take your car to the shop."

"Thanks," Devon said, as they climbed back into Ted's truck. He hoped it was something as simple as the car dying and nothing more sinister. His palms were sweaty, and his heart decided now would be a good time to jump around his chest like a ping-pong ball.

"Breathe, bro. We'll find her."

They drove down the road for about five minutes before Ted finally turned left into an unmarked driveway. Devon never would have found the place himself, because the entrance was hidden.

They approached a smaller one-story rancher with only the porch light brightening the entrance way. Everything else was dark and gloomy. There didn't appear to be anyone home. His spirit sank further into hell.

"Sorry, I thought they'd be here," Ted said. "No one said anything about them going away or anything."

"Do they go away a lot?"

"Usually only in the winter. What should we do next?"

Devon shrugged his shoulders. He had no idea. There was no point in calling Karen again because Emma wouldn't have made it back there on foot. And if her phone was off, there was no tracking her down on Snapchat.

"Should we call the cops?" Ted asked.

"We can't, not without letting the cat out of the bag."

"Right."

And he didn't exactly want everyone to know about them yet. He wouldn't have told Ted if it weren't for the fact that she was missing. He needed someone on his side in case things went sideways. Could there be something he was missing? His eyes suddenly widened.

"Take me back to the car."

"Sure thing. Chris will probably be there already. Business tends to be slow."

Sure enough, the tow truck was there, hooking their car up to the hitch.

"One second," Devon yelled to Chris as he rushed to the Mazda. He looked all over the interior and breathed a huge sigh of relief. "It's empty."

"Uh, we already determined that before, didn't we?" Ted asked questioningly.

"I mean, she took her phone and her purse with her."

"You think she left of her own accord?"

Devon nodded, and for the first time all night, his heart slowed down. Chris looked between the two of them with a puzzled look on his face.

"Don't worry about it, Chris. Just haul this junk into the shop and see if you can fix it," Ted said.

They watched as the man drove away, his taillights disappearing into the darkness. "You'd think that the police would have given you a working car, at least."

Devon chuckled. "It's probably a car they impounded from a drug dealer or something."

"Come on. I'll take you home. Maybe she's back now."

"One can hope."

They drove in silence the rest of the way. Devon didn't want to talk. He was afraid it might jinx them, and she would really be gone. Nothing scared him more than losing her completely.

When Ted turned into their driveway, Devon held his breath and crossed his fingers. He would have crossed his toes if they had the ability. When they approached the house, he slammed his hand on the armrest. It was just as dark as when they had left.

Shit!

This couldn't be happening. A life without her spiraled through his mind, and his spirit went down a deep, dark path. The very same path that Leila, his ex-wife, had saved him from.

"You can go, Ted. I'll handle it from here," he said, his voice cool.

"I don't know what you're thinking, bro, but I'd say by the look in your eyes that it's not anything good."

"If you know what's good for you, you'll leave now."

"Let's go inside and have a drink first. It might take the edge off."

Devon grabbed the man by the shirt collar, pushing him up against the car. "Damn it. Don't you know when to leave?"

Before Devon knew it, Ted had wrestled him to the ground, sitting on top of him. "You may be tough, bud, but you don't mess with ex-military," the man said, patting Devon on the head.

He tried to buck Ted off his back, but the jerk just laughed and held him there. Ted wasn't going to be laughing once Devon got his hands on him.

"Get off me."

"When you calm down, I will."

Growling, Devon reached behind him, trying to grab something. Anything to pull the man off him, but to no avail. He let out a string of expletives, smacking the ground in frustration. "I need to find her."

"And we will, but you need a level headfirst."

"I am level, damn it!"

"About as level as a sand dune," Ted replied, continuing his reign on Devon's back.

"We're wasting time."

"I'm not going to let you do anything that'll wind you up in jail."

"My life is my business," he mumbled.

"Think about Emma."

That was all he could ever do. His mind didn't let him do anything else. No matter where he was or what he was doing, she was all he could think about. And now she was gone. And for all he knew, she could be dead.

With every ounce of strength he had, he tried to buck the man off his back, but Ted was like an immovable mountain. "You are pissing me off, man!" Devon yelled.

"Fine, be pissed off, but be cool about it. You aren't going to help Emma by going off on a rampage."

"What do you know about it?"

"I lost my entire brigade by being stupid and losing my cool. I won't let you lose your family the same way."

Devon's breath hitched when he heard the word *family*. He desperately wanted to be a part of Emma and Skye's family. The last few weeks had given him a taste of what it was like living with her, and he loved it, despite her fighting the feelings she had for him.

He had to play it safe. He had to be smart for her. Taking a few deep breaths, he allowed his muscles to relax. Enough so, that Ted stood up and held his hand out to him.

"That's all I was waiting for. Come on. Let's go have a drink and decide what to do next."

Standing up, Devon bopped him on the shoulder. "That's for sitting on me."

Grunting, Ted said, "You had it coming!"

"Shut up," Devon grumbled as he stepped into the house. It didn't sit well with him that he wasn't out looking for her. But he had no idea where to start. She could be anywhere, with anyone. Did her disappearance have anything to do with the two boys from Vancouver? He should have gotten their names and had a friend of his do a search on them before he willingly let Skye stay over there.

"Whatcha thinking?" Ted asked.

"Do you, by any chance, know the names of Karen's oldest son and his friend?"

"Her son's name is Ashton, but I'm not so sure about the other kid."

Pacing the living room with a drink in his hand, he asked, "Can you tell me anything about Ash?"

Ted crossed his ankle over his knee as he sat on the couch. "Not much to tell, really. Strait-laced. Just joined the Delta police force."

Devon stopped in his tracks, his stomach bellyflopping into his groin. "Are you serious?"

Ted nodded. "Graduated top of his class, from what I hear."

Placing his drink on the coffee table, he grabbed Ted by his shirt and hauled him up off the couch. "You're going to drive me over there."

Ted shook himself loose from Devon's grip. "Easy there. Her kid wouldn't hurt a fly. I've known him since he was a baby."

"Humor me."

"Fine, but I will be saying I told you so."

As they stepped outside the house, they saw a vehicle coming up the driveway.

Chapter Nineteen

Emma swallowed hard as she stepped out of the vehicle. Devon was racing toward her. He had jumped off the porch, didn't even bother to use the stairs. She couldn't tell what kind of mood he was in. The darkness that surrounded them hid his face.

When he reached her, he swept her off the ground and spun around in a circle. "You scared the hell out of me."

Her ribs crunched as he tightened his grip on her. "I can't breathe," she gasped.

Putting her down, he framed her face with his hands and kissed her hard, like he hadn't seen her in a hundred years. "I thought I was never going to see you again."

"What's gotten into you?" She looked over his shoulder and saw Ted standing behind him. "Why's he here?"

"He was helping me look for you."

Confused, Emma scratched her head. "I don't understand."

"He thought you dropped off the face of the earth," Ted said.

"My car died, so I walked to their house." Emma pointed to the couple who had stepped out of the car. She'd been driving home when the engine cut out, and she couldn't get it started again.

"I thought so," Ted said, chuckling. "Hi, Gen. Hi, John."

Ignoring them, Devon looked at her. His eyes the color of a midnight storm. "Why the bloody hell didn't you answer your phone?"

Taken aback by his anger, she snapped, "Because it died, you dickhead."

Ted could barely stifle a chuckle, and that earned him a glare from Devon. "Why are you still here, Ted?"

"Tell me Em—Tara," the man quickly corrected himself. "What do you see in this guy again?"

Her heart stopped. "I...uh..." Emma looked at Devon questioningly. How did Ted find out her real name? Her fake husband's expression gave nothing away, except for the fact he was ticked off. She turned to Genevieve. "Thanks so much for your help and the wonderful dinner. You really didn't have to do that."

The older, plump, gray-haired woman moved toward Emma and hugged her tenderly. "It was my pleasure, dearie. I hope you'll stop by again soon. I enjoyed our chat."

She loved the countenance of Genevieve, an honest to goodness, wholesome lady. Even her husband was the sweetest guy on earth. When they had picked her up and stopped off at the nearest restaurant in town, he had offered his arms to both of them as they headed inside. Emma wandered over and gave John a hug.

"Be careful about going out at night again, especially in that car of yours," John said. "A pretty lady like you shouldn't be wandering the streets in the dark."

After she released him, she looked over at Devon, his face taking on the look of a prodded bull. Emma shivered. "I guess we should be getting inside. Thanks again."

"I guess I'll get going, too. Glad you're all right, Tara," Ted said, winking at her.

Emma watched as Ted climbed into his truck, severely puzzled by his reaction. Shaking her head, she wandered toward the house, only to be captured by Devon and thrown over his shoulder again.

"Devon," she squealed. "Put me down."

"I thought I'd lost you tonight, so no can do."

"Don't be silly. Nothing happened." She gasped when she got a look at the living room. He had set up candles everywhere. Roses and chocolates were sitting on the coffee table, and next to the chocolates was a bottle of wine, which now sat in a puddle of water instead of ice. "Wow."

Every ounce of fight fled her system as she stared at his handy work. Devon went through so much trouble for her. Warmth spread through her heart. "I can't believe you did all this for me," she said.

Slowly lowering her to the ground, his hands came to rest on her waist. "I'd do anything for you."

Suddenly, she remembered everything he had told her earlier that day and pulled away from him, wrapping her arms around herself. How could he leave his wife for her? Why would he even do that, knowing she was married and off the market? *I'm a home wrecker.* A cry burst through her lips, and she turned to flee up to her room. She didn't even get two steps before she was up over his shoulder again.

"Not this time, sweetheart."

"Put me down," she demanded.

"Nope, not until we talk," he said, sitting down with her on the couch, keeping his arms firmly wrapped around her.

Wasn't *talking* from a guy's perspective a euphemism for let me charm your ear off so we can have sex?

"I don't want to." She tried to squirm out of his hold.

"Tough."

"You're mean," she grumbled.

"You terrified me tonight," he said softly as he leaned in, brushing his nose against her neck. Her body trembled deliciously.

"That wasn't my intention. I tried to get home, but the couple insisted on taking me out for dinner."

"You should have called."

"I know. You're right. I just didn't think about it since my phone died."

"Please call me next time, okay?

"Okay," she said, trying to get up again.

"Nope, you aren't free to go yet. I want to know why you were about to run off again."

She didn't even know where to start. She wanted to scream at him for leaving his wife because of her. Who was she to break up another family? That was not something she wanted on her conscience. And seeing him every day, knowing his kids were missing him because of her, made her sick to her stomach. It was a burden she didn't want. A burden she didn't think she could live with.

"When this is all over, Dev, I want you to go home. Go back to your family and forget about me."

"There is no forgetting you, Em," he said, as his fingers danced like electricity on her thigh.

She pushed his fingers away, her tears flowing. There didn't seem to be any way to get through to him. "Don't you get it? I refuse to be a home wrecker. I wouldn't be able to live with myself."

"So, you want me to live with a woman who doesn't have my heart and not give her the chance to find someone who will give her theirs?"

"You had children with her, Dev. That ties you together forever. I refuse to live my life as the other woman."

"You are not the other woman. You are *the woman*. The one I never should have left."

"But you did."

Devon ran his thumb over the ring on her left hand, appearing deep in thought. She glanced at her ring and wondered if there was anything she could have done differently in her life. What if she had brought up the bad feeling she'd had that afternoon before Peter left? Would he still be with her today? Would she and Devon even be talking now?

Emma sighed, her heart tearing into two all over again. If she had spoken her mind back in the day, would it have been Devon she had married instead? She had spent so much of her time going with the flow and not standing up for herself and her needs. She wanted other people to be happy and often brushed aside her own needs to meet theirs.

"I was stupid," he said bluntly.

"Sometimes I wish I was more outspoken."

"You are perfect."

Emma scoffed in disagreement. "Did you know that I felt something in my spirit the day that Peter left for work?"

Devon stayed silent, letting her speak. And for that, she was grateful.

"I should have recognized it, because it happens any time something bad is about to happen."

"You couldn't have known."

"I knew, but I didn't say anything. When the cops came to my door, they didn't even need to speak. I already knew," she said, her mind traveling back to that day. "Did you know I dreamed about it? I knew what was going to happen, and I said nothing."

"It was a dream. It wasn't your fault."

"I dreamed he was going to run into someone, and he did. How is that not my fault? I could have told him to watch out for people on the road, but I didn't. I didn't want to sound like I was insane. I didn't want him to put me down again." Her tears fell thickly, like a waterfall. "Just like I could have told you how I really felt, and then maybe you wouldn't have left."

"You aren't in control of the universe, Emma. You are only in control of what you do right now. We have a second chance. Those don't come around very often."

Burying her face in the crook of his neck, she whispered, "I didn't want you to leave."

Devon rested his head against hers. "I know. That's why I hated myself so much. I love you, Em. You mean the world to me, and I want to spend the rest of my life proving that to you."

She turned toward him and placed a hand over his heart. As she looked up at him, her big hazel eyes filled to the brim with passion. "Make love to me," she whispered.

Emma's words took him by surprise. Devon never expected her to utter them tonight of all nights. He had taken sex off the table, wasn't even going to make a move.

"You sure?" he asked, treading carefully.

Stupid. Stupid.

She was offering herself to him. Why was he even asking? Anyone else and he would have likely jumped on the offer like nobody's business, but he wasn't about to jinx his future with her. "There's no going back if we do."

"I know."

"I don't want you to regret it."

Framing his face with her dainty hands, she said, "Kiss me before I change my mind."

Emma didn't even give him a chance to respond before her soft, tender lips, tasting as sweet as honey, claimed his. There was something different about this kiss. Something more real than any other that had come before. Her lips were the same. She was the same. But this time she was giving herself freely through no fancy coercion. And nothing could have been sweeter than that.

Getting up off the couch, he picked her up and cradled her in his arms, making his way to the stairs. Her lips left his and trailed across the cleft of his chin, hitting the sensitive spot beneath his ear lobe.

"I've wanted you for so long," he said as he kicked the bedroom door open. The lustful look in her eyes told him she felt the same. Desire flooded him, pulling him into another world and away from all the troubles that plagued them. Tonight, he wanted to give her everything he never had the chance to before. Everything that had once been denied.

"Then have me," she murmured.

He slowly slid her down his body, so she was standing on her own again. The friction against his cock made him groan with anticipation. This time, he wouldn't tie her up. He wanted her hands all over him, wanted to feel her fingers wrap around his growing erection.

There were no ifs, ands, or buts about it. He knew he had made the right decision in trying to win her back. Before the end of their stay, the ring that was hidden in his suitcase would be on her finger, and she'd belong to him forever.

Pulling her shirt over her head, he paused when he saw her blue laced bra underneath. His favorite color. "I swear you're trying to kill me," he moaned with appreciation as he lightly brushed her breast with the back of his hand.

Her cheeks reddened under his perusal. Emma closed the distance between them impatiently and wrapped her arms around his neck, linking her fingers together as she pulled his lips to hers. Desperately wanting to feel all of her, Devon cupped her bottom and pressed her against his swollen cock.

"Killing you? He feels quite alive to me," she said, her lips curling into a grin against his.

"Achingly so." Lifting her off the ground again, he carried her over to the bed and gently laid her down. Her breasts arched upward, enticing him. He grabbed the waistband of her pants, and soon she was lying there wearing only her bra, her womanhood visibly wet. "You look good enough to eat."

Devon stood up and removed his clothes with the speed of a jaguar and then kneeled on the bed, his erection pointing toward the ceiling. She lay there, waiting, smiling that womanly smile of hers.

"Please, Devon, hurry," she begged, opening to him as she ran her fingers over her clit, "Before we get interrupted again.

He loved seeing this side of her, free and willing, holding nothing back. He could only hope that things would be different from here on out. Taking her hand away, Devon replaced it with his own, lazily circling her clit.

"Don't tease me," she cried hungrily, bucking into his hand.

Slipping his fingers between her folds, he found her wet and ready. Swallowing a groan, he fought desperately to control his own needs. He wanted to plunge deep inside her. Something he'd been waiting to do for as long as he could remember. And seeing her on his bed like this, eagerly waiting for him to make a move, was almost enough to knock him off the precipice he was balancing on so precariously. But she deserved to be spoiled first.

He loved her and everything about her, from her long gangly toes to the tip of her cute button nose. Even loved the new creases that formed by her eyes when she smiled. For as long as he lived, she'd be his heart, his soul. Everything he could possibly want or need.

When his finger dipped inside her, she clenched the sheets on the bed and moaned his name. "How do you do that?" she asked breathlessly.

"I have the magic touch." He licked his lips as he watched his fingers disappear inside her, his cock hardening with anticipation.

"I never would have guessed," she said, her voice hitching slightly as he brushed up against her sensitive spot. "Holy fuck. You like that spot."

"So, you can swear after all," he said, chuckling.

"Mhmm," she murmured, her eyes closing as a dream-like expression passed across her features.

Her muscles trembled around his finger, letting him know she was close. He lazily circled her clit as he increased the pressure of his fingers moving inside her. Emma's breathing quickened as she arched her back, giving into the sensation that was steamrolling through her body with each flick of his finger.

Flashes of light ebbed and flowed behind her eyelids, matching the intensity of the feelings coursing through her. It reminded her of a star twinkling in the night sky. A supernova about to explode.

No other feeling in the world came close to the magic he was creating inside her, literally. Her and Peter's love life—

Emma shook her head.

She wasn't going to go there. Not right now. It was time to live in the present moment. When Devon's lips closed around her clit, she bit her tongue to stop from crying out but didn't succeed. The moan came out somewhat garbled, enough to make him chuckle.

Swirling her clit with his tongue, he moved his fingers in a come-hither motion inside her, harder and harder until she could no longer hold back, and her muscles convulsed around him. She cried out, gripping the sheets until her knuckles turned white.

Before she even came back down off the high, he positioned himself at her entrance and thrust himself deep inside. She cried out in ecstasy as they joined together for the first time, her muscles still quivering from her orgasm.

"You feel so warm and so god damn good," he said, burying his face in the side of her neck.

She froze in his arms. Afraid that if she moved, it would spoil the magical moment she found herself in. When he pulled back and plunged in again, she wrapped her legs around him, saying, "Don't move."

Lifting his head, he looked at her as a goofy grin played on his face. "That's kinda what you're supposed to do."

Emma rolled her eyes. "I know, silly. I'm not ready for it to be over yet."

"You don't think I can hold off?"

"I just want to sit like this for a while."

"And here I thought we'd get through this without interruptions this time," he said, laughing.

She felt the vibration of his laughter inside her, renewing the ache that had barely had a chance to ease. She didn't want it to be over yet, so she tightened her grip on his hips.

"I assure you the night has only just begun." He turned his puppy dog eyes on her, moving slightly inside her. "Please," he begged.

This was like a dream and had an unrealistic quality to it. Almost like she was watching the events unfold on television. Throughout all her life, she had never imagined that they'd ever be in this situation.

Releasing his hips, she allowed him to move. He moaned with pleasure as they rhythmically moved together to a beat that only the two of them shared in their minds. Faster and faster, he plunged inside her, sweat beading on his forehead as they reached for the next crescendo.

The fire built inside her, balling together like a raging inferno between her legs. She rode the tsunami-like sensations as they crashed through every nerve in her body. Emma gripped the headboard and tilted her hips, taking him in deeper. She wanted all of him, needed to be one with him fully and completely.

"I love you, Emma," he cried between breaths, diving off the deep orgasmic ravine, his body shaking against hers. She quickly joined him with her own release, taking her to a place she had never been before.

Tears formed in her eyes, even as her body continued to tremble. "I love you, too," she whispered.

He framed her face with his hands and kissed her softly. "I'm the happiest man in the world."

"I—"

The cell phone on the headboard rang, interrupting Emma. Devon didn't move a muscle and was still inside her when she reached for the phone.

"Tara, it's Karen."

The tone of her voice made Emma's insides shrivel in fear. Motioning for Devon to get off her, she sat up. "Is everything okay?"

"She's gone. Hailey's gone," Karen blurted.

Chapter Twenty

"What do you mean she's gone?" cried Emma. "It's after midnight."

"I'll call Ted," Devon whispered, squeezing her arm as he pulled out his phone.

"I'm sorry," the woman bawled.

"Maybe she is just with your daughter somewhere?" She crossed her fingers, hoping for the best.

"Julie's...with...me," Karen said between sobs.

"We'll be right there." Emma hung up the phone and quickly stood up, her eyes blacking out. She sat back on the bed, her throat closing as her breaths came in short frantic gasps.

Devon kneeled in front of her, taking her face in his hands. "Breathe with me, Emma. Focus on my voice." He counted for her as she took in a slow deep breath and then breathed it out. "We'll figure this out. I promise."

"Promises, promises," she whispered.

"I'll call the cops while you get dressed. Ted said he will be here as quickly as he can."

She looked from his body to hers. He was already fully dressed while she was wearing her birthday suit. Numb inside, she picked up a shirt and started to put it on, but Devon suddenly grabbed it, lifting it back over her head.

"What are you doing? You told me to get dressed," she snapped, pulling her shirt back down.

"I'm just trying to help. Your shirt is inside out."

"Leave me alone!" she cried, hitting him on the chest. "How...how could you let me leave her with them?"

He wrapped his arms around her and pulled her close, preventing her from hitting him. "We'll find her. I promise," he said soothingly.

"Let me go, Devon." Emma wasn't putting up with his games anymore tonight. Her daughter was in danger, while Emma had been here having sex. If she wouldn't have left Skye there to have a sleepover, against her better judgment, her baby girl would be with her right now. Not gone. It was all her fault.

After she put on her clothes, she choked back a sob as her legs gave out from under her. Her energy spent. Devon picked her up and carried her downstairs, sitting her on the couch. Agonizingly sweet, he grabbed her shoes and helped her put them on.

An image of her daughter laying dead somewhere popped in her head, and it hit her hard, bile filling her mouth. Slapping a hand over her mouth, she dashed for the bathroom. Her stomach churned as she leaned over the toilet.

"No...no...no," Emma cried between the dry heaves that racked her body. Skye couldn't be dead. *Dear God, don't let her be dead.* Her baby girl was her only reason for living. She wouldn't be able to survive without her, wouldn't want to.

Her head spun like the puke in the toilet. She slid the rest of the way to the ground, leaning with her back against the bathtub. What if they couldn't find her? What if he had her? She should have listened to her gut, but she didn't. All because a certain someone kept making her lose focus. If she lost her only link to Peter, she wouldn't be able to live with herself.

"Emma?" Devon called with uncertainty in his voice.

"I'll be out in a second," she yelled back.

"Lock the door and be quiet," he ordered. "And don't come out until I tell you to."

"W-why?" she stammered.

"Just do as I ask, please," he begged. And then there was silence.

"Devon?"

"Shush," came his reply.

Emma's heart pounded against her ribs. She leaned her ear up against the door and listened for anything that might help her make sense of his words, but all she could hear was a ringing in her ear.

"Devon?" she called.

"Listen for once. I'll fill you in after," he said quietly from the other side.

She hated not knowing what was going on. Turning the handle of the door, she went to pull it open. A force from the opposite side slammed it closed again.

"Lock it, damn it! I don't have time for your nonsense."

"You're scaring me."

"Good, because you should be."

The cold tone in his voice tore through her body like an icicle. Turning the lock, Emma backed away from the door as a snake-like shiver wrapped itself around her spine. She sat down on the toilet, unsure of what to do, when a buzzing sound emanated from the lights. The next thing she knew, she was surrounded by utter darkness. She slapped a hand over her mouth to keep from crying out.

They weren't in the middle of a storm, so what happened to their power? Suddenly, it was like the walls were closing in on her, shadows assailing her from every side. Emma struggled to breathe as she was hit with the full realization of what was going on.

He's here.

Devon kept his back tight against the wall as he peeked out the window. The mask-wearing man was approaching the door with a gun held to Skye's head. He probably should have told Emma that he was going to kill the power, but it was a spur-of-the-moment thing. Something he'd hoped would give him an advantage over the shithead who was advancing on the house.

As he dialed security, he tightened his fingers around the gun in his hand. One he'd kept hidden from both Emma and her daughter. He'd had a feeling it would come in handy if things ever came to a head.

No answer.

What good was security if they didn't answer his calls? Growling, he tossed the phone on the couch. There only appeared to be one guy, which evened the odds considerably.

"I know you guys are in there," the man yelled. "Come out, or I'll blow this pretty little head into smithereens."

He didn't doubt the man's word. When you worked with lunatics, you never knew what they were capable of. He'd seen enough in his day to learn that pretty quickly. "Let the girl go," Devon yelled.

"Give me Emma!" the asshole yelled back.

"What did she do?"

"Her whole family deserves to pay."

"Were you the one who threw the rock in the window?"

"No, it was my twin brother." He could hear the eye roll in the man's voice. "Of course, it was me. Now shut up and bring Emma outside."

"She's not here," he said, trying to stall for time.

"Do you really think I couldn't hear that frenzied love making of yours earlier?"

Shit. He'd been around longer than Devon thought.

"I'm going to count to three. If I don't see Emma out here, I'm going to blow the girl's head off."

"How'd you find us?" he asked, hoping that the man's ego would make him brag.

"Fairly easy. I went snooping in McGregor's files, when lo and behold, this address appeared. I wonder what your darling woman's going to do when she finds out that you planned this little mini vacation."

Devon heard a gasp from behind him and knew that Emma, against his wishes, had left the washroom and was standing right there.

"You don't know what you're talking about," he replied warily. This was not going to end well for him. He looked at Emma and shrugged his shoulders. She went to speak, but he covered her mouth with his hand, praying she'd stay silent. "Who are you?"

"That wouldn't be smart of me to tell you now, would it? Let's just say I'm a close friend of the cop that her husband almost killed. I'm here to return the favor."

"Her husband is already dead. It's over and done with." Devon peeked his head out the window again and saw that they'd moved a little closer to the house. A small cry bubbled in Emma's throat, but she kept the noise to a whimper.

"Hide," Devon mouthed to her.

She shook her head. "I'm not going to let that creep hurt my daughter."

"It's not done. And it won't be done until his entire family pays the debt in full," the masked man said.

Under the light of the full moon, she saw the man press the muzzle of the gun flush against her daughter's temple.

"No!" Emma cried, making a mad dash for the door.

Devon's arm wrapped around her middle, and he pulled her back to safety. "Don't be an idiot. He'll kill you."

"Skye," she said, her voice breaking.

"I'll save her. But I can't watch out for you both. Just stay out of sight."

"If your husband wasn't so stupid, my dad—my friend would still be fine." Skye's captor stumbled over his words.

The two of them looked at each other and mouthed the same word. "Dad?"

"Shit. Shit. Shit," the guy yelled to the blackened sky.

Emma's mind went back to the funeral service to the young red-haired man who had tended to the injured cop. He had stared at her with pure hatred in his eyes. If she remembered correctly, his name was Victor.

"I'm sorry for what happened, Victor. It was a horrible accident," she said with as much care in her voice as she could muster.

"No." The man tightened his grip around her daughter's neck.

"Let me go, please," Skye gasped.

"Shut up, both of you. They let you off easy, but I'm here to fix their oversight. You need to pay."

"Your dad was the one who stepped—"

Devon put a finger over her mouth. "Don't argue with him. It'll only make him angry."

"But it's the truth. His dad stepped in front of my husband as he was driving down the road."

"I understand, but arguing with him is not going to help. We need to outsmart him and keep him talking until help comes."

"Where are the security guards?"

"That's what I'd like to know," Devon muttered. "Maybe I can distract him long enough for you to run to the trailer."

"I'm not leaving my daughter," she refused adamantly.

"I can't very well do it and leave you here alone. If you run out the back door, he'll likely not even know you're gone."

What if she left, and he shot her daughter because she wasn't there? She couldn't take that chance. "I can't. I won't leave her."

Turning, Devon took Emma's hands in his. "This might be your daughter's only hope. Stay in the shadows. When you get out the back door, run toward the tree line and make your way through the forest. Stay parallel with the house until you get to the guard's trailer."

A strangled cry fell from her lips as she pulled away from him. Slipping into the dark shadows, she disappeared out of his line of sight. She didn't want to go anywhere. But what else could she do?

As she neared the back door, she spotted a baseball bat and grabbed it. Skye must have been playing with it earlier. Testing the weight of the bat, she gave it a light swing. If she could sneak up behind him, maybe she could hit him before he got a shot off. That didn't seem likely, but it appeared to be their best option.

War raged within her. Should she listen to Devon or follow her gut? Emma stared at the bat in her hands. Her daughter's life was in danger and every minute counted. There may not be enough time to go and get security. She swallowed the rock growing in her throat. Why couldn't there be one easy decision? She wanted to scream. Let the whole world know her fear and her pain.

They were at a standstill, and if Devon wasn't going to do anything, then she would. She tightened her grip on the bat and slipped out the back door.

Chapter Twenty-One

"I'm not going to wait forever," Skye's abductor roared. "Where's Emma?"

Devon moved to the back of the house and looked out the kitchen window, trying to catch a glimpse of Emma running through the trees. There were no shadows moving in the darkness. His shoulders tensed, and his muscles quivered. He had a sneaky suspicion that she didn't listen to him.

Heading out the back door, he glanced around, to no avail. Where the bloody hell was she? He couldn't call out to her, and it was driving him insane. His finger rested next to the trigger, not wanting to accidentally set it off. He hadn't used it in years. Hopefully, his aim was still sharp. His hand shook as he held it up in front of him. Sticking close to the wall, he side-stepped in the shadows, making his way along the west side of the house.

That was when he saw her, moving along the tree line, approaching the opening of the driveway, where Skye and her abductor stood. *Damn it, girl!* He sucked in a breath. He should have tied her to the bed and dealt with this himself.

"What are you thinking, Em?" he muttered. How was he

supposed to help her when she didn't include him in her plans? Being left in the dark was a death trap. He had to give her credit where credit was due. She wasn't making a sound, and he wouldn't have known she was there if the idea of sticking in the trees hadn't been his in the first place.

Staying absolutely still, Devon watched the scene unfold before him. Moving silently, his little ninja warrior approached Victor, her skills showing with every soundless step. That's when he remembered she'd had some martial arts training in the past. But his heart was still in his throat. One wrong move and things could go horribly wrong. "I hope you know what you're doing."

Despite her flawless execution, Devon held his breath. Hoping to help her out, he stepped out from his hiding spot. His gun trained on the interloper. "Hey, dude."

"I wouldn't do that if I were you, man." Victor clicked the safety off.

"I won't do anything if you don't," he replied, holding up his free hand in mock surrender. "This isn't going to change what happened."

"No, but it will feel fucking good. My dad was set for a promotion. Now, he's a paper pusher, all because of her husband."

"Look, I know it sucks ass for him, but at least he is alive, which is more than I can say for her husband. Don't you think they've suffered enough already?"

"I'm not going to feel sorry for her. I had to watch my mom stress about my dad's recovery, wondering if he would survive. I had to listen to her cry every night, and it drove me insane. No one in your family deserves to live."

"Think about your parents. Do you think they'd be proud of you for taking a little girl hostage? If you wind up in jail, won't that add to their stress?"

"I don't plan on going to jail."

"You will if you harm them. I'll make sure of it myself."

Emma was only a few steps behind the guy now. Devon watched her reach out, and it was like everything happened in slow motion, frame by agonizing frame. As soon as she tapped the man on the shoulder, headlights lit up the yard. Victor pivoted, hesitating for a brief second, appearing unsure of whom to target first. Skye wasted no time and dropped like a rock.

Taking the bat, Emma brought it down hard on his arm, knocking the gun out of his grip, but not before it went off. Victor howled in pain as he grabbed his dangling wrist. Taking the butt end of the bat, she drove it into the man's chin, dropping him to the ground.

Devon raced toward them as he watched her continue to pummel the guy.

"You bastard!" she screamed, hitting him over and over. "You're never going to hurt anyone again."

Once he reached them, Devon pulled Emma off Victor. "He's down, Emma. You did it."

"Not good enough." She struggled to get loose, trying to kick the guy with her feet.

Ted pulled his truck to a stop, and a cop car pulled in behind him. Devon finally let Emma go, and she rushed to where her daughter was sitting on the ground. She wrapped her arms around her baby girl. "Oh, Skye. Are you okay?"

"I'm fine," Skye replied, crying and hugging her mother tightly. When they pulled apart, her daughter's hands were covered in blood. "Mom?"

Emma tenderly touched her left side. When she withdrew her hand, it was covered in blood, too. Meeting Devon's gaze, her eyes widened with shock. "Oh," was all she said before she collapsed.

"Mom? Mom?" Skye cried, shaking her. "Mommy, wake up."

Adrenaline surged through his body, fear bowling over him like a hurricane. "Call the paramedics," he roared to the cops. "Ted, go check on the security guards. Find out why they didn't come."

"The paramedics are already on their way," one officer said as he kneeled beside Emma, checking her over. Devon watched as the officers worked on his one true love, and his heart lodged in his throat. Her face was as pale as a ghost in the moonlight.

"Please be okay," he whispered to his tender angel. His gut twisted with regret and remorse. It was because of his own selfishness she was lying on the ground, shot and dying. He was the one that had convinced Constable McGregor to let him be Emma's fake husband, so he'd have a chance at winning her back.

As he looked down at her, he realized she was better off without him. Damn it all to hell. Who was he to think that things were any different now than they were back in high school? If she died, it would be because of him. He had failed to protect her. A man's most basic duty.

If he had been the one to think of the idea first, she wouldn't be on the ground bleeding to death. It was just like when he lost Jack, his best friend, over a dumb get-rich scheme that they should never have been involved in. It was the same situation all over again. He didn't want to bury her, too. Devon shook his head, refusing to think of the worst-case scenario. His heart couldn't handle the thought.

It didn't take long before a helicopter touched down in the yard and an ambulance pulled up the driveway. Ted rushed toward them, huffing and puffing with exertion. "The guards are dead."

"Some use they were," Devon mumbled.

A cop walked over to him. "Can you tell me what happened here?"

When he started talking, another car drove up. Karen and her whole family climbed out, including a young man. Hell, the entire world was here. That kid had to be Ashton.

"One second." Devon walked over to them, his attention solely on the young man. He slammed the boy up against the car, his forearm across Ashton's neck.

"What the hell, man?" the young man gasped, trying to push Devon off him.

"Were you a part of this?" he demanded coolly.

"No. I promise. I had no idea."

"Trevor, please," Karen pleaded, "let him go."

"The name's Devon," he seethed.

Two of the cops converged on Devon and pulled him off the boy, making him sit on the ground a good distance away.

"Will someone tell us what happened here?" another cop demanded.

Devon clenched his fists as he nodded toward Karen's son. "Ask him about it. He knows the creep that shot my girl!"

Ashton held up his hands as everyone looked at him. "I swear, he never said a word."

"Is she going to be okay?" Karen asked, as they loaded Emma into the helicopter.

"She had better be," Devon said, his voice hardening.

Figuring it would be better to separate them. One cop took Devon into the house while another spoke with the other family outside. He watched as Skye climbed into the helicopter to be with her mom. Thankfully, the girl escaped unscathed, and it was all because of her mom. Emma was incredible, but he wished he would have been the one to come up with the idea. He should be the one on the stretcher. Not her.

She shouldn't have been here at all. He dug his nails into his palm as he tightened his fist. "This should never have happened," Devon muttered. He needed to get as far away from her as possible. He wasn't good for her.

The cop came and stood beside him at the window. "She's in good hands. Can you tell me what happened?"

Starting from the beginning, he filled the cop in on everything that had happened up to this point, and how the man who'd been threatening them was the injured cop's own son.

"He kidnapped her daughter from Karen's place and then came here, hoping to kill Emma," Devon said.

"And Karen's son?"

His heart burned with fury as he glared out the door. "I really don't know, but he was the one who drove that crazy asshole out here."

"To your place?"

"No, into town. They were apparently staying at Karen's house. Victor found out where we were staying, and I guess convinced Ashton to bring him out here." He still couldn't figure out whether Ashton was involved or just an innocent bystander.

"Sounds like quite the mess."

"You, sir, have no idea." Devon watched the helicopter take off, and with it, went his heart. "Do you know where they are taking her?"

"Winnipeg Memorial Hospital."

"Is she going to be okay?"

The cop's eyes followed the helicopter instead of looking at Devon. That's when he knew her situation was grave.

"I hope so," the guy replied.

They carted Victor off in the other ambulance. Seeing him in handcuffs made Devon feel a little better. Their lives would finally have a chance to return to normal, but he had no idea what that was going to look like for them. He couldn't imagine going back to not talking to her again. But after the mess he got her in, it would be the respectful thing to do. She deserved that much. Emma would probably never want to see him again, anyway, knowing his plan to come out here just about got her daughter killed.

Methodically, Devon gathered their belongings. He had a feeling their stay at their temporary home was almost over. As he picked up her clothes, his heart twisted, and nausea rolled around in his gut. What if she didn't recover? That was something he didn't even want to think about. Yet it overwhelmed his mind and flooded his soul with guilt. He grabbed the last of their stuff and hauled it outside, putting it on the ground. *Shit.* Their car was in the shop. "Ted, I need your truck."

His friend tossed him the keys. "Sure, bud. We have a spare back at the house."

Cops were still milling about the site, taking pictures. He locked up the house, tossed their stuff inside the truck, and walked over to them.

"Is it okay to go?" he asked one of the officers.

"Go ahead. We'll call you if we have any other questions."

"Do you need inside the house at all?"

"No."

Just before Devon drove away, he contacted McGregor to brief him on what had happened. The man apologized profusely. "I had no idea that it was an inside job, or I would have sent you somewhere else."

"I appreciate what you tried to do, sir."

"Did it work? Did you get her back?"

Devon rubbed the back of his neck as his eyes drifted to where Emma had collapsed on the ground. "I'm letting her go."

"You're what?" the cop asked incredulously.

"I'm no good for her."

"Baloney."

"If I would have just let her go, she wouldn't be fighting for her life right now," he replied, gripping the steering wheel tightly.

"You don't know that. He could have found her another way."

"I chose to do this. I'm responsible."

"Don't make me come down there and kick you in the ass."

"Thanks for the use of your house. It's locked up tight. I'll give Skye the key to give back to you."

"Devon," the cop said with a warning tone in his voice.

"You aren't going to change my mind. My mind is made up."

Constable McGregor sighed. "Stubborn mule."

If being stubborn meant keeping Emma alive and in good health, then that was exactly what he was going to be. He knew his arrival had upset her, and she didn't want him around, anyway. It gutted him to be giving her up a second time, but he was doing the right thing, just like he had when he left her in high school. He didn't deserve her. He should never have opened the can of worms by texting her.

Putting his car in drive, he started his trek to the hospital to say one final goodbye.

Chapter Twenty-Two

Devon entered the emergency room and rushed to the triage desk. "I need to see Emma Praught."

"And you are?" the nurse asked, glancing up at him.

"Devon, Devon Matthews. Is Emma okay?"

"Are you a relative?"

That was a perplexing question, to say the least. "We were in the witness protection program as husband and wife. I was with her when the situation went down. I need to see her."

"She's in recovery, but you should be able to see her once she's back in her room."

"Where's her daughter?"

"With her mom."

"Thank you." He fought to keep the frustration out of his voice. "Do you know when she'll be out of recovery?"

"I'm afraid not, but you can wait in the waiting room down the hall." She pointed to the right.

It was the last thing he wanted to do. He just wanted to see her and say his goodbye, not stick around and give his brain time to think of all the reasons why he shouldn't go. He would always love her, but he wasn't healthy for her. Never has been. And never will be.

Grabbing a coffee from the machine, he sat in the oversized chair tucked in the corner. Hitting the power button on the remote, the television burst forth with life. And the first thing he set eyes on was a picture of the house that had been their home for the last while.

Devon found it surprising that the story had already hit the news. No reporters were there when he left, and the drive hadn't taken him overly long. Having lived through the scene, he turned off the television and laid his head back against the seat. He had thought they made it through the incident unscathed until he saw the blood.

A chill slithered through him. Why the hell did he allow her to go off like that on her own? He should have guessed that she'd try to be the hero. Devon ran a hand down his face. It should have been him, but she beat him to it.

Damn her.

It was a joke to think they could have had a life together. They were lucky this time that it was only her past that came back to haunt them. Next time, it could be his. And his was darker than hers. So much so, he could never be mistaken for an angel boy. And he never wanted to risk her life again. Devon sighed and closed his eyes, totally exhausted. He didn't open them until his phone rang, startling him.

"I just heard the news. Are you guys okay?" Leila, his ex-wife, asked.

"Emma's hurt. No thanks to me."

"What do you mean?"

Devon groaned. He didn't want to tell the story all over again, but that's what he found himself doing as he gripped the armrest of his chair.

"There's no way you could have known, sweetheart," she said softly.

"I was supposed to keep her safe. I promised to keep her safe."

"She's alive. That's what counts."

"How are my kids?" he asked, changing the subject.

"They've been asking about you. Do you want to talk to them?"

He could hear them in the background, making loud squealing noises. "Sure, why not," he said. A weary smile spread across his face when his daughter answered the phone first.

"Daddy, Daddy, guess what."

"What?"

"I know how to swim."

"You'll have to show me when I come home."

"Can I get a mermaid tail? Clarissa's mom bought her one. She looks like a real mermaid."

He could literally hear her bouncing off the walls with excitement. Brianna's news didn't surprise him, though. She was his water baby, absolutely took to the water like a fish. His son, however, howled any time you tried to get him to pick his feet up off the pool floor.

"We'll talk about it, okay?"

"Yippy, I'm going to be a mermaid," she gushed, clapping her hands. He couldn't help but smile. In a way, he was thankful to be going home soon. He missed his little rugrats.

"When are you coming home, Daddy?"

His heart squeezed a little tighter at her wistful tone. "Soon. I just have to stay here a little longer. Love you, munchkin."

"Love you, too."

After a bit of muffling on the other end, his son came on the phone. "Hey Dad."

"Hi, Jake, how are you doing?"

"I'm surrounded by girls," the boy huffed.

Devon chuckled. "Don't worry. You'll enjoy that one day."

"Ya, right."

"You mean you don't want to get married yet?"

"Ew, no." After a brief pause, Jacob asked, "Can I go play outside with Jimmy?"

"What does Mommy say?"

"I have to clean my room first," his son muttered. "Why can't I live with you?"

It was one of the harder questions he'd had to contend with since the divorce, and it almost always broke his heart. "I wish you could, but I work a lot so that Mommy can stay home with you guys."

Devon heard Leila ask Jacob to hand her the phone, telling him it was time to clean his room.

"Save me, Daddy," Jacob begged.

"I can't help you with this one. You better go do what she says."

Muttering away, his son gave the phone back to Leila.

"Thanks for backing me up," she said.

"Anytime," Devon answered. "Hey, I just wanted to say sorry."

"What for?"

"Not having given you the life you deserved and for being so selfish."

"Dev, I knew what I was getting into from the beginning. You were upfront about everything. When I got pregnant, all you wanted to do was the right thing. *I* was the selfish one for agreeing to it."

"Stop being so nice," he groaned. "I don't deserve it."

"Would you rather I be the ex from hell?"

"That would make me feel better."

"Tough. Anyway, keep us posted."

Devon shook his head. He had got lucky in the ex-wife department, excluding her family. They hated his guts, but for her sake, he stayed cordial with them. "Will do. Talk to you soon."

After he disconnected the call, a nurse walked into the room. "She's been moved to her room. You can see her now, but she is sedated, so she probably won't be awake much."

He stood up and stretched his back. "That's okay. How's she doing?"

"Dr. Peterson believes they were able to locate all the bullet fragments. The bullet damaged her lung and shattered a rib. Thankfully, they were able to implant a prosthetic rib and stabilize her lung. She's quite the lucky woman."

His heart kicked against his ribcage. It was worse than he had thought. What was going to happen to Skye while her mom recovered? There was no way she could stay with him. He had no guardianship over her.

"Have you called Emma's parents?"

"Yes. They are flying in tomorrow."

The nurse led him to a room, and he paused at the door. The love of his life had tubes and wires attached everywhere, hooked up to every machine he could think of. One tube, filled with blood, hung down beside the bed.

With his heart racing, he turned to the nurse. "Is it supposed to look like that?"

"I know it looks awful, but that's normal. The machine is sucking out the extra fluid around her lung."

He let out the breath he hadn't realized he was holding. It looked anything but normal. Skye looked up from the chair she was perched in, her eyes red. Standing up, she ran over to him and crashed against his chest, her arms closing around him in a death grip.

"I'm scared," she cried, her voice muffled.

"She'll be okay," he said with as much confidence as he could muster, wrapping his arms around her. She had to be.

"I can't lose her, too. I just can't," she cried, her breathing ragged and rushed. The sound of her crying filled the room, drawing the attention of the nurses at the desk.

"Has she been able to speak with anyone yet?" he asked the nurse, giving a head nod toward Skye. "She's been through a lot."

"The counsellors will be in in the morning. And speaking of which, we usually only allow one visitor at a time in the ICU, especially this time of night, so I'll give you a few minutes, and then you'll have to come back later."

Skye's eyes widened, and she tightened her hold on him. "Please don't make him go."

"I'm sorry. It's hospital policy."

"He's the closest person I have right now. I need him," she said adamantly. "My mom would want him to stay."

"Sweetie—"

Skye squared off with the nurse, her hands on her hips, giving the woman dressed in blue scrubs a death stare. "Don't call me sweetie. If you make him leave, I'm going to scream."

"I'll ask my supervisor if it's okay." The woman scurried out of the room.

"You've mastered the stare I see," he said with half a smile.

Her eyes lit up slightly, and the corner of her lips twitched, but she didn't smile. Instead, she turned her attention back to her mom. "She shouldn't have tried to help me."

"I don't think there is anything your mother wouldn't do for you."

"I'd rather die than be alone," she said, her voice hitching as tears filled her eyes.

His heart ached for her as though she were his own child. Resting a hand on Skye's shoulder, he gave it a gentle squeeze. "She'll pull through," he said, forcing conviction into his tone.

Emma's condition was life threatening, and that opened a pit in his stomach that was quickly filling with fear and dread, but he had to present a strong front for Skye. And for the first time in his life, he was struggling to do that. Tears of his own threatened to breach the surface. He cleared his throat, trying to take the focus off his burning eyes.

What if he had allowed her to leave when she was adamant about going into the witness protection program? What if he wouldn't have convinced McGregor to allow him to tag along? Would she still be okay?

Shaking his head, he turned away briefly to compose himself. He had one motto in life. Never look back and never dwell on the what if questions. But now, he found himself lost in that world, falling deeper in the confines of its maze with each passing second.

Unable to hold back, he cried, his fists tight by his sides. Trying to stay silent, he swallowed the sob that fought like an army to get out.

That's when he felt Skye's thin arms slip around his abdomen, and it made him crumble. He couldn't hold back anymore.

"She's going to be okay. She has to be," he whispered as he turned to wrap his own arms around her, resting his chin on the top of her head.

Please, let Emma be okay.

Emma found herself in a haze, like she was watching the world through a cloud. No matter what she did, she couldn't get her vision any clearer. She heard muffled sounds, but nothing that she could make out clearly enough to understand. Dark shadows moved around her on all sides, but she couldn't touch them. Couldn't touch anything. Not even herself.

She tried.

And it annoyed her to no end. Was she dead? Was she in limbo—the spot between heaven and hell? All she knew was that she was trapped and stuck in this bubble with no sense of time, floating on a cloud of who knows what. She didn't seem to exist in any particular world, but rather was stuck in the middle. If she had somehow pass over, this wasn't exactly what she was expecting from the afterlife. Waving her unseen hand, the particles of mist in front of her rippled outwards, but it didn't give her a clear view of her new world.

"Hello," she tried to say, but no sound came from her mouth. It was like she existed and didn't exist at the same time. Here, but not here. The heart that should be pounding inside her chest was oddly silent.

"Someone help me, please," she begged silently. What was she doing here? Did it serve some sort of purpose? Maybe she was dying, and this was the waiting room while God decided her fate.

She had lived a moral life. She was sure of it. She hadn't killed anyone. She wasn't a thief, although she did accidentally steal a candy that she didn't even realize was in her hand when she walked out of the store. She had stayed faithful to Peter through thick and thin.

"God, are you out there?"

Emma kicked her non-existent feet in a fit when there was no answer, wishing she could break herself free from this jail. The last thing she could remember was Victor turning around as a car came up the driveway. Beyond that, nothing. Only whatever this was.

Skye!

Was her daughter still alive? Did she survive the psycho? Why couldn't she remember anything? "Let me go back to my baby," Emma cried. "She needs me."

Her new world reminded her of the movie, *The Mist*. Looking around, she made sure that no creatures were coming to take her away. The shadows, whatever they were, seemed to be on the other side of the wall of fog. She didn't like this place. Not a single bit. It was strange to be alone.

Scary.

Clicking her non-existent heels together, she wished to be back at home with Skye and Devon. She couldn't believe he had gone through so much trouble to try to prove himself to her. On one hand, she was mad that the trip was a farce. Yet no matter how harsh she was toward him, he appeared determined to be with her. And it was true, they had been in danger and needed to hide out. It wasn't Devon's fault it didn't work out according to the plan that had been cooked up. She knew he couldn't have known what was going to happen, so none of this was his fault.

Had she found out weeks ago that he'd planned this, she would have skipped out on him without a second thought. Her heart had been too broken to even consider entering into a relationship with him. Now she found herself wanting to give him a chance.

And she would.

All she needed to do was find her way out of this misty maze.

Chapter Twenty-Three

Devon pulled the chair close to Emma's bed. He had a few minutes alone with her while Skye went out with her grandparents to get something to eat. They had all corralled around her bed, watching and waiting for her to wake up. A few days had passed since the incident, and he had yet to see her look up at him with those gorgeous hazel eyes. The doctor said she was doing great, and her body was healing. But guilt had made a nest inside his heart.

"I should never have brought you out here," he said sadly, tracing the lines on her palm with the tip of his index finger. "This is all my fault. I just wanted more time to convince you that we belong together, but it looks like you were right all along. I'm sorry."

Bracing himself on the bed, he leaned over and kissed her forehead, tears forming in his eyes. "I can't believe I'm about to do this again to the only woman I've ever loved," he said, brushing a stray hair away from her face. "You are so beautiful. You captured my heart the moment you walked into the computer room. I can still remember the day like it was yesterday."

She'd been wearing jeans and an oversized shirt, but it was her eyes and her smile that blew him away. There was a radiance about her. A purity that didn't seem to belong in this fallen world. Yet what attracted him to her was the same thing that intimidated him the most. Now here they were, twenty some odd years later, and he was still captivated and just as intimidated.

"Oh, god, I don't want to go, but I know I don't belong in your world." He swiped at the tears falling down his cheeks. "You need someone who can keep you safe. Someone who knows how to do everything right, instead of a pinhead like me. I won't waste anymore of your time."

His chest burned with the regret of what he was about to do, and his stomach fought against the meal he'd eaten not that long ago. Placing a hand over his stomach, he tried to ease the rising turmoil as he stared at his sleeping beauty. "I love you more than you will ever know, Emma Praught."

Devon turned over her hand and placed a small wine-colored box in her palm. After he curled her fingers around it, he made sure the sheets covering her kept it securely in place. "This will always belong to you."

Down the hall, her dad's voice echoed off the walls, making his presence known. Devon stood up. He didn't feel like having Joshua tower over him, knowing full well how angry her dad was at his choice to leave. As the man rounded the corner, Devon could already feel the heat of his gaze as the hairs on his neck stood up.

"You can go now," Joshua stated bluntly.

Realizing he wasn't going to get a cordial farewell, he walked toward the door. Skye was staring at him, begging him to stay with her eyes. He mouthed, "I'm sorry," and then, as he gave Emma one last longing look, he stepped out of the room.

With his hands balled into fists, he began the long torturous journey down the hospital corridor. He was walking away a second time from not just his girlfriend, but his lover. His best friend. His heart and soul. Each step was arduous and difficult, his lead feet growing heavier with each passing second. Same with his heart.

He paused at the elevator, glancing back at the open door to

Emma's room. The dam hiding behind his eyes threatened to burst open right there in the hallway, with everyone looking at him. Damn it. Frantically glancing around, he spotted a sign leading to the stairs and took off toward it.

As soon as the door slammed closed, there was no more holding back. The tears flowed without his consent. He sat down on the top step. How was he supposed to live without her?

"It's for the best," he muttered. His heart didn't believe the words, but it's what he had to accept, regardless of how much he wanted to be with her. To hold her. Touch her. Claim her.

"Goodbye Emma," he whispered in the empty stairwell before disappearing down the stairs.

Emma groaned and tried to open her heavy-lidded eyes. It was like peeling the back off a sticker. Sucking in a breath, she gasped when a sharp pain hit her in the side and her nose filled with the smell of antiseptic.

"Skye," she cried, reaching out for something. Anything. Images of recent events flooded her mind, ending with her blood-stained hands.

"Easy, baby," a familiar feminine voice said, as soft, warm fingers wrapped around her hand.

"Mom?" she asked, her voice raw and weak. When she finally opened her eyes, she blinked rapidly, trying to clear away the white haze that had settled in front of her.

"I'm here," her mother, Irene, said.

Emma turned toward the sound of her voice and recognized her mom's faint outline through the haze. She squeezed her eyes closed and rubbed them with her palms. "What happened? Where's Skye?"

"Skye's fine. We're all fine. Do you know where you are?"

Dazed, she looked around the room, ears honing in on the

beeping of the machines around her as her heart raced. She shook her head just as a man dressed in a white coat entered the room.

"Hi Emma, I'm Dr. Peterson. How are you feeling?

"Like I got hit by a truck."

"Not quite, but it's not surprising you feel that way." the doctor told her. "You were shot."

"Shot?" she replied, as she looked down at her body, unable to recollect that particular moment.

"Do you remember anything about what happened?"

She stared up at the white ceiling, grimacing as she tried to get comfortable. "I remember trying to rescue my daughter. Where is she?"

"She went with your dad to get something to eat," her mom said.

"And Devon?"

Irene's lips pressed into a thin line, and she looked away.

Her eyes may be blurry, but Emma could see well enough to draw a conclusion. "He's gone, isn't he?"

"We'll talk about him later."

"No need. I know what that means." She waved her hand in dismissal, her chest aching.

"Do you know today's date?" the doctor asked.

Emma shook her head. "How long have I been here?"

"It's been a week and a half now," he replied.

"Say what? Why can't I remember?"

"You were sedated to give your body time to heal," her mom told her.

"Let's try to sit you up so I can listen to your chest," Dr. Peterson said, raising the head of the bed.

When she attempted to lean forward, she cried out in pain. "Shit, that hurts. Oh, sorry, Mom. I didn't mean to swear."

"I'm just glad you're okay," her mom said, waving off her apology as sorrow filled her eyes.

The doctor checked out her heart and her lungs. "Sounds better.

I'm going to get the mobile x-ray unit up here so that we can see how that lung of yours is doing."

"My lung?"

"When the bullet entered your side, it shattered a rib and pierced your lung."

Leaning back against the bed, Emma lifted her shirt and saw the tube sticking out of her side. Her eyes followed it to the machine it was attached to. "What's this?"

"The bullet caused your lung to collapse. We had to perform a Thoracostomy. The tube is removing all the air and fluid from around your lung to give it room to heal and expand."

"And my rib?"

"We had to create an artificial rib to replace the shattered one. But don't worry, you shouldn't even notice the difference," the doctor said with a smile. "I would like you to try and walk around the unit today. I'll have the nurses come in with some pain meds."

Nodding, Emma laid her head on the pillow and closed her still blurry eyes, exhausted. The activity was taking a toll on her body as was her inability to take a deep breath. An oxygen tube was still sticking in her nose, but it didn't seem to help with the shortness of breath. It just made her nostrils tickle. She rubbed her nose, and her eyes caught the glint of her wedding ring.

A quick dream-like sequence played in her mind, and it had her asking, "Do you have it?"

"Have what?" Irene asked, a puzzled expression on her face.

"Whatever it was that Devon gave me."

"I have no idea. Devon left over a week ago."

With her forehead furrowing, Emma stared at her empty hands. "I swear that he gave me something."

"When?"

"I-I don't know."

"It could have been a dream, Emma."

She opened and closed her hand. "I can still feel it. He said...he said, this will always belong to you."

It was almost like she watched it happen from above the bed, like she was hovering there. She couldn't remember anything else, other than that. She couldn't remember what it looked like or what it was exactly, but she knew he'd given her something.

Her mom shrugged her shoulders and held her hands out, palms up. "If he did, I don't know anything about it."

Soon the nurse came in with more meds, adding them to the intravenous tube. "This should help with the pain."

"Thank you."

"Maybe when your father and Skye get back, we'll try to go for a short walk," Irene suggested.

"Maybe..." Emma·said, her voice fading as her eyes closed, too exhausted to stay awake. Hopefully, she'd have more answers when she woke up again.

Chapter Twenty-Four

"You can't ignore her forever, you know," Leila said.

"I don't know what you're talking about," Devon mumbled as he watched his son glide across the ice. "He's improved a lot."

"Don't change the subject on me, Mister."

He ran his hand across the back of his neck. "I don't want to talk about her with you. It's weird."

"I still don't understand why you left her in the hospital without waiting until she was awake to say goodbye. I didn't take you for a coward."

Devon had no defense. It was a cowardly thing to do. But he knew that if he waited around and tried to say goodbye when she was awake, he'd cave. Her tear-filled eyes would have made him stay. At least, this time around, he had said the words before he left, even if she couldn't hear them. It pained him that he went back on his word, but when he saw her lying there on the hospital bed, it made him realize she deserved better than anything he could give her. That's why, when she woke up three weeks ago and tried to call him, he didn't pick up his phone.

As he sat there on the bleachers, his phone buzzed again, and her lovely face lit up his display. A pang of guilt riffled through him as he shoved it back in his pocket. Leila shook her head, rolling her eyes.

"Are you really going to make me go there and get her?" she said, challenging him.

"Stay out of this."

"No can do, honey bunch. You talk with her, or I will."

"You wouldn't?"

"You bet your batootie I would. She's perfect for you, and you're being a jackass again. If you won't do it, someone else is going to have to."

"Just leave it alone. I'm warning you."

Leila let it drop, but he could tell by the look in her eyes that this discussion was far from over. Turning away, he watched his son shoot the puck into the net.

"Way to go, Jacob!" he cheered. "The kid's a natural."

"Practicing with his daddy certainly helps," Leila said as she placed her hand on his arm. "They really missed you."

He smiled and gave her hand a pat. "I missed you guys, too."

"Are you still up for taking the kids tonight? If not, you can come over and hang with them at our place."

As much as he wanted to wallow in self-pity, he knew he had to get back into the swing of his normal life, and that included every other weekend with his kids. And considering they haven't had a weekend together in a while, he wasn't about to pass it up.

"I want to take them. Besides, you deserve some me time. Go to the spa or something."

"If you're sure..." she said hesitantly.

"Yes, I'm sure. Go have fun tonight."

Leila gave a shout as their son started up the ice with the puck again before turning back to Devon. "Don't take them swimming or anything, though. Brianna still has her cough."

"Is that why she didn't come to the game tonight?"

"Ya, she's at home with Naomi."

"How long has she been sick now?"

"Two weeks."

"I'll plunk her favorite movie in the Blu-ray and cuddle with her tonight."

"She'd like that," Leila said, smiling.

He returned the smile. She was a beautiful woman in every way, with her short, bleach blond hair and emerald eyes. If circumstances were different, he could have easily spent his life with her. But she wasn't Emma. No one could be Emma, but Emma.

"You should go get her."

Her voice broke him out of the endless circle his brain kept trying to trap him in.

"What?" he asked.

"Go get Emma. You know you aren't going to be happy until she's back in your arms."

"You don't understand."

She shook her head, her lips curling into a rueful smile. "You're so handsome, yet so stupid."

Devon glared at her. He knew she meant well, but he wished she would quit meddling. He didn't want to talk about Emma. It was hard enough that her face was at the forefront of his mind every minute of every day, and his arms ached to hold her. Man, he was pathetic. He wasn't about to tell his ex-wife that, though. She would gloat big time because she felt comfortable enough to do so. They had too close of a relationship sometimes.

"Shut up," he said good-naturedly.

She tapped his shoulder and then returned her attention to the game. Only a few seconds remained. Their son's team won the game easily. A huge improvement from last year. Devon walked down the bleachers to the bench where his son had just stepped off the ice.

"You were awesome," he said to Jacob, giving him a high five.

"Did you see my goal, Dad?"

"Yep." Devon nodded, ruffling his son's hair. "A future NHL star in the making. We should celebrate by getting ice cream."

"We'll need a rain check. I don't want Bri catching a chill," Leila said, shaking her head at Devon.

"Why don't you head home and get her ready? I'll run Jacob by Dairy Queen for a quick snack."

"We should wait until Brianna can go, too. It's only fair."

"You always ruin my fun. I wish I didn't have a sister," Jacob whined, stomping his way to the locker room.

Leila shook her head. "You sure you want them?"

"Maybe I'll go back to Winnipeg," he replied, laughing.

"Take me with you," she begged, her eyes sparkling.

"Let the kids fend for themselves?"

She laughed. "Yep."

Once Jacob emerged from the locker room, they began the drive back to Leila's place. Jacob rode with Devon and chattered non-stop about the game. He tried to focus on his son, but his mind kept wandering to Emma.

"Dad, are you even listening?" his son huffed.

He scrambled to remember what his son was talking about, searching his mind for anything that sounded familiar. Finally, a word popped into his head. "A tournament?"

"Can you come?"

"I'll have to see—hell, hold on," he yelled, as headlights were coming straight for them.

"Emma, you need to eat something," her mother said.

"I don't want to," she replied, burying her face in her pillow. "I'm not hungry."

"I'll just place the tray on your nightstand, then."

She heard the clink of the metal tray and then the soft click of the door as her mom left the room. Bracing herself for the pain, she cringed as she rolled over to grab the painkillers that she knew accompanied the food. It was getting easier to move, but her body felt so heavy these days and her mood *blah*.

Swallowing the painkillers, she buried her head in the pillow again. The hospital had released her over a week ago, but she was still bedridden. If it wasn't for the money she had received from her husband's death, they would be struggling financially right now. She had received the settlement while she was in the hospital.

She picked up her phone and scrolled through her Facebook profile, her heart skipping a beat when her eyes fell across Devon's name. He was ranting about a close call he had on the road the other day and how they'd landed in a ditch. His son had apparently thought it was the most exciting adventure ever.

Emma clicked on Devon's name, which took her to his profile. She scanned his recent posts, but there was no mention of her or their own adventure. It was like it had never happened. Tears threatened to gather, but she pushed them away. She was done crying over him. However, her heart still didn't seem ready to let go.

She was certain that he'd given her something before he left. But given that nothing had turned up since then, it was likely her own imagination wishing for more. A dream that had no bearing on the truth. Why would he put her through all this again? Why not let bygones be bygones? It didn't make sense. *He* didn't make sense.

"Okay! Time to buck up, Emma," she muttered. Grimacing, she swung her legs over the side of the bed and sat up. Life had to begin again sometime. Her chest and side still hurt like mad, but it was getting easier to get up and move around. It was her heart that was in the worst shape of all.

She had allowed herself to dream of a future with him. And he had left her. Again. The sad part was she had actually believed him when he said he was there to stay. He'd been so persistent. Now she realized he had only wanted to have sex with her. Why else would he go back to ignoring her again? She couldn't believe she'd been so stupid as to give in.

"Stupid. Stupid. Stupid." she mumbled, smacking her forehead twice.

The dickhead.

She was never going to believe anything he had to say again. Her finger hovered over the unfriend button. It was truly time to say goodbye. Seeing his name pop up everywhere was too painful to handle.

Sucking in a deep breath, she clicked unfriend. And for the first time since joining Facebook, she no longer had her ex on her friend's list. She had hoped to feel relieved when his name disappeared, but a heavy feeling wrapped itself around her heart and mind instead.

Why did she still care about him? This should have been the final nail in his coffin. It should have been easy to bury their friendship. But it wasn't. Putting her phone down, she stood up and wandered into the bathroom.

Resting her hands on the marble counter, she stared at herself in the mirror. She had matted hair and red eyes. Her face ghostly pale, matching her cracked lips. For the first time in her life, she wished that make-up was a part of her routine. A touch of rouge and lipstick would go a long way in making her look alive again.

But—*blah*—might as well look as lousy as she felt. It's not like she was going anywhere or expecting any company, except her parents and her daughter. She wanted to sleep until she was a hundred years old. Her energy levels had been completely non-existent since the incident.

Just as she was about to crash on the bed, Skye flew into the bedroom like a whirlwind. "Come on, Mom. No more lying around. We're going out."

"I'm not up to going out. Why not ask your grandma?"

"It was her idea. Come on." Her daughter wandered over to Emma's dresser and pulled out a pair of pants and a loose-fitting t-shirt. "Get dressed."

Grumbling, Emma got dressed and followed her daughter into the living room. Her mother was leaning over and tying her shoes as she looked up. "Good, you're out of bed."

"Where are we going?" Emma asked.

"It's a surprise," her mom replied, a huge smile on her face.

Within twenty minutes, they were standing outside a beauty salon.

"What are we doing here?"

"We're getting a make-over," her mother announced.

"It's a waste of money. There's no point."

"Yes, there is. I want to spoil my daughter for once."

Emma crossed her arms and stared in the window, watching a woman get a facial. "This is stupid. Let's just go home."

"We can't. We've got a lunch date."

"With who?"

"You'll find out soon enough," her mother said mysteriously.

Skye was grinning from ear to ear.

"Can't you guys just let me wallow in misery in my bedroom?"

Her mom pulled open the door. "Enough wallowing. Life is too short to wallow."

Crossing her arms, Emma followed the two conspirators inside. They sat in the waiting area and skimmed through magazines, trying to determine the best look for Emma's hair.

Skye pointed to a pixie cut. "Mom, you'd look good with this one."

"The last time I tried that style, I looked like a boy. No, thank you."

"What about this one?" her mother asked, pointing to a bob cut hair style that curled under the chin.

"That does look cute. I've had a similar one done before." Emma closed the magazine, having made her decision.

"Have you ladies decided on what you want done yet?" a stylist asked.

All three of them nodded and followed the three stylists to their chairs. After a grueling hour and a half, they were finally finished and on their way out the door.

"Do I have lipstick on my teeth?" Emma asked, feeling certain she did.

"Nope, you're good, darling," her mom said as they climbed into the car. "Now for our next stop."

Irene pulled out of her parking spot, and after another ten minutes, they were at their next destination—a small café that served soup and sandwiches.

"We got all gussied up to come here?"

"You'll see why," her daughter said mysteriously.

Something about this didn't feel right to Emma. The two of them had something up their sleeve. She knew it by the way they were looking at each other. Nerves gathered in her stomach, making it churn.

"I hope this isn't an attempt to fix me up with someone," she said, cautiously eyeing the cute guy in the window, who chose that moment to look over at her and smile.

"Just get your butt inside," her mom said, rolling her eyes.

Skye took Emma by the hand and pulled her through the doorway. "Relax, Mom."

When they stepped inside, a lady with short blond hair, sitting in a corner booth, raised her hand in greeting. Her mother sashayed around the tables, heading toward the unknown greeter.

"Come on." Skye said, pushing Emma in the same direction.

The woman stood up as they approached the table and held out her hand. "Thanks for meeting with me. I'm Leila, Devon's ex-wife."

Emma's eyes narrowed a smidgeon, her lips pulling to one side in uncertainty.

Leila gestured toward the empty chairs. "Please, have a seat."

When Emma hesitated, her mom squeezed her hand and said, "Sit down. You'll be okay."

"I come in peace," Leila said, smiling. "Honest."

A waitress came, and they placed their order. As she walked away, an awkward silence filled the air.

"You're probably wondering why I'm here."

"Just a little," Emma muttered.

"Part curiosity and part hope, I guess. I'll cut to the chase instead of dragging it out. I love Devon."

"I'll make this easy and quick for you. You can have him." Emma stood up and had every intention of leaving when Leila grabbed her arm, making her sit down again.

"He loves you," the blond said.

"I find that hard to believe."

"He's got this notion in his head that you are better off without him. But you aren't, are you? I can see it in your eyes."

"It doesn't matter what I think. He's made his choice," Emma said as the waitress placed a hot chocolate in front of her. "Thank you."

"He only left because he felt responsible for you getting hurt."

"So, he decides to hurt me more by leaving?"

"He's hurting just as much, trust me. He felt like he had to leave to keep you safe. Look, I know it makes no sense, but it does to him. I probably shouldn't be telling you this, but he lost a close friend in a drug deal gone wrong and has blamed himself ever since. I think what happened to you reminded him of that, and he got spooked. You mean more to him than anyone else in the world. He loves you."

"He has a funny way of showing it," Emma said, unable to believe she was having this conversation with Devon's ex-wife.

"You love him, don't you?"

"Yes."

"Then don't let him push you away."

"Why didn't you fight for him?" Emma asked.

"I did, for a while anyway. But my battle was lost before we even got married. I just didn't realize it until after. He married me because he felt it was the right thing to do, and I let him because of my own selfish reasons."

"You guys have kids together. You should be together," Emma pressed further.

"That was the excuse I used, too. But I'm glad it turned out the way it did, otherwise I never would have met Curtis. We're getting married next summer." Leila held up her hand, a diamond ring sparkling on her finger. "Look, the love that you two have is a once in a life-time love. Don't let it go."

"He made his choice."

Leila pressed her palm against her forehead in frustration. "I can see why he picked you. You're as stubborn as he is."

Her mom wrapped her fingers around Emma's forearm. "Honey, listen to Leila."

Emma leaned back in the chair, pressing the pressure point on the back left side of her neck, trying to stem off the headache that was making its presence known. "I'm not stupid enough to put myself in a position to get rejected again."

"Did you bring it, Irene?" Leila asked.

"Bring what?" Emma asked, looking between the two women.

"Your dad is going to kill me once he realizes that I've given this to you."

Confused, she asked, "Give me what?"

Her mom reached into the pocket of her red jacket and produced a small wine-colored box. Placing it on the table, she pushed it toward Emma. "You were right."

Emma stared at it, her heart racing. "About?"

"Devon did give you something."

Reaching out, Emma picked up the box and a flood of images from the hospital overwhelmed her. *I love you more than you will ever know, Emma Praught.* His voice echoed in her mind as though he were right beside her, saying it again. Tears pricked her eyes as she covered her mouth, smothering a sob. "This will always belong to you," she whispered.

"Sometimes us women have to fight for what we want. Some men are too prideful to admit when they're wrong," her mom said, grabbing a napkin and handing it to Emma.

"I came down today because Devon hurt himself at work by being too distracted. He needs you, even if he doesn't realize it," Leila said.

"He hurt himself?" Emma asked.

"He broke his arm, falling out of a tree."

"Guess he doesn't make a very good monkey, eh?" Emma said, sniffling and chuckling at the same time.

"That's my girl," her mom said, patting Emma on the hand.

"Don't let Devon know that I came down here today, okay? He'd kill me," Leila said.

"He won't hear it from us," Skye said, pretending to zip her lips closed.

Emma opened the jewelry box and gasped. Safely cocooned inside was a silver ring with a dazzling blue diamond. The glass chandelier above the table made the ring glitter. "How could he afford this?"

"It was passed down from his grandmother. He was told to give it to the woman of his dreams."

"Did he give it to you?" Emma asked Leila.

"Nope."

Emma looked at her mom, puzzled. "How'd you get it?"

"Before Devon left, he placed that in your hand. I guess your dad thought he was doing you a favor by hiding it."

"Men!" Emma growled. Why did the men in her life feel like they could control everything and make decisions for her? It was time to take back her life, this time on her terms, not theirs.

"You won't hear me argue," Irene said. "I found it hidden in our closet the other day and confronted your dad about it."

"So, what are you going to do, girl?" Leila asked.

"Can I swat them up the side of the head?" Emma muttered.

"Be my guest." Devon's ex-wife laughed as she looked down at her watch. "I better get going. It's a long drive back."

"Thanks, Leila. I owe you," Emma said, giving her a quick hug.

"Shall I tell him you're coming?"

"No, don't say anything. I have an idea."

"Just a fair warning. Devon is going to be stubborn," Leila warned her.

Emma grinned. "Not as stubborn as I'm going to be." The man wasn't going to know what hit him. "Come on. Let's go."

Chapter Twenty-Five

Two weeks after meeting Leila in the café, Emma finally felt well enough to take a trip to Alberta. But before she left, there was still one more thing she had to do.

Pulling into an empty parking spot at the cemetery, she turned off the engine. This was the first time she'd been back to this place since it all started. She grabbed the flowers off the passenger seat and climbed out of the car.

Passing under the archway, she made her way to Peter's grave and kneeled down, placing the flowers in front of his tombstone. Emma sat there silently and ran her fingers along his name engraved in stone, tears pooling in her eyes.

"I thought that when I got here I'd have so many things to say, and now my mind is drawing a blank." Emma sighed as she wiped the tears from her eyes. She wanted to tell him all about Devon and everything that had happened to them both, but she could just picture him rolling over in his grave, grumbling.

There was no getting around it. As hard as she tried, she couldn't stop thinking about the hard times that had befallen them prior to his accident. Most of their conversations before he had died revolved around how much his life sucked and how he hated his job. Yet he had refused to do anything about it.

Had she done something wrong? Could she have made things any better for him somehow? She'd withdrawn into herself and focused more on being a mother than she had on being a wife. It was the only way she managed to keep her sanity and hide herself away from the painful truth of not being able to make him happy.

She would always love Peter. He was a hard-working man and did what he could to provide for them, but emotionally, he just wasn't there. There was too much going on in that head of his to make room for them. That had hurt almost as much as his death, but she'd always buried her emotions and focus on loving him, because divorce wasn't an option in her mind.

In all the time they were together, they had never had the same connection as she had with Devon. The bond they developed in high school never really disappeared. It was always there, waiting below the surface. She had felt it every day. Maybe that was why she couldn't be what Peter needed, couldn't make him happy. And why she couldn't refuse Devon when he reappeared in her life. In a way, she could understand why he felt so strongly about letting Leila find her happily ever after.

But she refused to think of her life with Peter as wasted time. They'd had a decent life, and if they wouldn't have got together, Skye would never have been born. And if Devon wouldn't have had his time with Leila, his kids wouldn't be here either.

And now, Peter was flying free, no longer shackled by the turmoil of life while she, on the other hand, had a life to live. One that she wanted to live with the man of her youth. The man who had once again claimed her heart, taking back the piece she'd always reserved for him.

"I've met someone. Well, not really met. We used to know each other."

Oh, god! What if he thinks I cheated on him?

"Don't worry. We didn't talk much while you and I were

together, besides saying happy birthday. But he breathed life into my body after you were taken from me, and I-I love him." She blurted out the last bit rapidly, afraid that she'd chicken out.

Emma rolled her shoulders and ducked her head into a protective position, expecting God to strike her with lightning. "I tried not to. I tried to push him away, but he's in my heart, Peter. He always has been. I don't have the strength to fight it anymore. And honestly, I don't want to. He makes me feel alive, makes me feel young again."

She looked down at Peter's ring as she twisted it around her finger. The weight of Devon's jewelry box in her pocket intensified. Once she removed her wedding ring, it would mean the end of an era. She never thought it was possible to love two people at once, but now she realized she'd been doing it all along.

Her love for Devon had always remained, sitting in the sidelines while she lived her life with Peter, waiting for the time when it would be reborn or let loose on the world again. And what once had caused her grief and guilt now made perfect sense. They were the two men who were always meant to be in her life, just at different times.

Emma knew it was because of their past relationship that things had heated up so quickly. Devon wouldn't have made it onto her radar otherwise. It was like their passion for each other had been waiting for a time such as this. But all of it would have been for not if she couldn't convince the stubborn ape to take her back.

Standing up, Emma brushed the dirt off her slacks and adjusted the shoulder strap of her purse as she gave his gray tombstone one final glance. "I'll never forget you, Peter. I love you."

And with that, she walked away, determined to move onto the next stage of her life with a man who has never failed to be more than a message away. Her heart still stung knowing she'd never grow old with the man who had been with her for half her life, but she found peace knowing he was finally at rest. No more pain. No more depression, just peace and rest. And as much as it hurt that he was gone, the knowledge that he was in a better place made her feel a little lighter.

Climbing into her car, she headed home to prepare for her trip.

>I heard about what happened. Are you okay?

Devon stared at her text message and, as hard as he tried, he couldn't stop the grin that spread across his face. *Déjà vu central.* Was she going to go to the same lengths he had?

Giving his head a rueful shake, he placed his phone down on the counter. There wasn't any point in playing along. It wasn't like it was going to go anywhere. He knew they couldn't be together for her own safety.

Soon, his phone dinged again.

>Please talk to me. Let me know you're okay.

A chuckle escaped him before he realized it, much to his annoyed displeasure. She really was going to go there, exactly like he had. *Frustratingly cute little minx!* Devon had no idea how to proceed. He was baffled. How did she find out about his accident?

"Leila!" he groaned, smacking his forehead with his cast. "Oh, that smarts." Devon rubbed his forehead. He couldn't wait to get the darn thing off.

His ex-wife must have squealed, but how? It's not like the two girls could get together easily. They lived miles apart. And he never gave her Emma's number.

He clicked on his ex-wife's name and typed out a message.

>What have you done, Leila?

Her reply came quickly with feigned innocence.

>What makes you think I've done anything?

>I know you told Emma.

>Told her what.

>Forget it.

He smacked the send button with his finger.

Devon tossed his phone on the couch and got up to grab a beer from the fridge. "Meddling woman," he muttered. It was hard enough staying away from Emma as it was without Leila getting involved. He'd thought Emma had finally given up on contacting him, as he hadn't heard from her for a while.

Desperately needing that drink, he opened the can and guzzled half of it before placing it on the coffee table. Hearing his phone ding again, he picked it up and stared at the screen, unsure of whether he should laugh or groan.

>You better answer me, bucko.

Laying his head back against the couch, he pinched the bridge of his nose. Didn't Emma understand the willpower it took to stay away from her? It didn't matter how much time had passed. He still wanted her. Needed her as much as ever. It was for that reason he couldn't answer her. If he did, he likely wouldn't be able to stop.

He should never have accepted her friend's request on Facebook again. And now, he couldn't very well delete her, not without hurting her again. He definitely missed the day when the internet didn't exist. It made things so much easier.

Desperate for a distraction, he turned on the television, and the first thing he saw was a movie, Sleeping Beauty. She was lying there on the bed, and Prince Charming was leaning over to kiss her. She looked so much like Emma that it had him squeezing his eyes closed. He was seeing her everywhere.

Damn it.

Devon picked up his beer and swallowed the rest. He was in for a long night. His hands itched to respond to Emma's text, and it made him fiddle with the tab on the top of his beer can to keep his fingers occupied. Changing the channel, he settled on an action movie, The Fast and the Furious.

Soon, he had a warm glow in his belly from the drink, and the anxiety inside him began to ebb. There was nothing like a fast-moving movie with a bunch of explosions to easy the twinge in his gut. His phone dinged again, and he couldn't help but glance at it. It was Emma.

>I never thanked you for watching out for us.
>Some good I was.

>It wasn't your fault, Dev.

Placing his phone on the couch, he rubbed his eyes, which were beginning to burn with tears. Man, he was such a weakling.

>I made the choice to face him. That's on me, not you.

He should have tied her to the bed or locked her in the bathroom, but you know what they say about hindsight being twenty-twenty. In an effort to end the conversation, he sent a quick message.

>Please, Emma. I don't want to talk about it.

>Tough. I do.

>Good night, Em.

>Don't you dare disappear on me!

>I need to sleep. I work tomorrow.

>No, you don't. You're trying to push me away. I'm not stupid.

>If you want someone like me, you are stupid.

The minute he hit send, he felt like someone punched him in the gut.

>Sorry, I didn't mean that.

>Maybe I am stupid, but at least I'm not chicken to go after what I want.

>Touché.

Even as he said the word, he knew he couldn't pick up the gauntlet that she'd thrown down. He had to keep her welfare in mind and stick to his guns.

>Good night.

>Dev, don't do this. We need to talk.

He grabbed another beer and turned his divided attention back to the movie. He couldn't give in to her, not if he wanted her to move on with her life. But when another ding caught his attention, he couldn't help but look at the screen again.

Pathetic.

>If you ignore me, I'm going to come down there.

He stared at her text. There was no way she was in any condition to show up on his doorstep like he'd done when he said that very thing, so he decided to play her game.

>Then come.
>Okay.
>No.
>Yes.
>No.
>Sleep well, Dev.
She added a devil emoji at the end of her comment.

Oh, god. His little minx was up to something. And he wasn't sure he was up for whatever she had planned. Standing up, he wandered into his bedroom and collapsed on his bed. Their little exchange had left him weary and exhausted.

Sleep quickly claimed him, and Emma—the woman of his heart—quickly claimed his dreams.

Devon rolled over in bed and picked up his phone off the nightstand, checking to see if he had any messages. His phone had stayed strangely silent all night. He found himself checking it whenever he woke up, which happened to be a million times throughout the night.

Climbing out of bed, he stood up and stretched his back and his neck, working out the kinks from a restless night's sleep. It surprised him that she had remained silent and didn't even send him a good morning text.

He grabbed a towel out of the closet and went into the washroom. Having a shower was the most annoying thing in the world right now, with the cast on his arm. Thankfully, he didn't have much hair to wash, so one arm sufficed. And since he wasn't allowed to get the cast wet, he wrapped it in plastic and jumped under the steamy shower.

There was no way he was going to miss his daily shower. It helped ease the ache in his muscles that arose from his line of work. Today, it was to ease the ache in his neck from over thinking.

If she showed up at his house, he wouldn't be able to resist her, not with her sweet, luscious curves and come-hither eyes. The dreams he'd fought with throughout the night had left him aching. He knew he would never stop wanting her for as long as he lived. That meant he would be one of those miserable old bachelors who whined about people stepping on their lawn.

No other woman would ever be able to satisfy him. There wasn't even any point in trying. He wasn't getting any younger and couldn't stand anymore heartbreak in his life.

"Sorry, fella," he said, glancing down at his morning woody. It had been crying the blues ever since he'd disappeared on Emma. He could remember the feeling of being buried deep inside her warm, wet—

He hit the wall with the palm of his good hand. *Stop it!*

His mind was trying to get away on him again, something it did very easily where Emma was concerned. Holding his cast out to the side, he leaned over and turned the water off. He couldn't believe he had to keep the cast on for another few weeks. The thing was a damn pain in the ass.

As he reached for the towel, someone knocked on his front door. Drying off in record speed, he wrapped the towel around his waist and stepped out of the washroom. The visitor knocked again.

"Hang on, I'm coming," he hollered. Holding his towel, he glanced out the peep hole.

It couldn't be. Giving his head a shake, he looked through the hole again. And sure enough, there she was.

"Open the door, Devon. I know you're in there."

He couldn't stop his lips from curling into a smirk. She was playing it exactly the same way he had. There was one difference, though. He was standing there, wearing only a towel. Not something that she would expect. So maybe he had the higher ground yet again.

Expecting to shock her, he yanked open the door and said, "Nice shoe—"

When he laid eyes on her, his jaw dropped, as did his towel.

Chapter Twenty-Six

"Will you marr—"

The question that Emma had been rehearsing died on her lips when his towel hit the floor. "I...uh," she stammered, frozen in her kneeling position, her hand holding up the ring he'd given her.

Devon's eyes widened like hers did, and both their jaws hit the floor. He slapped a hand over his parts and dove behind the door. But not before she saw his naked body, which left her drooling.

A loud thud came from inside the apartment.

"Damn it," he cursed.

"You okay?" Emma asked, struggling to get up off her knee. She grunted when a sharp pain hit her side.

"Ya, sure," he muttered.

She poked her head around the door and found him face down, with his butt sticking up over the seat of a chair that had fallen over.

Slapping a hand over her mouth, she tried to prevent a giggle from escaping. "Oh, gosh."

"I'm glad you find this so amusing," he grumbled, attempting to push himself up with his good arm.

Howling with laughter, Emma walked over and slapped him on the bare butt. "Very much so."

He reached out to grab her, but she side-stepped away.

"Just wait till I get my hands on you."

Leaning on the side of the couch with her hip, she crossed her arms over her chest and grinned. "And then what?"

"I'll think of something." He pushed himself backward off the chair, landing on his butt. As he rolled into a kneeling position, his eyes sparkled with a predatory gleam. "You have one last chance to walk out that door."

"Pardon my expression, but hell no. I came here with a mission."

As he stood up, she caught a glimpse of his manhood as it slowly increased in size, apparently wanting to join in on their conversation. Emma swallowed hard as her insides warmed intensely, her underwear growing damp.

"I have my own mission," he replied.

"So does he, apparently," she said, pointing toward his cock.

"I think this is one mission that we're in agreement on."

"Do I have a say in the matter?"

"What say you?"

"Yes..."

As soon as she said that, he reached for her, but she stepped away and pulled the jewelry box out of her pocket. "On one condition."

Not even a second later, Emma found herself back over his shoulder, despite his arm being in a cast.

"We have time for that later," he replied.

"Hey!" she cried.

He slapped her on the butt. "Silence."

"Your arm."

Devon kicked the door of his room open. "My arm's fine."

This wasn't what he had in mind when he opened the door. He had planned to play it cool and be cordial and then send her on her way. But when he saw her there, kneeling in front of him, he had no hope in hell of being callus with her. Her eyes sparkled with joy and a soft smile played on her lips. And as soon as her lips parted, he knew exactly what she was going to ask.

Thankfully, his peep show halted it. The last thing he wanted to do was tell his friends that his high school sweetheart had proposed to him instead. They would rib him for being the girl in the relationship. He would never hear the end of it.

Reaching the end of his bed, he leaned forward, and she fell back onto the mattress with a giggle. "What do you think you can do with one hand?" she asked jokingly.

"You'd be amazed, darling!"

Her fingers curled around the fabric of his shirt, a wicked gleam glittering in her eyes. "Maybe I need to be the one to take charge this time." With a quick tug, she pulled him down onto the bed beside her and climbed on top.

Wrapping his good arm around her, he flipped her, so he was back on top.

"Hey!" She struggled to get out from underneath him, pouting.

"My rightful place." He grinned, leaning on his good arm.

"Now what?" Emma smirked, pointing to his free arm with the cast.

"I can still do this," he said, tickling her side.

She snorted with laughter. "You're so" —he tickled her again, making her snort a second time, her face turning red—"mean."

Devon buried his face in her shoulder, laughing. "You're priceless." When he lifted his head, their eyes locked. A world of emotion swam in the depth of her eyes, along with a beauty that no one could ever match. It didn't take long for his throat to tighten. "I don't deserve you."

"Deserve-smerv. Love isn't based on merit, Dev, or on what you deserve. Love just is or is not."

"You're like a lady Shakespeare."

She scrunched her nose and said, "To be or not to be, that is the question."

"And what are we going to be, Emma Praught?"

"The main characters in our own story."

"Have a title in mind?"

Chewing on her delectable bottom lip, she stared into space for a second. It didn't take long for a mischievous grin to spread across her face, her eyes lighting up like a Christmas tree, as she said, "Not You Again!"

Dev tickled her side mercilessly. "Smart alec."

Giggling, she pushed his hand away from her. "And you love me for it."

Running his fingers gently across her cheek, he said, "More than anyone else in the world."

"Then marr..."

"Shush, woman." He covered her mouth with two fingers. "That's my job."

She raised her eyebrows and gave him a look that said, 'well, ask me already before I bop you one.'

"Emma Praught, will you marry me?"

She framed his cheeks with the palms of her hands, tears sparkling in her eyes. "As in together forever?"

"And always!" he answered, his lips closing over hers.

"Sounds good to me," she murmured.

It may have taken them twenty years to reach this point, but you know what they say, 'fate takes its own time.' And for once, she wasn't going to argue with it.

"I love you, Devon Matthews."

"I love you more."

"Are you going to argue with me already?" Emma asked.

"That depends. Do you believe in make-up sex?"

"Just shut up and make love to me!"

"As you wish..."

Epilogue

Six months later...

"You can't be serious," Devon gaped at the small stick in his hand. "This isn't what I think it is, is it?"

Emma wasn't sure what to think as she stared at it herself. She was forty years old, and they had only been married just over a month. "I...uh...I think it means we're going to have a baby."

"You and me?"

"Who else would I be having a baby with, you big dolt!"

Devon sat down on the edge of the tub, first looking at the pregnancy test and then at her flat belly. "There's a baby in there?"

She couldn't help but laugh at the bewildered look on his face. They hadn't expected to still be able to conceive, as she'd started perimenopause already and didn't ovulate regularly.

"Well, unless you've figured out how to get pregnant..." Emma replied with a grin.

Grabbing her by the waist, he pulled her onto his lap, kissing her hard. "Always the smart alec."

"Always the charmer," she said, laughing.

"I can't believe I'm going to have a baby with you."

Emma stared at her stomach. Suddenly a thought dawned on her, and it scared the living daylights out of her. "What if we have twins?"

Devon's arms wrapped around her. "Two kids that look like you? I'll take that any day."

"I'm serious. They say the chance increases with age."

"Two, four, six kids, doesn't matter to me. I'm ready for whatever our lives throw at us."

"So says the man who doesn't have to carry them," she muttered.

"You are going to look so sexy carrying my baby," he said, placing a hand on her stomach.

"I don't think sexy and being pregnant go together."

"So says you. I think you'll be gorgeous."

"I hope you'll remember that when I'm as big as a house."

"You as big as a house? That I've got to see." He chuckled when she bopped him on the shoulder.

"Shut up."

The months flew by, and soon they were holding their newborn son, surrounded by family.

"What are you going to call him?" Joshua asked.

Devon smiled with pride. "Destin."

"That's unique," Irene said, unable to resist touching the soft skin of her grandson. "What does it mean?"

"His name means destiny, fate." Emma took her husband's hand in hers, smiling up at him. "We wanted something to remind us of what we went through, and that what is meant to be will be." She looked down at her newborn son. "And that no matter how much time has passed, life will always find a way."

Devon brought her hand to his lips, kissing it lightly. "That it will, my sweet wife, that it will."

Fairy tales don't always come true in this cruel world, but in Emma's case, her prince charming was standing right by her side.

Now and forever.

It's never too late to believe.

THE END

About the Author

Patricia Elliott lives in beautiful British Columbia with three of her children and her amazing, incredible partner. Now that her kids are all adults, she has decided to actively pursue her passion for the written word.

When she was a youngster, she spent the majority of her time writing fan-fiction and poetry to avoid the harsh reality of bullying. Writing allowed her to escape into another world, even if temporarily; a world in which she could be anyone or anything, even a mermaid. Dreams really can come true. If you believe it, you can achieve it!

For more titles and to join her newsletter, please visit Patricia Elliott's website:

https://patriciaelliottromance.com